WHO KILLED NETTA MAUL?

D1459119

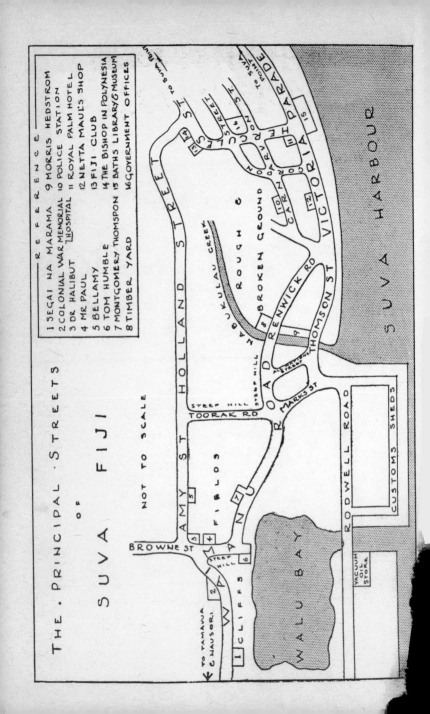

WHO KILLED NETTA MAUL?

A Story of Murder in the Fiji Islands

FRANK ARTHUR

Oxford New York

OXFORD UNIVERSITY PRESS

1989

TO STANLEY WEATHERBY

Oxford University Press, Walton Street, Oxford OX2 6DP

Oxford New York Toronto
Petaling Jaya Singapore Hong Kong Tokyo
Delhi Bombay Calcutta Madras Karachi
Nairobi Dar es Salaam Cape Town
Melbourne Auckland

and associated companies in
Berlin Ibadan

Oxford is a trade mark of Oxford University Press

© The Estate of Frank Arthur

This edition first published 1941 by Victor Gollancz Ltd.
First issued as an Oxford University Press paperback 1989

All rights reserved. No part of this publication may be reproduced,
stored in a retrieval system, or transmitted, in any form or by any means,
electronic, mechanical, photocopying, recording, or otherwise, without
the prior permission of Oxford University Press.

This book is sold subject to the condition that it shall not, by way
of trade or otherwise, be lent, re-sold, hired out or otherwise circulated
without the publisher's prior consent in any form of binding or cover
other than that in which it is published and without a similar condition
including this condition being imposed on the subsequent purchaser

British Library Cataloguing in Publication Data
Arthur, Frank, 1902–1984
Who killed Netta Maul?: a story of murder in the Fiji Islands.
I. [Who killed Netta Maul?] II. Title
823'.912 [F]
ISBN 0–19–282673–5

Printed in Great Britain by
The Guernsey Press Co. Ltd.
Guernsey, Channel Islands

03964708

CONTENTS

AUTHOR'S NOTE

THIS IS A work of fiction and all the people in it are fictitious. I have tried to make each character unlike anyone I knew in Fiji, and if I have used the names of people who exist, I have done so unintentionally. It is many years since I left Fiji, and I have remained completely out of touch with the colony and its inhabitants ever since. Although (while taking certain topographical liberties, and using my prosaic licence to delay closing time in the bars of Suva) I have used buildings that exist, I do not intend that any of my characters should be taken to be portraits of the owners, tenants or lodgers, past, present or future, of such buildings. Nor do I wish to suggest that the conduct, private or official, of such civil servants as I have portrayed, resembles the conduct of real Fiji civil servants.

I am grateful to Mr. F. A. Hornibrook for permission to quote from his valuable work, *The Culture of the Abdomen*, and to Messrs. William Heinemann, Ltd., for allowing me to make use of the Golden Pine Edition of A. C. Swinburne's poems.

FRANK ARTHUR

CHAPTER ONE

THE SCREAM AT NINE FIFTY-NINE

(*Thursday : 9.43–10.4 p.m.*)

INSPECTOR SPEARPOINT, OF the Fiji Constabulary, drove slowly down Waimanu Road, Suva, and pulled up outside the temporary residence of Mrs. Montgomery Thompson. If he could have entered the house and arrested her, he would have done so with pleasure; but as he had no warrant for doing that, he remained seated in the car. He did not like Mrs. Montgomery Thompson, and Mrs. Montgomery Thompson did not like him; but his daughter and her daughter were close friends, a circumstance which both parents had for eight years hoped would be temporary. It was thus by unspoken agreement of long standing that when Inspector Spearpoint came to drive his Muriel home from an evening with her Mildred, he waited outside in the car, and did not intrude on her hostesses; even his realisation that Mrs. Montgomery Thompson approved of this arrangement could not overcome his dislike of meeting that most formidable of Suva's matrons. It was by extremely plainly spoken command that his Muriel never kept him waiting beyond the stipulated time, which had been extended to ten o'clock ever since the Inspector had accidentally discovered that Mrs. Montgomery Thompson preferred her Mildred to be in bed by nine thirty.

Glancing at the dashboard clock—you will understand the sort of man Inspector Spearpoint was when you learn that even his dashboard clock did not dare to work inaccurately—he observed that he had nearly ten minutes to wait. He liked having ten minutes to wait; it gave him time to think, and he realised acutely that he needed time to think. A determined but modest man, Inspector Spearpoint. He deliberately cultivated his mind; he habitually composed mental exercises for himself; and, what is more, he worked them out. He was aware that he was not a clever man, that his brain functioned slowly, that he had no gift for repartee; after his professional interviews with the leading commercial men of the Colony or the young Oxford and Cambridge graduates who took turns as acting Chief Police Magistrate, he was painfully apt to feel that in their eyes at least he had appeared rather much of a fool. But he always justifiably consoled himself with the reflection that none of them had over-reached him yet, and that several had retired from contests with him looking particularly foolish in the eyes of all Fiji. Slow by nature, his determination to be sure made him doubly slow. By methodical habits and trained memory he had overcome the handicap of lacking a nimble brain; he relied on facts, and until he knew his facts, he would make no decision.

One of his favourite mental exercises for the casual moments he was careful to provide for himself, was to recall to mind all the people he had seen during the day, and where he had seen them. By this means, he had acquired extensive knowledge of the names, residences, places of work, associates, and habits, of most of the two thousand Europeans, and many of the ten thousand non-Europeans, of the capital. At the back of his memory were thousands of names and faces, the deposit of his fifteen years of study of the inhabitants of Fiji—a mental portrait gallery of which he made extensive and sometimes (to the originals) surprising use.

So he dismissed Mrs. Montgomery Thomspon from his mind and began to recapitulate the incidents of his brief drive. He had been making a friendly call on his own account in the upper stretches of Waimanu Road, and had left the house a little before twenty to ten; but it

must have been nearly a quarter to by the time he had
pressed the starter, as he had sat trying to recollect the
name of his host's Indian cook-boy. Then he had driven
slowly in order to catch glimpses of the faces of the people
he passed as his headlights picked them out: there had
been four natives in a group, hand-in-hand and singing,
leaping aside from the path of the car with unnecessary
energy and shrieks of happy laughter; then two in single
file and silent. He had overtaken an overweight volu-
minous-skirted Indian woman, spewing voluble chatter
at her undersized man in dirty dhoti and towel turban,
who was preceding her by a couple of yards; and he had
himself been overtaken by a Gawd saloon car, going at
considerable speed. It was No. S63, Jim Camelback's
car; the driver, apparently alone, looked, as he slid past,
like Jim Camelback. ('Going to pick up some girl or
other.')

In front of the Colonial War Memorial Hospital Spearpoint had overtaken a rare bird—a European walking
for pleasure. This was a short, slight young man in his
middle twenties, wearing a cricket shirt open at the neck,
white shorts and tennis shoes, and carrying a stick. He
had looked round into the car's headlights, blinked a
little, and stepped closer to the gutter. ('Bellamy; stock-
clerk in Marryam & Cutt; the chap in Malua who discovered Cuthbert Goodchild-Boaned that night; nervous
kid; then he got transferred to Suva, and married Charlie
Booth's daughter—funny to see him alone; they're never
apart; oh, yes, she went off to Sydney on the *Aorangi*
last month; going to have a baby; and he must be baching
at home; rather do that than live at a pub; not a good
mixer; no friends but his wife.')

A hundred yards or so ahead of Bellamy, just before
Waimanu Road took a sharp turn downhill to the right
and Browne Street ran out at right angles uphill to the
left, the Inspector had overtaken Netta Maul. Swinging
her famous silver handbag, she had walked on without

looking round. Why should she look? You cannot recognise the driver of a car that passes you at night, and
Bellamy had displayed lack of self-control in not repressing
the instinct to look. Whoever the driver was, he would
recognise Netta Maul; and he would either stop and offer
her a lift (which she would decline, if she felt in that
mood), or else he would be of the minority who would
have refused to offer her a lift in any circumstances (but
she would never have condescended to ask a favour of
anyone). Netta Maul had once been the prettiest half-
caste, indeed, the prettiest girl in Fiji. There is always a
prettiest half-caste in Fiji, who has her brief notorious
reign and is then forgotten in married respectability. But
Netta Maul had not married, and had not fallen into
oblivion. She was still good-looking at twenty-six; the long
tresses of which she was so vain were as black, her sun-
burnt complexion as smooth as ever; but she was un-
deniably fat. The dainty slenderness of the Netta Maul of
legend was a memory of the dim and sticky past. But such
was the force of her personality that she remained an
institution and a tradition; and raw newcomers to bachelor
quarters in the sugar districts round the coast found themselves confronted on their inauguration with two obliga-
tions: to provide a dozen of beer and to listen to stories
about Netta Maul.

As he took the right-hand turn down Waimanu Road,
Spearpoint glanced left up Browne Street, in case a car
was coming out. Until he drew level with Browne Street
his view in that direction was obscured by the cliff along
whose side that portion of the road is cut. Just round
the corner, on the far (right-hand, and thus the wrong)
side of the road, a car was parked, facing inwards. It
was drawn well into the side, under the overhanging
garden hedge of Dr. Halibut, the acting Police Medical
Officer; a figure stood behind it, obscuring the number.
In the deep shade, on this dark night, and with the momen-
tary glimpse he had, the Inspector could not be certain

whose car and whose figure these were, but he received the impression (though he distrusted mere impressions) that it was Camelback's car and Camelback's figure.

Jim Camelback might be calling on Dr. Halibut, or he might be waiting for Netta Maul. Well, if Jim Camelback wanted to speak to Netta Maul, it was no business for the police. But it was a matter that would interest all the scandal-mongers of that most appreciative scandal-mongering town, the capital of Fiji. Netta Maul and Jim Camelback had each been chief actor in the outstanding scandal of the other's career. His association with her had all but cost him his position in the Government Audit Department. Her association with him, leading one of her admirers to suicide and another to the verge of murder, had all but cost her her life. Punctuated by hot-tempered quarrels, their friendship had lasted for three years, but it had ceased abruptly some twelve months earlier. In the Thomson Street Parliament and elsewhere, rumour had it that the Governor himself had intervened to uphold the reputation of his civil servants; and rumour had it also that his threats had served merely to convert the open affair to a surreptitious one. Inspector Spearpoint knew that in the first case rumour was correct, but believed that in the second case she was mistaken.

On his downhill drive, he had next passed a Government surveyor driving uphill, and finally, an Indian laundryman cycling down, balancing his unwieldy bundle of washing on the handlebars.

As he sat outside Mrs. Montgomery Thomspon's, recalling these people, the Inspector was passed by two taxis proceeding uphill. One was empty; the other had indistinguishable occupants; and he speculated on the identities of the Indian drivers, reasoning from the number plates to the owners and the usual drivers.

Then his thoughts reverted to the Europeans he had seen earlier: "Jim Camelback; Bellamy; Netta Maul. Only this morning I saw Bellamy coming out of her shop.

And he doesn't smoke. What would he be doing in a tobacconists'? If Netta Maul had been coming down Waimanu Road she would have passed me by now. Perhaps she stopped to talk to Camelback. She might have gone up Browne Street, and along Amy Street, or entered a house there. Bellamy lives in Amy Street; and as Amy Street runs parallel with this section of Waimanu Road, I could see his house from here. I wonder if he's home yet."

He turned and looked up the unpaved, weed-covered cul-de-sac beside Mrs. Montgomery Thomspon's house, across the muddy paddock that separated her imposing residence from the tiny bungalows of Amy Street. There were twelve of these bungalows, which were built on a soapstone ridge, considerably higher than the soapstone foundation of middle Waimanu Road. The field between was a swamp in the rainy season, and a horse pasture in the other (or wet) season, an irregular, hoof-pitted surface, dotted with eccentrically-trunked palms and stately mango trees. It was private property, and little used in the daylight. Inspector Spearpoint, however, had information about people who sometimes resorted to its solitude for supposedly secret (although not illegal) pleasures. He knew that a certain path which looked like the side entrance to Dr. Halibut's house on the corner of Browne Street, actually led to the paddock, and, being far less conspicuous than the cul-de-sac in Waimanu Road, was much favoured by the patrons of the field. Netta Maul, for example, might have gone along the narrow passage to a rendezvous in the field: or even via the field and Bellamy's back garden to Bellamy's house—a fantastic thought; but you never can tell: still waters run deep, and policemen have reason to be cynical. Bellamy's house was the—the fourth from Browne Street. The first was occupied by the prosperous Chinese merchant, Sing Wong Toon (who, before his recent marriage, had borne the name of Kum Sing Long); the second was empty. The third was Joe Nomore's. The fourth was Bellamy's. There was no light in the fourth house yet, though, had Bellamy proceeded straight home, he should have been indoors long since.

In the third house was light enough. There lived old Joe Nomore, his cross-eyed wife, and his cross-eyed twin daughters. Joe Nomore received a cheque at the end of each month from the leading draper of Suva, and was one of the characters of the town. It was probably from his sitting-room that the faintly-heard gramophone was bawling 'Little man, you've had a busy day.' No one could say that old Joe was a little man, and no one had ever known him to have a busy day; the fact was that his employer hated to change old habits, and one of the oldest of his habits was to stand at the door of his office and stare at Joe Nomore, hands in pockets, propping up the mercery counter with his paunch. It was Pencarbon who did all the work in that department.

Then, as in answer to the thought, Stanley Pencarbon appeared. It was Stanley Pencarbon all right, although his features were hidden by his sun-helmet—it was extraordinary for a man to wear a sun-helmet at night—and he kept sedulously in such black shadows as trees and shrubs afforded. He even made a detour to avoid coming within range of the headlights of Spearpoint's car (or so Spearpoint assumed), but when he turned into the cul-de-sac and, by the light of a pocket torch, picked his way daintily along the kerbstone to the gap in the barbed wire fence, the set of his sloping shoulders and his prancing gait revealed his identity beyond a doubt. He was coatless and his cricket shirt was rolled above the elbows and open at the neck. Diagonally across the strengthening at the base of the front opening Spearpoint had observed the usual laundry-mark, unreadable at the distance, but evidently long enough to contain nine letters. (It is common in Fiji for men to carry their names printed thus across their solar plexi.) Stanley Pencarbon, thought the Inspector, boards at the Royal Palm Hotel; so does Netta Maul.

Some months ago they had been frequently seen together; lately there had apparently been a coolness between them; but to-night their paths seemed to converge. It was more likely that she was awaiting him in the paddock than that she was walking along Amy Street, or talking to Bellamy.

A group of Fijians, men and women, talking and laughing loudly, passed, upward bound.

Inspector Spearpoint glanced again at the dashboard clock: three minutes past ten. That girl of mine will hear of this, he thought; and wondered whether he should break his rule and seek her. Then he remembered that he was driving, not his own car, which was under repair, but one borrowed from a Government official who was on leave. It was a car of the same make, but of a different colour, and with a less reliable clock. He consulted his wrist-watch: one minute to ten; and as he twisted his arm back to its normal position, he heard a shrill scream, which broke off suddenly. So sudden and so unexpected a yell was it, that he found himself holding his breath and scrabbling at the leather of the seat with his fingers, waiting for a repetition, or for succeeding sounds. But no sound followed. Silence, except for a car honking in the town, and the winches of the *Waiwuri*, the sugar-boat loading at the wharf. Even the gramophone had ceased.

So far as he could judge, the scream had come from the direction of the field, beyond Joe Nomore's house, nearer the back of Dr. Halibut's; it was probably a woman's voice, but whether the woman was European, Fijian or Indian, he could not decide. But so deceptive to the senses is a sudden brief noise, that he was not certain it had not come from the Fijians who had just passed.

His attention was distracted by the streak of light from the opening of Mrs. Montgomery Thomspon's front door, and the appearance of Muriel. Most of the light was immediately blocked by the massive form of Mrs. Montgomery Thomspon; most of the atmosphere was immediately occupied by her deliberately-raised voice, saying, "Good night, my darling; and give my very kind regards to your dear mother, won't you, Muriel? Tell your dear mother I hope she is keeping as well as can be expected in the circumstances, won't you, my dear?"

The circumstances alluded to, the Inspector assumed, consisted solely in her being married to him, since he knew of no particular reason why his wife should not be well. He smiled grimly as Muriel climbed into the car, but retained sufficient command of himself to ask, "Had a good time?"

"Yes, thank you, daddy."

He pinched his daughter's arm affectionately, and felt for the gear lever, but an approaching car tempted him to pause and glance instinctively at its number: S96; a Rattler; Mr. Montgomery Thomspon's car. But there was no time to observe whether the driver was Mr. Montgomery Thomspon. If it was, he was driving with uncharacteristic recklessness—swishing up the hill at a pace which few Suva motorists would have dared under the eye of the District Inspector of Police. Moreover, he did not stop at the house of the car's owner, but slashed furiously past.

" Are you going to chase him, daddy?" asked Muriel, hoping he would accept the hint.

"I'll get Sharpe to. have a word with him in the morning," was the disappointing, prosaic and practical answer. "Did you see who it was?"

"No; he was going too fast."

"It didn't look to me like Mr. Thomspon's driving. Was he at home, by any chance?"

"Mildred said he was at the Club. I shouldn't think he would drive like that unless he was drunk."

Spearpoint smiled at the idea of an inebriated Mr. Montgomery Thomspon. The Fiji Club was on the other side of the town, in the direction from which the car had come; but it was unlikely that Mr. Thomspon would be so excited as not to know his own house. He still dallied with the gear lever, realising that something was worrying him, and forgetting what. Ah, yes: the scream! He looked across the field: and, as he looked, the lights went on in Bellamy's house. Eight minutes past ten by the dashboard clock.

CHAPTER TWO

THE BODY IN THE BAG

(Friday : 6.4–6.56 a.m.)

At four minutes past six the next morning, Inspector Spearpoint lay flat on his back on his front verandah. He was clad in pyjama trousers only. Both the knees were bent; the soles of the feet were on the floor and about twelve inches apart, with the heels close to the buttocks. Both the hands were flat on the floor. Raising the hips about two or three inches from the floor, he swung his body vigorously from side to side, keeping the shoulders flat on the floor, so as to tilt each hip upwards alternately. If the reader forms the idea of swinging in a hammock with somebody checking the movement suddenly, he will have a clear conception of this exercise, says the author of *The Culture of the Abdomen,* a copy of which delicately-worded essay lay on the verandah ledge.

What checked the Inspector's motion, however, was the strident summons of the telephone bell. As an unexpected modesty had caused him to prohibit his houseboys from entering the building until 6.15, when his abdomen had received its daily equivalent of T. S. Eliot and Fra Angelico, Spearpoint was forced to answer the telephone himself.

"Hullo," he growled, rubbing against his left ankle the right big toe he had just stubbed on an unlawfully projecting chair.

"Is that you, Inspector? Cherry here. I'm down at

the wharf." Cherry was a Customs officer with a reputation
for practical-joking.

Spearpoint became suspicious. "Well?"

"You'd better come down here at once, I think."
Cherry sounded urgent.

"What for?"

"I've got a couple of Chows here with a bag, and
there are feet sticking out of it."

"What do you mean: feet?"

"Don't you know what feet are? What you stand on,
of course. F-E-E-T: feet. A girl's feet, with shoes on.
These Chows were out fishing and they fished out this
bag and there's a body in it, and I've got the Chows
and the bag and the body here in the Customs shed
waiting for you. It weighs half a ton. Now will you
come?"

"I will; but if this is a joke, you'll be for it."

"Put a jerk in it, then. The *Niagara* will be in in an
hour and we'll have the wharf jammed with people."

The Inspector prided himself on being a man of action
when action was necessary. By 6.15 he was clad in khaki
shirt, khaki trousers, khaki sun-helmet and canvas shoes,
and was running towards his garage with his jacket half
on and half flying behind him. He drove to the Customs
shed at a speed which would have earned him the vigorous
censure of the District Inspector of Police, had he wit-
nessed it, rising and falling in his seat like a horseman
as he careered over the potholes of the waterfront road.
Yet, as he alighted from the car and stepped on to the
wharf, he was conscious of an exhilaration at the beauty
and freshness of the morning: the sheltered waters of the
harbour like a steel mirror, the mile-distant tumbling surf
like a dazzling white wall, the olive-green hills opposite,
a land of mystery.

The excited Cherry came running from the further
shed, his face white and his manner agitated. "It's not a
joke, Inspector," he kept repeating, as they strode along;

"it's not a joke. There's a girl in the sack, all right. She's dead all right. She's dead!"

"All right, old man," returned Spearpoint, half believing him. "Calm yourself. Who is it?"

"I don't know. You can only see her feet. But she's dead, all right. They fished her off the edge of the reef. It's not a joke this time."

Cherry spoke the truth. In the office of the landing waiter he indicated two silent Chinese and a knobbly sack. The Chinese were sitting calmly on a packing case, but they rose to their feet when the Inspector appeared, and remained standing in his presence. Ignoring them, Spearpoint made for the sack, which was large, bulging and dripping wet. From it protruded two human feet, wearing light feminine walking-shoes, with lumps of gravel still adhering to the insteps. The ankles were tied tightly together with cord which did not hide the ornamental ankle chains under the thin silk stockings. The mouth of the sack had been tied, but the knot had come partly undone, and the feet had apparently forced themselves through.

Spearpoint rubbed his chin and reflected what to do. Cherry, hovering anxiously in the background, was muttering:

"It's murder, all right, Inspector, it's murder. Who is it, do you think?"

"Is it murder?" thought Spearpoint. "I'd look a nice fool if I brought Dr. Halibut in to examine a dummy!" and he decided to satisfy himself that this was no hoax. He cut the string still loosely securing the mouth of the sack, bent, lifted the corners at the closed ends, and shook until the contents tumbled on to the floor. It was the trussed body of a plump girl, fully clad, with the knees drawn up to the chin, the arms doubled at the sides, and with a dirty nail-bag over the head. She had been tightly and efficiently bound, and she fell in a lump, on her back, rolling sideways, so that the Inspector found himself confronted with the generous curve of a pale blue, slightly muddied frock, which seemed familiar.

There was now little doubt that this was Inspector Spearpoint's first European murder case, but a natural curiosity impelled him to confirm the victim's identity. He cut the cord which fastened the nail-bag round the head, and, with some slight difficulty, peeled the bag off. The face was not a pretty sight; it had been slashed several times with a sharp instrument, but the cuts, although deep, had not bled much. The hair, which was black, had been hacked short, and the ends stuck out dishevelled and matted. Nevertheless, recognition was instantaneous. Death had paled the even tawniness of her complexion and glazed the almost irresistible lure of her dark eyes; the instrument of death had ravaged her shapely features and pillaged the glory of her hair; but this was undoubtedly the corpse of Netta Maul, the most famous beauty of the South Pacific Islands.

Another fact was evident also: the murder was a crime of passion, the crime of one who hated her for her alluring beauty and her long, lustrous hair.

Even as he recognised the victim, Spearpoint felt himself sickening. Cherry, after one glance at the ghastly face, ran headlong from the shed. Doubtless he had often desired to kiss those dead lips, to clasp that voluptuous body in his arms, to hold the scornful queen at his pleasure; probably he had not achieved more than the desire. Here she was, helpless and fallen; and his emotion was horror. The Chinese burst into their own cluttering language, but their faces betrayed nothing of their feelings.

Spearpoint took control of himself, considered a moment, and then went to the door and called unsympathetically to Cherry, who was sprawling at the edge of the wharf, with his head over the water: "Must you have this shed to-day?"

Between his spasms the retired practical-joker intimated that its use was imperative: the *Niagara*, from Honolulu, might be sighted at any minute. He implored the Inspector, with irrelevant emphasis, to have the corpse removed without delay.

Spearpoint returned to the office and addressed the Chinese in Fijian, asking what time they had found the body. One shrugged his shoulders and grinned; the other answered in a jargon which Spearpoint found incomprehensible until he realised that the man was trying to speak English. Even then, the reply seemed so involved that Spearpoint decided to wait for the interpreter to prepare a report, and asked, again in Fijian, for help in putting the body back in the bag.

Both grinned at this, and the linguist said, "Me helpee," and picked up the sack. Spearpoint replaced the nail-bag on the head of the corpse, pushed the body head first into the sack, and retied the mouth, leaving the feet sticking out much as he had found them. He felt more comfortable when that face was hidden, and even as he was deciding on his course of action, he began to wonder what had happened to Netta Maul's famous tresses. Her silver bracelets were still on her arms, her silver rings on her fingers, her silver chains on her ankles; only her silver comb appeared to be missing. It would appear that the murderer had not plundered as well as mutilated his victim.

He sent the Chinese to place the sack in his car and to get in themselves, and then turned to Cherry, who had almost recovered his composure, but was still white-faced and unnaturally meek. "Does anyone know of this, except you and the Chows?"

"No."

"Well, keep your mouth shut about it for the present. When the news gets all over the town, you can tell 'em what was really done. But keep it under your hat for a few hours. You'd better write out a statement of all you know about the finding of the—the sack. I'll send a boy down for it presently."

Ten minutes later, the half-caste corpse was locked in a cell at the Police Station, the Chinese were waiting in the orderly-room to make a statement to the interpreter, six sturdy Fijian constables in their blue serge tunics and white Vandyke-edged sulus, were marching in double column up Waimanu Road to take possession of the paddock behind the house of the Montgomery Thomspons, Sub-Inspector Sharpe was being routed out of bed by his Indian cook-boy, and Inspector Spearpoint was speeding along Victoria Parade to the Royal Palm Hotel, with two callow, bearded Punjabi policemen in the back seat. The Inspector had a brief interview with the landlord, took possession of his (secret) duplicate key to Netta Maul's room, satisfied himself that her bed had not been slept in, that her room was superficially in order, and that her famous collection of silverware was, at least largely, intact, and slammed the door, leaving a constable locked inside with strict instructions to touch nothing, but to remain hidden until he was relieved. The second constable was stationed to keep watch on Netta Maul's shop, which had only one entrance and that locked.

At four minutes to seven Inspector Spearpoint was flat on the back on his front verandah, the knees bent, the soles of the feet on the floor and about twelve inches apart, and the heels close to the buttocks. He had determined to give this system, as every other system he had tried, three months, and not even murder could prevent his daily indulgence.

CHAPTER THREE

THE STOLEN CAR

(Friday: 7.20-8.40 a.m.)

AT TWENTY PAST seven Inspector Spearpoint stood
in slippers and pyjama trousers in his bathroom, rubbing
lather into his chin and wondering whether he ought
to discuss with his wife the quality of the eggs that Indian
was supplying nowadays. He had already decided that
his first job, after reporting the murder, should be to
interview the men he had seen during his drive the
previous evening, and until he had heard their evidence
he refused to speculate on the identity of the murderer.
The telephone bell distracted him and he waited grimly
for the pattering bare feet of the Indian, who had twice
lately failed to answer before the second ring.

This time he did not delay; Inspector Spearpoint's
houseboys rarely did delay thrice. The boy returned
along the back verandah and knocked at the bathroom
door, calling, "Sahib!"

Spearpoint opened the door, saying, "Yes?"

"Mrs. Montgomery Thomspon on the telephone, sahib."

"What's she want?"

"She not say, sahib. She say she want to speak to the
acting D.I., sahib."

"Tell her I'll call her presently."

"She is holding the line, sahib. She say it is urgent."

"Tell her she must bloody well wait—but not in those
words, you blockhead."

"Yes, sahib."

In a minute the boy was back at the bathroom door.
Inspector Spearpoint had shaved his right cheek, and
glared round ferociously.

"Mrs. Montgomery Thomspon say, sahib, that she must speak to you at once, sahib. It is very urgent, she say, sahib."

"Did you tell her to go to the devil?"

"I told her you were engaged, sahib."

"And what did she say?" enquired the Inspector, carefully drawing the blade up the throat to the point of the chin.

"She say I must wake you up, sahib."

"The devil she did! And what did you say to that?"

"I said the D.I. was in the lavatory, sahib—shaving, sahib."

"You blithering fool! What the hell did you want to say that for? Go and hang up the receiver, you silly ass. . . . Why can't she give a message, like a Christian?" Spearpoint grumbled, as he wiped his face, and strolled along to the instrument.

He picked up the receiver and smiled as he heard the efforts of Mrs. Montgomery Thomspon to recall the exchange and to complain of having been cut off. After appeasing his ruffled senses for half a minute with the music of her impatience, he said, "Hallo!"

"Hallo! Hallo!" A change in her tone showed that she recognised his voice; and she seized the opportunity to ruffle his dignity. "What is the matter with this line? I want to speak to the acting D.I."

"This is the D.I. speaking. Who are you?"

"Oh, is that you, Mr. Spearpoint? I thought it was that stupid boy of yours again."

"This is the D.I. speaking. Who are you?"

"Oh, Mr. Spearpoint, I am so sorry to have to rout you out of bed, but my husband wants to get off to the office——"

"Who is your husband, madam?"

"Don't be ridiculous, Mr. Spearpoint! You know perfectly well who I am!"

"I beg your pardon, madam, but all the people whose

telephone voices I am acquainted with are well aware
that I was confirmed in the position of District Inspector
almost two years ago. Perhaps if you will tell me who
you are——"

But Mrs. Montgomery Thomspon had no intention
either of conceding his proper title or of announcing her
identity. It is doubtful whether she heard his speech as
she was simultaneously delivering one of her own: "If
the police did their job properly instead of lounging in
bed half the morning, respectable citizens might perhaps
be able to get to work at a reasonable hour. The in-
efficiency of the Suva police force is notorious. I wonder
the Governor stands for it. I wouldn't! My husband is
going into town by taxi and he will send the bill to you
personally."

They paused, the Inspector because he saw no sense
in speaking without an audience and the lady because,
having uttered half as many words again as he had, she
was slightly out of breath. She resumed first, however,
demanding peremptorily, "Now, will you look into the
matter at once?"

"What matter?"

"Why, our car, of course."

"What's the matter with the car?" But, even as he
asked, he remembered the circumstances in which he
had seen it the previous night.

"If you would only listen, I would tell you. It's been
stolen."

"Well, it can't be far away," he pointed out; this was
before the coastal roads were constructed, and there were
few car roads on the Suva side of Viti Levu. "If you'll
tell me its registration number, I'll have a search made.
You'll probably get it back to-day. Where did you
leave it?"

"I didn't leave it anywhere," retorted Mrs. Montgomery
Thomspon, accepting the obvious question as an implica-
tion that she was the sort of absent-minded person who

left motor-cars lying about. "My husband parked it in the cul-de-sac beside our house last night, and now it has gone. Will you kindly see that it is returned immediately."

"What time did your husband park it?"

"Shortly after 11.15."

"Are you quite sure of that time?"

"Of course I am."

"Did you yourself see it there after 11.15?"

"Of course I did not, you silly man! Do you think I go walking about the garden at midnight to see that my husband has parked the car properly?"

"I wouldn't put it past you," thought the Inspector. He said, as he scribbled a note for his assistant, "You haven't told me yet who you are, or what the number of your car is."

But she was not to be drawn; and answered, "You know my car well enough. Now, hurry up and send it back. I expect some of your so-called policemen have been having a joy-ride. And, remember, I shall hold you personally responsible for any damage."

"I will attend to the matter," he capitulated, and rang off. He sent the houseboy across the garden to the Police Station with the memo, and went to dress.

Normally, Spearpoint shaved and dressed before breakfast, and afterwards, sat on the verandah, smoking and reading overseas newspapers until the stroke of eight called him across the garden to his office. But to-day was decidedly abnormal. He had eaten unshaven; and he sacrificed his digestive smoke in favour of hurried visits to the Chief Police Magistrate, the Inspector-General of Constabulary, and the Colonial Secretary.

Arriving at his desk some ten minutes late, he observed fretfully that Sub-Inspector Sharpe had not yet appeared. He glanced hurriedly over the routine matters arranged for his inspection, telephoned to Dr. Halibut, and, finding him out, left a message asking for him to visit the Police

Station as soon as possible, and sent for Sub-Inspector Clubb, to whom he handed over all his own duties and the duties of Sharpe until further notice. Then he dismissed daily routine from his mind and settled down methodically to write what he could remember of the sequence of events on his drive down Waimanu Road the previous evening.

He had barely written, in column form, the names of the Europeans he had seen, when his assistant entered. Sub-Inspector Sharpe was the second tallest white man in Suva, a freckled-faced youth, with a downy moustache which was not yet so much as promising, and high eyebrows which gave him an air of perpetual wonder, as if he was astonished to find himself so dignified a person as a policeman. So pronounced was his air of surprise that those who met him for the first time when he still lived in his native London, judged him to be born for the position of poster-writer for an evening paper. He treated Spearpoint with a mixture of deference and impudence which none of the other subs would have dared to assume, and Spearpoint, after a doubtful first month, had decided that he liked it.

In answer to his superior's scarcely polite nod, Sharpe reported respectfully, "I've just brought along Montgomery Thompson's car, sir. It was abandoned in the timberyard by the creek. Singh gave me your note about it, sir. Shall I take it along to Thompson's office?"

"No; don't let him have it yet. We'd better be careful about that car. Let's have a look at it." Busy as he was, Spearpoint could not resist the temptation to take a close personal interest in any crime that concerned Mrs. Montgomery Thompson.

They walked into the courtyard and inspected the car together. On the back seat they found a cheap electric torch, pillar shape, and an almost new lipstick in a good white-metal holder. On the floor under the driver's seat was a black tin trouser button. Spearpoint impounded these articles, deeming them more likely to be relics of the borrower than of the owner. They saw nothing remarkable about the car until they came to examine the steering wheel for fingermarks. There were no marks on the wheel at all.

"That's extraordinary," exclaimed Spearpoint, "whoever borrowed this car not only wore gloves, but he wiped off all the other fingermarks. Now who in this town would so much as possess a pair of gloves, let alone wear them?"

"I put on gloves to drive the car here, sir," said Sharpe. Gloves were a part of his ceremonial uniform, which had not been designed by one who had any consideration for the comfort of a man living in the Tropics. "You know, I always do when a car is stolen. There would be rubber gloves in the power house, sir——"

"Yes, of course, I know that. But people in Fiji don't go about carrying gloves. It looks as if whoever took this car went out intending to take a car. We ought to try and catch him. There's been too much of this car-conversion lately. Find out if any of our men saw the car in town late last night. Let's see if we can find any fingermarks anywhere."

On the inside handle of the offside rear door was a perfect set over which Sharpe (who was the Suva police force's fingerprint expert) was jubilant. On the outside handle of the same door were fainter, less complete marks.

"They'd both be a man's, sir. That's a good set. We might be able to trace him. But all these little bits of marks on the fittings in the back seat, they're hopeless. Besides, they probably belong to the family."

Spearpoint brightened at the idea of forcibly taking Mrs. Montgomery Thomspon's fingerprints in order to compare them with the marks in the car, but regretfully abandoned the project, and said, "These marks on the handle suggest that he didn't wear gloves, but that he wiped the wheel carefully afterwards. Funny he forgot these handles. Or perhaps these were made by someone else, earlier, and the thief never touched the back door. Anyway, we'll find that out later. Whoever made these prints on the inside was inside when he made them; I suppose one set was made getting in and one set getting out. Probably not the chap who drove the car. Well, get up these prints and photograph them. Measure the petrol. Tell old Thomspon we've found his car. Ask him how much petrol was in the tank. He won't know, but ask him. And give him back the car. And hurry up; we've got a busy day in front of us."

He turned to go back to his office, and then wheeled round as an idea struck him.

"By George! Sharpe," he exclaimed, "we must be careful about this car. It may have something to do with the murder."

"Did you say 'murder,' sir?" enquired Sharpe, shocked.

"Oh, of course, I haven't told you yet. Netta Maul's been murdered."

"M-m-m-murdered?" stammered the Sub-Inspector, whose experience of crime had so far been limited to petty theft, unpaid dog-licences and slovenly hand signalling by automobile drivers. As the news sunk into his consciousness, his eyebrows seemed to go higher, and he looked more like a poster-writer than ever. The fingers of his right hand twitched like those of a man burning to scrawl in six-inch letters the catchpenny words: 'Netta Maul Sensation.' Then he recovered himself and added with an air of nonchalance, "Netta Maul, eh? Properly this time? Good business!"

"No friend of yours, eh?"

"Rather not, sir. Who did it?"

"You won't be the last idiot who'll be asking that, my lad," replied Spearpoint, tartly. "It's our job to find out. Now, listen. She was fished out of the harbour, over by the reef, early this morning, by a couple of Chinese fishermen. She was doubled up and trussed, with her arms at her sides and her knees up to her chin. She was in a sack, with a nail-bag over her head; her throat had been cut and her face slashed and her hair cut off. She still had her bangles and her anklets, so she was killed in passion and not for robbery."

"Blimey!" muttered the Sub-Inspector; and, then, recovering himself, he added, "Nice work."

"Now I saw her about a quarter to ten last night, near the hospital, walking down Waimanu Road. I drove past her. Incidentally, Jim Camelback passed me just before, and must have passed her, too. We were all going the same way——"

"—Home," interpolated Sharpe, impulsively.

Spearpoint glared at him and continued, "Camelback pulled up outside Dr. Halibut's house; he may have been waiting for her. At exactly one minute to ten I was in my car outside Montgomery Thomspon's house, and I heard a scream from that direction. Yes, and directly after that, this car of Thomspon's was driven up Waimanu Road at a hell of a lick."

"But if she screamed like that when Jim Camelback cut her throat," objected Sharpe, "Conky Thomspon would have arrived too late to add his quota to the good work. Or do you think it was Conky who cut her hair? I think he'd make a rotten barber."

"I don't think at all," responded Spearpoint impulsively.

Even the irrepressible Sharpe dared not rejoin to that, and Spearpoint hastily amended, "I mean, I don't theorise on slender knowledge. I wait for facts. I've told you all the facts I know at present. Camelback may have had nothing to do with the matter. This car may have had nothing to do with the matter—and, by the way, it was not necessarily Thomspon driving. I saw the car, not the driver. It wasn't Mrs. Montgomery Thomspon, either, because I'd seen her at her own front door not more than a minute earlier. What else is there? The only other Europeans I saw were Bellamy—the clerk in Marryam & Cutt's, not the P.W.D. Bellamy—who was following her down Waimanu Road, and Pencarbon, who started to walk across the paddock from the cul-de-sac a few minutes before the scream."

"That's four suspects," responded Sharpe; "four already. Camelback—Conky Thomspon—Bellamy—and Pencarbon. I give you two to one on Camelback."

"Exactly where was this car when you found it?" asked Spearpoint, ignoring him. "Drive me back—in my car;" and, leaving a unit from his unlimited supply of Indian constables in charge of the stolen car, he and his assistant bustled along Renwick Road to the timberyard by Naboukulau Creek. Here Sharpe indicated, so far as he could remember, the position of the car when he had found it; and Spearpoint drew this in his notebook, showing it in relation to the uprights of the wooden embankment which projected above ground level. Meanwhile, Sharpe, idly eyeing the fishermen's rowing boats moored on the other side of the creek, had an idea. "Suppose, sir, the—the body," he suggested, using the word with relish, "was brought here in Conky's car. Then it could have been dumped in one of those boats, and rowed silently out to sea at dead of night, as it were, and tipped overboard."

Spearpoint considered this, and agreed to send a sergeant to enquire whether any of the boats had been tampered with. As they drove back to the Station, Sharpe speculated, "Looks to me like a plot between Jim Camelback and Conky Thomspon. Camelback struck the foul blow, and Conky delivered the goods."

"It's too early to theorise," warned Spearpoint, "we must gather our facts first."

"Interrogate the Big Four, eh? I've a good mind to make a book on it. Two to one on Camelback: I saw her talking to him near the Rewa Hotel last week. Four to one, Pencarbon: he's what they call a dag, where he comes from; he might easily murder her for fun. Ten to one, Conky: he wouldn't murder a flying-cockroach.

Twenty to one, Bellamy: he's a quiet one, he is; I'd be safe on twenty to one, Bellamy. What do you say, sir? Who's your fancy? If you don't speculate, you can't——"

Spearpoint came out of his reverie to say, "We'd better make a more careful examination of the car. But first we'll have a look at the sack, to see whether there are any traces of it in the car."

They alighted; he despatched an Indian sergeant to interview the boatowners, and then led the way across the yard to the cell where the corpse had been deposited, warning Sharpe, as he unlocked and threw open the door, "Come in, and close the door. We don't want too many prying eyes.—She's a nasty mess, you know, my lad."

"She always was," grinned Sharpe, a little unnaturally, his gaiety becoming sobered at the prospect of the actual sight of bloody murder. Spearpoint was quite unimpressed by his proximity to the gruesome corpse, being over-whelmingly conscious that he was faced with the most important problem of his career, but he realised that his assistant might have an attack of nerves if he was not kept actively employed, so he said, "Take the sack by the top corners and lift it, and shake her out. She's darned heavy—about eleven stone, I reckon."

"These half-castes always get bloody fat, in the end," grinned Sharpe, with affected indifference, as he bent down, grasped the top corners of the sack firmly, and heaved them up with a tremendous jerk. Netta Maul tumbled out on to the concrete floor with a thump, and rolled over into the corner.

"Steady on," admonished Spearpoint, too late. "I didn't tell you to chuck her about and bruise the body. Come out of here now. We'll have a look at her later. The sack's the thing." He relocked the door, and held up the sack in the strong sunlight of the courtyard. It was a flour bag, apparently standard in size, in good condition, but long disused.

"This bag was inside out," he said, turning it round and examining it carefully; "yet there's not a trace of flour on it."

"Salt water would wash it all off, sir," suggested Sharpe, diffidently.

"Probably. What's this stain? That's not seawater. Looks like oil to me; and this is earth." He pointed to a cranny by the seam. "It's a long time since this held flour." He began to turn it inside out, and as his hand grasped the bottom he felt something metallic. Eagerly he completed the reversal and brought to light Netta Maul's silver head-comb, bent, almost snapped in two, and entangled in some partly-detached fibres.

There was nothing else in the bag, but the brand was now visible. It was that of a famous Australian firm of millers. Above, in cruder and less distinct letters, appeared the mark, 'M & C,' which the policemen assumed stood for Marryam & Cutt, Ltd., one of the leading companies of general merchants in Fiji, and the importers of that brand of flour.

"Bellamy works for Marryam & Cutt," Sharpe pointed out, unnecessarily.

"But he's hardly likely to buy sacks of flour from them," Spearpoint retorted. "Let's see if we can connect this sack with the car."

They opened the side doors and peered in, offering excellent opportunities for any daring and sportive Fijian constables who might desire to catch their officers bending.

"Look here, sir, this is earth!" exclaimed Sharpe, excitedly, pointing to a few dark crumbs on the floor.

"Oh, well," answered Spearpoint composedly, "it's common enough to find bits of earth on the floor of a car. But these are shreds of sacking, I think." He pulled three or four threads of dirty fibre from a slightly-protruding screw that helped to secure the back floor-covering.

"You'd better bring up and photograph every finger-print you can find," he ordered, when their search failed to reveal anything else. "Go over this car with a fine tooth-comb."

"Sorry, sir, I've lost my tooth-comb. Would a fine tooth-pick do?"

Spearpoint glared at his assistant. "Don't rot! This is your big chance to make some use of the knowledge you're supposed to have of fingerprints. Get everything there is in this car. If it's just a car-conversion case, the prints may help, especially if they're Indians. If the car was used for a murder, the prints won't help, because whoever it was remembered to wipe the wheel. Now, that wiped wheel ought to tell us something. I suggest it shows that whoever took the car and whatever his purpose was, it was not an Indian. Although all Indians, whether they can read and write or not, know quite well that finger-prints are certain means of identification, I doubt if any of them realise that smooth surfaces retain their prints, and that the prints can be dusted up and photographed and studied. They're too familiar with the inky rubber-stamp pad to realise that fingerprints can be taken any other way."

"Some of our Indian bobbies know, sir; but I don't suppose they'd split."

"Well, take all the prints, anyway. I'll get on to Thomspon, and find out what he knows. It won't be much, but we'll have to make the best of it. Come in as soon as you've taken the photographs. I'll just measure this petrol."

CHAPTER FOUR

MONTGOMERY THOMSPON, THE FURTIVE MAN

(Friday : 8.40–9.15 a.m.)

WHEN INSPECTOR SPEARPOINT returned to his office, he was informed that Dr. Halibut had telephoned to say he could not reach the Police Station before a quarter past nine, so he asked the exchange for Mr. Montgomery Thomspon and told that ornament of the legal profession that his car had been recovered and that a personal interview with the District Inspector would be useful for securing the apprehension of the thief.

Then he completed his records of the previous night's drive, adding, so far as he could remember or calculate them, the exact times at which each person he saw would have arrived at each point on his presumed route. He puzzled over the unusual fact of Netta Maul being on foot near the hospital, at the opposite end of the town from her hotel and the places of amusement; and headed a list of matters to be enquired into with: "What were N. M.'s movements prior to my seeing her?"

When inspiration failed, he turned to examining the button, the torch and the lipstick, but was unable to arrive at any conclusions concerning them save the obvious ones that the button was probably a trouser button, the torch cheap and of a kind commonly used in Fiji, and the lipstick both new and fairly expensive. The button and the torch might have belonged to the same person, for the torch suggested an owner who was either poor or economical; but the lipstick implied wealth or extravagance. It might have been Netta Maul's lipstick; for, although her tobacconist's shop was expensively run and not particularly remunerative, her admirers had notoriously found it pleasant (or at least expedient) to make her handsome presents at frequent intervals. The button, however, could not have been hers; nor could it have fallen from any white man except an artisan in his working clothes. An artisan would be wearing white in the evening. No one wearing trousers of a kind likely to harbour a cheap tin button would be likely to sit at the driving wheel of Mr. Montgomery Thomspon's car—except an Indian garage attendant. The button might be a relic of a recent overhaul, and unconnected with the theft or the murder. Whoever it was who had driven the car up Waimanu Road last night, he was not the owner of the button; Spearpoint was certain that the driver was in white. For residents of Fiji a torch is as essential a possession as an umbrella. Outside of Suva, street lighting does not exist and the roads are not smoothly surfaced. Ruts and puddles obstruct the walker. Even in the capital there are pavements only in the two business streets. Those whose walking will take them off the tarmac carry a torch at night; Pencarbon, for example, had brought one to light his route across the tussocky paddock. The fibres appeared to have come from the sack—at least, they came from a similar flour bag; and the murderer's sack was torn in places.

Sharpe entered to report that he had taken his photographs and to ask whether he should develop and print them.

"Wait a bit," advised Spearpoint. "There'll be more before we've finished. Wait and listen to what our visitor has to say. He was in conference, or so he said. But once he starts he'll run all the way here."

Sharpe laughed at his chief's humour, and asked, "Will you offer a reward, sir?"

"Not at this stage. I fancy we can get all the information we want to-day without paying for it."

"No, sir, I didn't mean that. I mean, shall we give a reward to the man who did it—rid the Colony of Netta

Maul? Most public-spirited act since the Mayor put in the electric-lighting plant."

"The only reward he'll get," returned Spearpoint, grimly, "is hanging, whatever he may deserve. We may not think she was much loss; but it's our job to catch the fellow and hand him over to the judge. That's our job, Sharpe. Mai!" The last was a command in answer to a thump on the door. A Fijian orderly put his fuzzy head into the room and announced, "Misser Montgomery Thompson, sir!"; and, then, at the D.I.'s nod, he opened the door fully and ushered in the husband of Suva's most formidable matron.

Mr. Montgomery Thompson was five foot three inches tall, and thin; he had a weak, straggly moustache, a weak, indecisive chin, weak blue eyes, and thin mouse-coloured hair. His one strong feature was a Roman nose of more than ordinary proportions, a nose which had caused him to be known throughout Fiji for thirty years past as 'Conky' Thompson. Despite his considerable wealth, derived partly from well-considered speculation and partly from inherited Australian company shares, and hardly at all from his solicitor's practice in Suva (which was ostensibly his only interest in life), he was a nervous and shamefaced little man, without authority in appearance or confidence in manner. He habitually dressed according to Mrs. Montgomery Thompson's taste in well-cut cream gaberdine trousers and an expensive brown blazer with rolled gold buttons. He changed his silk shirt for a clean one three times a day. Yet he always contrived to appear ill-dressed, and his bow-tie was surpassed for slovenliness only by that of the redoubtable Mr. Cutt, the managing director of Marryam & Cutt, Ltd.

Mr. Montgomery Thompson sidled in with an unhappy air and perched on the extreme edge of the chair Spearpoint indicated. His manner was nearer that of the Indian kitchen-boy charged with breaking and entering than that of the leading citizen calling to recover stolen property.

"We have a theory about your car, Mr. Thomspon," began Spearpoint, using the plural in the royal or editorial sense to mean himself, rather than himself and his assistant. "And it would help if you could come with us, and show us exactly where you left the car last night."

"Certainly. Certainly," murmured Mr. Thomspon. "I—er—I——" and he lapsed into silence. Spearpoint wondered whether he had forgotten what he had to say, or whether he had decided that it was not worth saying.

"First, though," continued the D.I., taking up his pen, "perhaps you wouldn't mind answering a few questions? What time did you last see the car?"

"Oh—er—fairly late—well, no, not so late as that. Say, eleven last night."

"We thought it was nearer 11.30," suggested Spearpoint, at random, sensing from the wretched man's manner that he could have answered more precisely had he cared.

"Well, as a matter of fact, it was about 11.30, now I come to think of it."

"We presume you came home about that time and ran the car into the unmade road beside your house, and left it there?"

"Er—yes."

"Did you come home alone?"

Thompson hesitated, and then plunged, "Well—er—yes."

"Was there anyone else about? Anyone see you park the car?"

"I didn't see anyone at all." For the first time, the answer was clear and decided, but the little man continued to look uneasy, and his glance roved around the room and rarely found the faces of the two policemen.

"Did you cover the bonnet at all?"

"Cover the bonnet? Why, no."

"We found this sack in the car—at least, we found it in circumstances which made us connect it with the car. Recognise it?" Sharpe, at a gesture from his superior, displayed the sack. Montgomery Thomspon's weak eyes studied it for a minute; then he mumbled, "No, it's just a sack. I've got a tarpaulin, anyway. It was a fine night. What would I want to use a sack for?"

"There were a few other things found in the car," continued Spearpoint. "This button. I suppose that's yours?"

"That's a black button," returned Thomspon, with some show of interest. "That can't be mine. All my buttons are white." He made a gesture as if about to prove that all his trouser buttons were white, but the Inspector waved his purpose aside.

"No, I expect it came from the fellow who stole your car."

"Looks like an Indian," suggested the lawyer, sagely. "A lot of the Indians wear black buttons on their trousers. All the white men wear white buttons. Only the blacks wear black buttons."

"That's reasonable, isn't it, sir?" broke in Sharpe; "white men, white buttons: black men, black buttons." Then he added, sorrowfully, "All my buttons are khaki."

Spearpoint ignored him, and asked, "Was the car overhauled recently? Could there have been a mechanic at the wheel yesterday?"

"No; it had not been to the garage for some weeks. It was an Indian that took the car, all right."

Spearpoint grunted, and holding up the torch, asked, "Yours?"

"Certainly not," answered Mr. Thompson, almost with indignation. "That's an Indian's torch, that is. I have a torch, certainly—but mine's a powerful torch, not like that thing."

"And I suppose you don't claim this, either?" and Spearpoint held up the lipstick.

The little man eyed it with hesitation, and then asked, "What is it? A thermometer? A silver pencil? Not mine, definitely."

"It's a lipstick."

"A—a—a lipstick?" Mr. Montgomery Thomspon's voice died away, and his face changed colour. "I suppose you don't recognise it?" asked Spearpoint, unemotionally, placing it back on the desk.

"Er—no; it's not mine," returned Thomspon, slowly. Then he added, firmly, "Definitely."

"You—er—don't use——" began Sharpe, mischievously; but Spearpoint's glance silenced him.

"May be Mrs. Montgomery Thomspon's," suggested Spearpoint.

The little man looked up in alarm and shook his head violently. "No! No!" he exclaimed. "Not my wife's. Definitely. It is certainly not hers. It's no use asking her. She—she doesn't use lipstick."

It was an obvious lie, but Spearpoint let it pass, and asked how much petrol had been in the tank when the car had been left last night.

"There was exactly two gallons." This correct answer came promptly and a little defiantly.

Spearpoint thought it curious that Thomspon should appear to resent the question, and enquired smoothly, "You measured it, I suppose, before turning in?"

"Well—er—yes, as a matter of fact I did." This came with reluctance, and with no offer to explain why it had been measured. But, as Spearpoint continued to wait, he went on, "I'm keeping records of the performance of the two brands of benzine. Er—I check every night. Last night there was exactly two gallons."

"That's curious. There are two gallons there still. Sharpe drove the car from the timberyard by the creek to the Police Station, about a quarter of a mile. That wouldn't use much. It looks as if the car was driven only from your house to the creek—about half a mile. Did you hear anyone start it up in the night?"

"No. Nor did my wife. Definitely."

"Were you asleep soon after you went in?"

"We were both asleep by a little after twelve,—er—more or less. My wife is a very sound sleeper. But I am a poor sleeper. The bedroom is on that side of the house, and I confess I cannot understand how the car was removed without my hearing it."

"You heard nothing?"

"Nothing at all. Well, the usual sounds, you know. Occasional cars passed. But not my own car being started."

Spearpoint considered, fidgeting with the lipstick. Thomspon watched him anxiously, following his movements. It almost seemed as if the little man knew more about the removal of his car than he dared admit. When the Inspector looked squarely at him, Thomspon turned hastily away.

"It's a bit of a puzzle," said Spearpoint, at length, reflectively; "but there's one fact we do know——" He made a further unavailing effort to catch the little man's eye. "There was a girl in your car last night."

"N-no, there wasn't, I assure you," squeaked Thomspon. Then he clinched the denial with, "Definitely."

"And we have good reason to believe," continued Spearpoint, ignoring him, "that it was Netta Maul."

Mr. Montgomery Thomspon stood up in great agitation. He took two steps towards the D.I., turned and looked at Sharpe, who met his gaze unwinking, and then clasped his hands together, and unclasped them, licked his lips, leant over the Inspector's desk, and gasped, huskily, "No—no—no, I assure you. She was not with me last night. Definitely. I don't know where she was last night. I didn't see her last night. Definitely." Then the words came in a torrent. "Just because she has been seen in my car once or twice—I don't see how anyone could have seen her more than twice, at the most—you think she was there last night, but she was not, not last night. If that lipstick is hers, then she did not leave it there when I was there. She may have put it in after I had gone to bed. Yes, she might easily have done that. But

I swear to you I did not see her last night. Definitely."
He paused, then added fiercely, "Does she say she was
with me last night?"

"No. She doesn't say it, and we don't say it, either.
We only say she was in your car when it was driven down
Waimanu Road."

"She was seen? Then the driver was seen? She was
with an Indian?" The change in Thomspon was tremendous. He was excited and almost hysterical.

"Now, look here," remonstrated Spearpoint, "sit down
and be reasonable. What is there to shout about? Anyone
would think you were being accused of something. The
position is that your car was stolen last night, and we
are trying to find who stole it. Now, we know that Netta
Maul was concerned in the affair, but we don't know
how. I suppose she would know where you park the car
over night? Everyone in Suva knows, of course. We know.
By the way, I suppose it was right up the cul-de-sac, as
usual?"

"No, it wasn't. It was only just beyond the line of the
fence,—just far enough not to obstruct the roadway."

"Netta Maul would know where you park the car?"
Spearpoint asked again.

"How should I know what she knows?" retorted
Thompson, rather warmly—for him.

"Well, you've given her lifts, on occasion, you know,"
suggested Spearpoint, and continued, confidentially, "You
know, we don't go about the place with our eyes shut.
We see a lot of things that are no actual official business
of ours, and we keep them to ourselves, of course; but we
do know what goes on. We have reason to believe, for
example, that you have sometimes gone out for an hour
or so in the evening, and found Netta Maul in your car
up the cul-de-sac, and sat there with her, quietly, without
anyone in the house knowing anything about it. That's
true, isn't it?"

"If you know it," said Thomspon, wildly, "there's no

need for me to tell you whether it's true or not. I'm not in the witness-box, anyway."

"Still, it is important. You were out for a while last night, weren't you?"

"Yes, but not up the cul-de-sac. I was at the Club."

"How long were you at the Club?"

"All the evening. But I don't see what this has got to do with my car."

"You'll see presently. Can you tell us precisely during what hours you were at the Club?"

"Between eight and eleven."

"And you were there all the time? You didn't leave the place at all between eight and eleven?"

"No. I was playing bridge."

"All the time?"

"All the time. But I don't see——"

"And between eleven and eleven-thirty? It wouldn't take you half an hour to get home from the Club?"

"I don't see why you should question me so closely," protested Thomspon, weakly. "I didn't steal my own car."

"No, but it's important to trace your movements last night. I suppose Mrs. Thomspon could vouch for your arriving home at 11.30?"

"Yes, she can. It was exactly 11.30, if you want to know." (Evidently, thought Spearpoint, Mrs. Montgomery Thompson had commented on the time.)

"And you did not see Netta Maul between 11 and 11.30?"

"Definitely not. I've told you once that I didn't see the girl last night."

"Will you tell us when you did see her, then?"

"I have not spoken to her for a week or more."

"But when did you last see her? Did you see her yesterday at all?"

"Not yesterday. I saw her—in the street—a couple of days ago. I did not see her last night. Definitely. Why do you question me so closely about the girl?"

"I saw her myself at a quarter to ten last night," explained Spearpoint, slowly. "I saw her again at half past six this morning. Between those hours she had been murdered."

Thomspon jumped to his feet again. "Did you say murdered?" he screamed, his voice soaring and cracking on the last word. "Murdered? Then she's dead! Thank God for that!" His manner was one of genuine surprise and relief, and he had never been suspected of ability as an actor. "When did this happen? Who did it?"

"It must have happened last night," answered Spearpoint. "We don't know who did it. Her body was found in this sack."

Mr. Montgomery Thomspon gazed at the sack in stupefaction, while the policemen waited for what he would say. Presently, he put out his hand and fingered it, touching it with fascinated reluctance, as if it were itself a corpse. Then he looked up, and made the obvious remark, "Why, it's wet. How did it get wet?"

"We thought perhaps you could tell us that," responded Spearpoint, blandly.

"I? How could I tell you? You're not accusing me——?" He shrank back in the chair, and seemed to shrivel, so terrified was he.

Spearpoint smiled. Although he despised the wretch, he had for him (without realising it) something of the sympathy which Mrs. Montgomery Thomspon professed for Mrs. Spearpoint. "Why, of course not, Mr. Thomspon. We wouldn't expect to find you doing a thing like that. But you know from your professional work that people do the most uncharacteristic things at times; and as there are fibres from this sack on the floor of your car, it seems probable that your car was used to transport the body; and as she was last seen alive near your house, and you have some sort of secret association with her, and you are so reluctant to explain your movements last night, we thought you might be able to tell us something about the matter. At least, perhaps you will now see the wisdom of letting us know exactly what your movements were last evening, and exactly where your car was."

The little man thought over this, and then objected, "Anyone might have taken the car."

"Quite. But we must prove that someone did. You don't think we're going to publish your statement in the *Fiji Times*, do you? You want to give the police all the help you can, don't you?"

"Well," began Thomspon, slowly. "I was playing bridge at the Club from eight until half-past ten."

"Half-past ten?" queried Spearpoint, sharply.

"Yes," he affirmed, and hurried on. "Then I came out——"

"But you said earlier you left the Club at eleven?"

"Well, between 10.30 and 11. It's difficult to remember the exact time. I got into the car——"

"Wait a minute, though. This half-hour is the important one. Are you certain that you were playing bridge at, say, ten o'clock?"

"I said so."

"I know you said so."

"Well, I was, then."

"And where was your car between, say, 9.45 and 10.30?"

"Why, outside the Club, of course."

"All the time?"

"Of course."

"You actually saw it there?"

"No, of course not. I was inside at bridge."

"Who were you playing with?"

"Cutt, Dummfish and Carnarvonshire."

Spearpoint made a note of the names. Dummfish was a young District Commissioner. Carnarvonshire was a doctor in private practice.

"You four were playing from eight until 10.30?"

"Yes, about that. Actually, Dr. Halibut was playing

for about an hour; then he dropped out and Dummfish took his place."

"Did Halibut stay in the Club?"

"He watched us for a while, and then went on to the verandah and sat there reading."

"Was he there when you left? Could he verify the time you left?"

"He might—in fact," continued the little man, unwarily, "he commented on the time the last rubber had taken, and asked if I'd had more luck with Dummfish than with him."

Spearpoint could not resist the temptation to diverge by asking, "Had you?"

"No, worse. It's no good playing against Cutt. He's a proper devil, whatever cards he has."

"So as Halibut commented on the time you left, he would know it exactly?"

"I suppose so," admitted Thomspon, helplessly.

"Half-past ten, in fact?"

"Well, as a matter of fact," conceded the little man, "it was a quarter past."

"Good," said Spearpoint, "now we're getting at the facts. You got into your car and drove——?"

"To the Point," was the reluctant admission. The drive to the tip of the peninsula to catch the breeze was a favourite one with Suva motorists, but they rarely went alone.

"Where you called on——?"

"No one."

"You went just for the drive?"

"Well, as a matter of fact," confessed the wretched fellow, explosively, "I took a girl with me."

"What, Netta Maul?" burst in Sharpe, excitedly.

Spearpoint glanced at him reprovingly, and he subsided; but his interposition was more effective than his superior's questioning, for Montgomery Thomspon replied, sulkily, "Well, if you must know, it was Bettina Bloggins, the little half-caste girl in——"

"Yes, we know her all right. Where did you pick her up?"

"Just beyond Holland Street."

"Practically outside the Club, in fact?"

"Well, it was beyond that Indian's hut on the corner of Holland Street," protested Montgomery Thomspon, quibbling over a hundred yards.

"Did you meet her by chance or by appointment?" pursued the Inspector.

"By chance, of course."

"But if you were beyond the Indian's house, you were going away from your home," Spearpoint pointed out.

"Well," conceded Thomspon, sulkily, "there was a chance she might be there."

"What time did she say she'd be there?"

"Ten o'clock."

"So you were about a quarter of an hour late?"

"Yes. I hesitated about going." He paused and went on hurriedly. "It was no pleasure—business. It's a hard job getting that sort of girl to give information."

Leaving this for a time, Spearpoint changed the subject promptly and asked, "When you got into your car at 10.15, was it in exactly the same place as you'd left it? Could anyone else have used it whilst you were in the Club?"

Thompson thought a moment, and then answered, "I didn't notice anything different. It seemed to be in the same place."

"Where was that?"

"Out in the road."

The Fiji Club grounds are on top of a twelve-foot cliff and the building is so far from the edge of the cliff that only the roof is visible from the road. Consequently, cars parked at the roadside are invisible from the Club. The main entrance faces a side road, which leads only to the Club, but there is another entrance at the top of a flight of steps leading up the cliff from the road. It was at the foot of these steps that Mr. Montgomery Thomspon had parked his car.

"Were there any other cars in the road?"

"Two or three."

"Did yours happen to be the last one? Or were there other cars both in front of and behind yours?"

"Mine was the first, just by the steps."

"Then," suggested the Inspector, "anyone who had wanted to borrow a car while you were in the Club would have been most likely to have taken yours; and could have done so without anyone in the Club knowing; and could have put it back without your noticing any-thing—provided it had been put back, as it was, by the time your game broke up, that is, by 10.15?"

Thomspon thought this out, and conceded that it was correct, adding, "It was 10.15 when I left the Club, exactly." He gave no indication of the reason for this decision to admit the exact time.

"And what time did you leave Bettina?"

"About a quarter past eleven."

"Whereabouts?"

"Along Victoria Parade—by Albert Park."

"Near her home," Spearpoint commented.

"Er—yes," Thomspon agreed.

"And then you came straight home, arriving at 11.30?"

"Yes."

"Stopping on the way to fill up the tank to just over two gallons?" asked Sharpe, suddenly.

Thompson darted a sulky glance at the young man and admitted that the surmise was correct. Spearpoint noted the times, which tallied closely enough with the route Thomspon must have taken, glanced at his wrist-watch, and stood up, saying, "Good. Later we'll get you to show us exactly where your car was, both when it was outside the Club and during the night. Take it now, of course; and you might examine it carefully and let us know whether it has been tampered with at all. I think that's about all the help you can give us at present."

Mr. Montgomery Thomspon accepted his dismissal with obvious relief and rose meekly to go, but at the door he turned, and said with hesitation, "Er—Inspector—you will, I hope, keep that to yourself—about my going to the Point, and so on?"

Spearpoint shrugged his shoulders. "Naturally, we can't promise that. It depends on whether your car was used by the murderer. But it won't come out unless it is necessary. We know much more about everybody in this town than we let on. We don't go blabbing all we know. We may have to ask you for a written statement; or you may have to give evidence.—On the other hand, we expect you to keep the news of the murder to yourself until, say, lunch time. It will be common knowledge by then."

"Oh, I will, Inspector, definitely." He half turned to go, and paused, with an unuttered question on his lips. Sharpe broke in with, "Which way was the car facing —outside the Club, I mean?"

Thomspon paused, and then replied, "Towards the steps."

"You're quite sure of that?"

"Definitely."

"Right-ho, then," and Thomspon went.

Sharpe shut the door behind him, and grimaced at his superior in criticism of the visitor. Spearpoint said, "That was a good point about the way the car was facing."

"Yes, sir; you see, what I thought was this: suppose he's telling the truth, and suppose he did leave the Club at 10.15. Of course, it's easy enough to verify that, so he's probably right about it. Then it was someone else you saw driving his car up Waimanu Road. Now, with the car facing that way, it would have been possible for anyone to jump in, drive forward down Hercules Street or Gordon Street to Victoria Parade, along Victoria

Parade and Renwick Road, up Waimanu Road, round
Browne Street, down Amy Street and round by Holland
Street back to the Club, leaving the car facing the same
way. How long would that take, sir?"

The route described would have taken the driver to
Dr. Halibut's house on the corner of Browne Street (the
point on it farthest from the Fiji Club) by way of the waterfront and the business part of the town, and brought him
back along the heights at the rear of the town; Holland
Street had no inhabitants, being a winding switchback
over the broken ground and filled-in gorge of the now petty
Naboukulau Creek.

"It would take about five minutes, I suppose, at the
rate he was going," answered Spearpoint, "allowing for
all the corners. Normally, something over ten. But can
you tell me why anyone but a bloody fool would want to
drive round Suva in a circle at fifty miles an hour?"

"Well, sir, that sort of gentleman is not unknown in
Suva. He may have been doing it for a bet. But, unless
that was the reason, there must have been a stop of some
kind, and the journey could hardly have taken less than
ten minutes. Anyway, it's plain that if Conky found it
O.K. at 10.15, it must have gone via Browne Street, very
shortly after the scream you heard, along Amy Street,
and Holland Street."

"Prove it."

"Well, sir, I suppose you went straight home, down
Waimanu Road and along Renwick Road?"

"Yes, except that I stopped at the garage by the creek
for some petrol."

"Well, then, if the car had gone back the way it came,
it must have passed you in order to get back to the Club
by 10.15. It didn't pass you, did it?"

"No. But it might have gone down Marks Street; it's
a longer way round, of course. Moreover, we don't yet
know for certain that it was back by 10.15. We can check
that idea of yours later. Meanwhile," and Spearpoint

pushed aside mere theorising, "I've got this appointment
with Dr. Halibut in a couple of minutes. I want you to
enquire of all the residents in Waimanu Road between
Montgomery Thomspon's and Dr. Halibut's—both sides
—and find out if any of them heard the scream I heard
at one minute to ten last night. Leave Amy Street for the
present. Find out what time it was, and which direction
it came from; and tell Bettina Bloggins I want to speak
to her at a quarter to ten sharp. Got that?" And Spearpoint hurried out, calling over his shoulder as he passed
through the doorway, "And be back yourself by a quarter
to ten."

"Er—yes, sir," muttered Sharpe, and his frown deepened
as he wondered exactly how many people he would
be expected to interview in half an hour.

CHAPTER FIVE

EXAMINATION OF THE BODY

(Friday : 9.15–10.15 a.m.)

In the entrance hall, Spearpoint found the acting
Police Medical Officer, sitting erect in the visitor's chair,
smoking a cigarette, and chatting in Punjabi with the
sergeant on duty. Dr. Halibut was a large, benevolent
man, with a large, benevolent face. He was generally
popular among the Europeans of the Colony, since he
did not appear to regard membership of the Golf Club
as a test of whether you were a human being or not;
and his garrulous habit of gossiping with everyone he
met (if possible in the other fellow's language) had won
him many unlikely friends among the Indians and the
Fijians. In the case of the Chinese he had had to be
content with a nodding acquaintance, unless they were

able to converse in English or Fijian. His besetting sin, if so amiable a man could be said to have a sin, was curiosity, and Inspector Spearpoint sometimes wondered whether the doctor cultivated his friendship in the hope of obtaining inside information on the scandals and crimes of the Colony. If this was so, Spearpoint reflected grimly, their social encounters must have caused the P.M.O. many pangs of disappointment. Nevertheless, as the chances of Government service had frequently stationed them in the same district, a certain intimacy, as well as a good deal of liking, did exist between the two.

"Well, old man," Spearpoint explained, "I'm afraid we've got rather a nasty job for you. A corpse to examine. This way." He marched out into the courtyard, picking up on his way the stretcher and sheet he had ordered to be placed in readiness.

"A corpse, eh?" The doctor's smile faded, as he followed. "How did you come by that?"

"Fished off the reef this morning. We've got it in a cell; but, for your benefit, we'll have it transferred to a table inside."

"Fished off the reef?" exclaimed Dr. Halibut, in astonishment, standing still in mid-stride. "What is it? A native?"

"No. I'm afraid it's Netta Maul. She's in here." Spearpoint was inserting the key in the lock as he spoke, and his back was towards Dr. Halibut, but the gurgling noise the doctor made caused him to glance round quickly. Dr. Halibut was staring at him with horror written all over his large countenance.

"Netta Maul?" he gasped. "Was she—drowned?"

"No." Spearpoint turned back to the door. "It appears as if someone cut her throat, shoved her in a sack and threw her into the harbour. She's a nasty sight."

"But did she float?"

Spearpoint shrugged his shoulders. "Can't say till I've examined the Chows who found her. But I shouldn't think she'd have floated on the surface. More likely she was carried on to a ledge on the reef, and left there as the tide went out."

The doctor pulled himself together with a visible effort and they entered the dimly-lit cell. Here, Halibut betrayed no uneasiness. With professional lack of emotion they placed the bundle on the stretcher and covered it with a sheet. Spearpoint called a couple of Indian constables and instructed them to carry the mysterious burden into the building. There, when the door of the room had been locked on the inside, the two set to work on their gruesome task. They untied the lengths of stout cord which bound together the ankles of the murdered girl, which bound her arms to her sides, and her wrists across her shins, and which pulled her chin as close to her knees as the plumpness of her body would allow. The cord was not new, and was of several lengths and qualities; Spearpoint put it aside for further examination. The two powerful men struggled mightily to straighten the limbs stiffened by several hours of rigor mortis and, before removing the sack from the head, they examined the clothes carefully. These gave no indication of a struggle, but there was a small piece ripped out of the frock, which was muddied at the back, and there were tears and ladders about the knees of the stockings. There was gravel but no mud on the shoes.

As they turned the body over, something fell from the front of the frock and clattered to the floor. Spearpoint stooped at once, but Dr. Halibut, although six inches taller, got there first, and their heads collided with a forcible impact which drew corresponding comment from the policeman. The doctor said nothing; he did not even rub his bald forehead, but stood turning the object over and over in his hand, with a stupefied expression on his usually smiling features. It was a cut-throat razor. He opened the knife, and fingered the edge of the blade. It was red, and already rusting in its sheath.

"Here," cried Spearpoint, "don't handle it like that. There may be fingerprints on it, man. That handle would retain fingerprints."

"Sorry, Spearo. I was so surprised to see it fall. And I lost my head when we bumped, I'm afraid. This is the weapon all right. This is blood. And it's sharp all right."

Spearpoint took the razor gingerly and ran his finger along the blade. It was old and thin and very sharp, and had obviously been ground and set many times since it had left the works of its Sheffield manufacturers. The handle was worn and polished, and bore no distinguishing marks.

The doctor remarked, "It looks a common enough razor. I suppose plenty of people still use 'em. Always use a safety myself." But Spearpoint was not to be drawn into discussion.

They carefully unrolled the nail-bag off Netta Maul's head, and revealed the horrid mutilation of her face. Death, the Inspector assumed, had obviously come from a deep slash across the throat, but there were numerous crossing cuts on nose, mouth and cheeks, none of which appeared to have bled at all copiously. Apart from an ugly bruise on the temple, and some faint bruises on a more fleshy part, the body bore no other marks of violence. Her long black tresses had been hacked off, roughly, close to the head, and the few strands that had escaped the shears served only to accentuate the ferocity of this out-rage; for Netta Maul's hair had been as famous in Fiji as her career. It had inspired the masterpiece of Leonard Rogers, not the least of the four poets who had written in the Colony—the other three being Rupert Brooke, Richenda Parham and Frank Arthur.

"Whoever did this, hated her like hell," remarked Spearpoint, dissembling his disgust.

"This was the prettiest wench in Fiji once," agreed Halibut, sententiously. "It was done by someone who hated her for her good looks, all right! And, incidentally, it was done by someone who didn't know much about surgery. That's a very clumsy cut throat. Might not have killed her at once. If I'd had her in my hands immediately after it was done, I might have saved her life. All on one side of the throat, and only just reached the vital vein—if you'll allow me to omit technicalities. None of these other cuts were dangerous. They'd have disfigured her, of course. Proper Australian trick, this face-slashing. Sort of present the Sydney razor gangs make to their former friends. I'll tell you, Spearo: the murderer held her head stretched out, with the neck taut, and then he sawed away at the windpipe; and blood would have spurted all over the place. He's bound to have it on his clothes. He'll be soaked in blood."

"Thanks." The Inspector had already thought of this.

After a moment's consideration, and a further conscientious examination of the wounds, Dr. Halibut turned his attention to the bruise on the forehead, and then straightened himself to deliver a short lecture on Some Causes of Violent Death.

"This is a very interesting case," he said. "This throat was badly cut; there's no doubt about that. All on one side; and you'll notice it hasn't bled much; I mean, of course, not as much as you'd expect from a cut throat. Now, it's very hard to tell exactly—at least, in this case—but I reckon that when these cuts were made she was already dead. All these cuts on the face were certainly made after death; see how little they've bled. And I think this one on the throat was, too. Not much after, certainly, but certainly after."

"Then what killed her?"

"This blow on the temple. To have the appearance it has now, twelve hours after death, it must have been delivered with terrific force—either a full punch from a very powerful man, or else a heavy blow from a club or some heavy blunt instrument. That would have been enough to kill her. Those other bruises were made before death, of course, but I can't say how. I should say the blow on the temple killed her. After that, the murderer slit her throat—perhaps to make certain—and later, did the rest of the business."

"The blow killed her, you think; and all the cuts were done after death?" asked the Inspector, who found it hard to believe.

"Yes; there's no doubt about that," returned the doctor, coming down firmly on the side of his theory. "And, further, she was tied up and bunged in the sack very soon after death—within half an hour, I should say. Incidentally, may I see the sack?"

The doctor took the sack and held it at arm's length, looking first at one side and then at the other. He lowered it, and put his hand deep inside as if to fetch something out, and his attitude reminded Spearpoint of a very different occasion when he had watched Dr. Halibut fumbling in the bottom of a sack—when the doctor had masqueraded as Father Christmas at a children's party a few months before. Father Christmas was a role that suited him better than examiner of murdered bodies. He turned the bag inside out, and scrutinised the brand and the stains. Finally, he laid it aside with the remark, "I was wondering what had happened to her hair."

"Do you think we didn't look inside?" laughed Spearpoint. "We found her comb there. But the hair's missing. And another thing that's missing is her handbag."

"Handbag? Did she have her handbag?"

"You know that blessed silver handbag of hers!" began Spearpoint and then cursed himself for an impulsive idiot. The two people most intimately concerned in the history of the handbag—its giver and its recipient—were both dead; but no one living had more cause to remember Netta Maul's famous handbag than Dr. Halibut. "She always carried it, you know," he concluded, lamely.

"So she was robbed and murdered?" enquired the doctor, quietly. He had swallowed hard at mention of the handbag, but he immediately brought his emotions under control.

"We don't know," Spearpoint answered. "We just know it's missing. Certainly most of her jewellery was left. She's wearing four rings—I think that's about the most she used to wear; and she's still got her anklets and bangles and ear-rings. And we found her comb. They're all solid silver, and worth a bit. I glanced at her room, too, and that seems to be undisturbed.—However, to return to business: what time do you reckon she was killed?"

The doctor considered. "It's very hard to tell, you know, to within a minute or so; the salt water would affect the state of rigor. But, as it's nearly ten now, I should say death took place—let's see—say, about eleven o'clock last night. Might have been a bit earlier, but I wouldn't put it as early as 10.30. I should think she was in the water seven or, at least, six hours."

"So far as we have been able to ascertain as yet," volunteered Spearpoint, slowly, "she was alive at a quarter to ten. She was seen then; and, by the way, she had her handbag with her."

"Was she, then?" mused the doctor. "Whoever saw her at a quarter to ten saw her in the last hour of her life. If I were you, Spearo, I'd be pretty suspicious of whoever says he saw her at a quarter to ten."

"If you were me, old chap," returned the Inspector, smiling, "you'd know that that person, at least, is innocent."

"Well, as you know, Spearo, I'm a detective-story fan; and in the stories it's always the character who seems most innocent who turns out to have done the job. But, of course, murder in real life is different. Next time I have an appendix to cut out, don't hesitate to offer to show me how to do it."

"Don't apologise; I reckon a man's an ass if he thinks he knows his job so perfectly that no one can teach him anything. But, so far as this suspect of yours is concerned, I'm positive he's innocent—one of the very few men in Suva we can say that of at the moment."

"How's that?" asked the doctor, interested.

"It's my business to suspect everyone until they're proved innocent. I may have to make everyone in Suva account for his whereabouts last night."

"Well, I was at the Club from eight till 11.30, so you can add me to the list of non-suspects," laughed the doctor.

"We are told," agreed Spearpoint, slowly, "that from eight until nine you were playing bridge—partnering Montgomery Thomspon against Cutt and Carnarvonshire. Then you dropped out and Dummfish took your place, and you sat on the verandah reading until about 10.15, when Conky Thomspon left, telling you he'd had even worse luck with Dummfish as a partner than with you."

Dr. Halibut's smile faded during this recital, and then appeared again. "I congratulate you," he said, obviously taken aback by this exact knowledge. "Might I ask if you can do that for everyone in Suva? And what did I do next?"

"We don't know," conceded Spearpoint, smiling also. "Tell us, what did you do next?"

"After Conky left I sat reading until 11.30, and then I got a lift home from Broone. I arrived home about 11.40 and went to bye-bye. Come, you tell me, what did Conky Thomspon do next?"

"You know Mr. Montgomery Thomspon as well as we do," parried the Inspector. "As a matter of fact, he gave us a precise account of his movements last night because someone stole his car, and we were trying to find out when and where he left it."

"And he says he left the Club at 10.15? Very precise, for him. I'll bet he wasn't as accurate about his other times."

"He was jolly vague about them, as you might expect. In fact, he only knew that one, because he remembered you mentioned the time to him. Was he right about that?"

"He was, as near as dammit. As he came on to the verandah I said, 'Have you finished that rubber already? It's only just a quarter past ten'; and he said, grumpily, 'Well, you know what it's like playing against Cutt.'"

Spearpoint laughed, and turned towards the door; then he looked round at the doctor and said, "There's another thing we ought to know, I suppose, about——" He nodded towards the corpse. "I'll leave you to find out."

The doctor looked puzzled; his thoughts were elsewhere.

"To put it bluntly," Spearpoint explained, "we ought to know whether she might have been murdered by a fellow who did not want to be the father of a quarter caste."

"Ah, yes, of course; but I'd prefer to do that up at the hospital. It's not a chance we get every day."

Spearpoint considered the significance of this last remark, and gave his consent with the hint, "We'd like her identity kept quiet until lunch time, say; but we would have no objection to your making the examination at the hospital. I'll have the—the exhibit sent up to you."

"At eleven, say—I'll be ready to receive."

"By the way," Spearpoint asked, as they passed into the courtyard, and, whilst locking the door, he remembered that the dead girl's assistant had been ill, "is Cecilia Snitch still up at the hospital?"

"Yes, poor kid; she'll be there a long time, I'm afraid. There won't be much of her inside left by the time we've finished with her. And I expect this affair will shake her badly; she's about the only person in the world who'll mourn this wench sincerely." He shrugged his shoulders, stifled a yawn, and added, "Well, so long for now, Spearo. Good hunting. See you at the inquest." And he climbed into his car.

Spearpoint, satisfied for the moment at having discovered a possible reason for Netta Maul's presence in the vicinity of the hospital, returned to his office with the sack, the razor and the dead girl's shoes. On the chair outside sat Bettina Bloggins, who eyed him a trifle resentfully. Saying politely, "I shan't keep you waiting more than another minute, Bettina," he went in to where Sharpe also awaited him.

"Look here, Sharpe, here's the razor that did the job. Careful: there are prints on it. And here are her shoes; there ought to be prints on them, too. Get up all the prints you can on these and photograph them. So you did notice where Conky Thomspon put his marks on the inkwell? Good work to get them! Old Halibut's been fingering this razor all over, the fathead. What do you make of this shoe?"

Sharpe took the shoe daintily and pored over it with the frown which indicated that his brain was, for a change, working.

"Yes, sir," he said at length. "There are two sets here. Both men, I should think. Large thumbs. And one seems familiar. Very familiar, sir. I'd bet my Sunday strides I've seen this one before."

"Well, hurry up. I want the shoes for another purpose. They're rather unusual, aren't they? Ever seen such silly little high heels? How could she walk in them?"

"She had an unusual walk, too, sir, if you ask me," chuckled Sharpe, preparing to go; "ever walk behind her?"

Spearpoint grinned and said, "Show Bettina in. Yes, and run up and see if you can bring Carnarvonshire here at once."

Although Netta Maul had hardly been the fallen star, Bettina Bloggins was certainly the rising one; but she would never rise to the fame of the murdered girl. There was about her a vivacity, a bubbling joyfulness, an innate friendliness, a warm-hearted dislike of hurting people's feelings, which doomed her to be for ever second-rate. She could never assume the cold, calculated scornfulness of her dead rival, that mocking, languorous half-smile with which Netta Maul had regarded her victims. Every man who met Bettina Bloggins, however casually, passed on his way with his self-confidence increased and his vanity plumed, because a pretty and charming girl had obviously admired him. But, delightful though she was, she could not attract men and suck them dry and break them with the impassionate ease with which Netta Maul had made her conquests.

Spearpoint himself liked Bettina, and he smiled at her as he motioned to her to sit down. She was unusually subdued, frightened perhaps, and therefore ready to lose her half-Irish temper.

"Now, Bettina, I just want you to tell me where you were last night," he began.

"It's no business of yours," she retorted. Then she softened, and said more cheerfully, "I wasn't doing anything you could do anything to me for."

"No, we know; but we just want you to corroborate what someone else has told us."

"Who told you?"

"Mr. Montgomery Thomspon."

"Oh, he's been telling you tales about me, has he?" she burst out. "Well, whatever he's told you is a pack of dirty lies, and you can tell him so from me."

"Come, come, Bettina. What he said was that he took you for a drive to the Point, picking you up about 10.15 and dropping you at 11.15. Is that true?"

"No, it isn't. I wasn't in his car last night. And I'll never be in it again. You can tell that to Mr. Conky Thomspon."

This was disconcerting, but she was so obviously lying that Spearpoint did not hesitate to tell her so.

"Now, Bettina, you know that's not true."

"Do I, then?"

"Of course you do; and I know it's not true, too."

"Well, Mr. Spearpoint," and here she gave him the broad and friendly smile which eighty per cent of the tourists passing through Suva on the mail steamers carried away with them on a certain best-selling picture-postcard, "if you knew I was with him, what did you want to ask me if I was for?"

"We want to make certain exactly what time he picked you up, and where."

"At half-past ten. Just past the corner of Holland Street, beyond the Bishop's House."

"And you drove out to the Point?"

"He drove. He won't let me drive." From the way in which she said this, there had plainly been some argument on the point. Spearpoint wondered that the little man had been able to summon up the determination to resist her blandishments to such an extent.

"And he put you down by your house?"

Bettina nodded, and added, smiling, "There's no hiding anything from you, Mr. Spearpoint."

"What time would that be?"

"About twenty past eleven."

She was as wax in his hands—perhaps, thought the Inspector. Twenty past eleven outside her home by Albert Park would enable the driver to be home by 11.30. The five minutes' discrepancy in the time of parting was immaterial; but there was a fifteen minutes' difference in the time of meeting. The house of the Bishop in Polynesia was separated from the Fiji Club only by the Girls' Grammar School Hostel and a field, and was situated on the corner of Holland Street; on the farther corner was the humble corrugated iron home of an Indian family.

"Are you sure it was half-past ten when he picked you up, Bettina?"

"Certain sure. By my wrist-watch," and she exhibited a shining new wrist-watch. The time on it, 9.55, agreed with that on Spearpoint's own watch.

"Was he waiting for you?"

"No—I was waiting for him—only a minute or two. I wouldn't have waited more than a minute or two," she added, suddenly remembering her dignity.

"You'd arranged to meet at half-past ten, then?"

"Yes. Half-past ten," she agreed. Then, feeling that she was not believed, she added, "I did so. You can ask my mother if it wasn't twenty-five past when I went out."

"All right. Now, do you recognise any of these things?" And the Inspector held up the button, the torch and the lipstick. She denied them all, blankly, and he could not tell whether she was lying. He was wondering whether to question her more closely when Sharpe came in to announce that Dr. Carnarvonshire was waiting. He decided that further cross-examination would be better postponed until he was able to disprove some of her statements, and said, "Well, Bettina, that's all for the moment. Go back to your work, and be a good girl."

"And the same to you," she retorted, quite at her ease now; and, twitching her nose in comradely banter, the now undisputed Queen of the Town departed.

Dr. Carnarvonshire was a sombre man of middle age who professed to hate Fiji and everyone in it, but who earned a sufficient income by his private practice to render him disinclined to leave. He accepted impassively the announcement of the murder, and confirmed Mr. Montgomery Thomspon's account of the bridge four, but he stated that it had been well after 10.15, possibly after 10.20, before it had broken up.

Spearpoint noted this further disagreement in the times, and then, as an apparent afterthought (but this was, in reality, his reason in sending for Dr. Carnarvonshire), asked if he would care to see the body, and give his opinion as to the time of death. He thought it desirable to get a second opinion, and, although he did not place much reliance in Dr. Carnarvonshire, who was in the habit of stating his opinions so emphatically that he invariably roused antagonism and distrust, yet he could hardly call in one of Dr. Halibut's juniors to contest his judgment.

"Death occurred about twelve hours ago, say at half-past ten last night," pronounced Carnarvonshire. "The body was not in the water long, perhaps a couple of hours."

"This bruise on the temple. Was that done before or after death?"

"Obviously before."

"Could it have killed her?"

Carnarvonshire shrugged his shoulders. "I doubt it. It would very probably have stunned her."

"We were thinking this blow knocked her out, and these other bruises were caused when she fell."

"Very likely."

"You think this cut in the throat killed her?"

"Obviously."

"Would you say it was skilfully done?"

"A surgeon could have made a neater job of it, but it served its turn.—Had the inquest yet? You can't keep this unburied much longer, you know."

CHAPTER SIX

JIM CAMELBACK, THE DEFIANT MAN

(Friday : 10.15–10.50 a.m.)

INSPECTOR SPEARPOINT RETURNED to his office, and found awaiting him the Chinese interpreter's report of the evidence given by the fishermen who had retrieved the body. It was brief: they had noticed an object half submerged and half stranded on a shelf of the reef, had made for it, hauled it aboard, realised its significance, and brought it ashore. They were vague about the time of the discovery, but it had evidently been about five a.m., for dawn had not broken until later.

Spearpoint consulted a tide table, which informed him that high tide had occurred at thirty-six minutes after midnight. If Dr. Carnarvonshire were correct in his estimate that the body had been in the water about two hours, then it had been put in about three a.m., when the tide was ebbing. The murderer might have calculated on its being carried out through the gap in the reef to the open sea, where it would doubtless have constituted a satisfactory breakfast for some early shark. Some cross current must have upset his calculations and swept the corpse against a ledge and imprisoned it within the reef. The fact that the sack was not weighted (and it bore no evidence that it had been weighted) suggested four possibilities to the Inspector :

(a) that the murderer had had no time to weight the body;
(b) that he had not thought of the desirability of weighting it;
(c) that he had expected it to be carried out to sea;
(d) that he had wanted it to be found in the harbour.

If Netta Maul had been in the water since three o'clock, she might have been dropped from a few points on the wharf in the confident expectation that the tide would carry her away; but only a murderer so unskilful as to overlook the play of currents against the wharf, or one fully conversant with this complicated matter, would choose the wharf for such a purpose. And this theory assumed that the murderer had access to the wharf, which was closed at night, and the ability to elude the watchman. There was no place along the sea wall of the town where the depth of water was sufficient at high tide for the launching of such a freight; and it seemed reasonable, therefore, to assume that the body had been dropped from a boat.

If Dr. Halibut were more correct in his estimate than Dr. Carnarvonshire, then this must have been done about 10.30 or eleven, that is to say, on the rising tide. This suggested either that the murderer had forgotten the tide, or else that he had wanted the body to be found in the harbour. (An inhabitant of a port could hardly be unaware of the existence of tides.) If he had forgotten the tide, he might even have dropped the body from a launch outside the reef—but the very act of navigating the launch would remind him of the tide. On the other hand, if he had wished the body to be found, why go to the trouble of trussing it, and placing it in the harbour? Presumably to mislead the police, either in order to perfect his own alibi or to incriminate someone else.

This raised the doubt: would a fresh corpse be carried by the tide? Spearpoint didn't know; but would the murderer know either?

What was plain was that, unless the murderer had desired the body to be found, he had been either criminally careless or extremely unlucky. Which was the fact did not matter to Spearpoint, whose main concern was to discover who was the murderer. After that, he had to prove that he had caught the right man. And the right man might be one who was ignorant either of the peculiarities of the tides in Suva harbour, or of the fact that tides had peculiarities.

As Spearpoint pondered thus, there entered the irrepressible Sharpe, camera in hand.

"Will you have your photograph taken, sir?" he asked, as he caught the Inspector's eye. "Look pleasant, please."

"Get to hell out of it!" retorted his superior, without malice. "Look: did you notice the discrepancy here? No, of course, you didn't hear what Bettina had to say. She stuck out that they'd arranged to meet at 10.30; but Conky was positive they'd arranged to meet at ten. One of them must be lying."

"Both, if you ask me, sir."

"Still, the time they arranged to meet is not so important as the time they actually did meet. She's sure it was a little after ten-thirty. He's sure he left the Club at ten-fifteen, and Halibut confirms this; but Carnarvonshire (if he's anything to go by) says Conky didn't go until twenty past. It wouldn't take him five minutes to get from the Club to the corner of Holland Street, so, if he left at ten-fifteen, he must have been there by ten-twenty."

"Well, we expect him to be vague, don't we, sir?"

"Yes, I realise that," agreed Spearpoint, slowly. "If they were vague about the time, you'd think it an explicable discrepancy; but the fact that both are quite positive suggests that they're trying to hide something—either different things, or else we caught them on a point where they hadn't agreed what tale to tell. But, mind you, Thomspon wasn't so positive at first."

"He must have thought of some reason for being positive, sir."

"Well, we'll clear it all up presently. We can get plenty of corroboration of the time he left. There are three more people I want to have a word with before this matter becomes public. The first is friend Camelback." He picked up the receiver and asked for the Government audit office.

"The other two would be Bellamy and Pencarbon, eh, sir?" asked Sharpe, intelligently.

Spearpoint nodded. "We can check Conky's time later."

"There's a point that's just occurred to me, though, sir," Sharpe pursued. "If the car came back via Holland Street, and it seems pretty certain it did, Bettina couldn't have been waiting there then, or she'd have recognised it. So the meeting must have been for ten-thirty."

"No. The meeting might have been for ten, and Bettina twenty minutes or so late. Besides, for all we know, she did see it."

The telephone bell rang, and Spearpoint said, "Hallo; put me on to Mr. Camelback, please. . . . Oh, hallo,

Camelback . . . Spearpoint here . . . Can you give me about a quarter of an hour? . . . Yes, right away . . . Well, if you're going off on the *Whitman* this morning, I must see you before you go. . . . It's very urgent. . . . To hell with your work! . . . Well, would you like me to get the Colonial Secretary to tell you? . . . Oh, yes, he would. He knows how urgent it is. . . . I can't tell you on the 'phone; come along here. . . . Yes, right away. . . . That's the stuff. . . . 'Bye."

He turned to Sharpe. "The blighter's going off to Lau on the *Whitman* at half-past eleven."

"Well, he'll be safe enough aboard her."

"We're not going to take any chances, though," decided Spearpoint. "Suppose you hop down to the wharf and have a word with Captain Stickithemud. Tell him from me that we've just got an important case on—for the love of Mike, don't let on what it is—and tell him that Camelback is going to be the star witness, and we shall want him brought back in good order."

"Camelback will hear that I've called on the skipper, sir," objected Sharpe, taking his khaki topee, nevertheless, and moving to the door.

"Can't help it if he does. I'm not taking any chances.— When you get back, come in here and listen to the story."

Sharpe went, leaving Spearpoint deep in a reverie from which the entrance of Camelback presently aroused him. Jim Camelback was rather below the average height, but he possessed broad shoulders and an exceptionally thick and deep chest. Now that his athletic days were long over, his abdomen had acquired an exceptional thickness also; and he appeared less like the gorilla he had been likened to in the days when, during a brief pugilistic boom, he had been middle-weight boxing champion of the Colony, and more like the walking barrel he was now compared with by the irreverent youth who knew nothing of his past except the legends of his numerous romances. Men admire the sportsman, but they envy the rake; and thus a man who has been both sportsman and rake will be remembered for his strenuous nights long after his strenuous days are forgotten. Camelback had the thick white hair of an American senator, the red face of the determined whisky drinker, the shifty eyes of the villain of the films, and a high, thin tenor voice which was his most unexpected attribute. He was not the approved pattern of the successful lover, but he was now past his prime, both as a man and as a Don Juan, and the fact that he had been for many years a highly-paid (and by no means thrifty) bachelor had had a considerable share in his past conquests.

He accepted with apparent unconcern the chair indicated by the Inspector, but he contrived not to look him full in the face. That indicated nothing, for Jim Camelback never did look anyone full in the face.

"Well," began Spearpoint, "we're sorry to have to worry you on your busy day, but I suppose you can guess what we've asked you here about."

"Haven't the faintest idea, old chap," responded Camelback, his eyes roving. "Has there been a defalcation in Lau?"

"No, but there's been a murder in Suva." Spearpoint brought it out softly, conversationally. Camelback received the news without emotion, so much without emotion, in fact, that Spearpoint believed that it came as no surprise.

"A murder, eh? Well, old chap, what's that got to do with me?"

"We have reason to believe that you were one of the last persons to see the murdered person alive."

"Was I? Who was he?"

"I didn't say it was a he."

"Well, she, then. I haven't heard of any murder, old chap. What are you getting at? Who's been murdered, and when?"

"Netta Maul. Last night."

At this, Camelback did show some sign of emotion. He stiffened in his chair, and, for a moment, his eyes fastened on the Inspector's. Then he laughed. "Netta Maul? Murdered, eh? Who did it? I thought someone would do her in sooner or later—poor kid," he added, as a pious afterthought.

"She was found dead this morning," said Spearpoint, slowly, watching his man closely. "And we were wondering whether you could give us any information likely to prove useful."

Camelback uncrossed his legs, and shrugged his shoulders. "Me? What can I tell you? I haven't spoken to her for a year. You know that."

"We thought you might be able to tell us something about her habits and associates."

Camelback laughed. Either he was acting very cleverly, or else her death meant nothing at all to him. "That's rich! You've come to the wrong shop, old chap. You want to try the rising generation. I don't doubt you yourself know more about her nowadays than I do. Why, I haven't spoken to her for a year."

Sharpe entered at this juncture, nodded carelessly to Camelback, and perched himself on a table, whence he had the visitor in profile. This entry made things more difficult for Netta Maul's one-time friend, who now had two pairs of eyes to avoid, and his mock-friendly manner turned to a sullen defiance.

"Have you seen her lately?" asked Spearpoint.

"No."

"Can you recall the last time you saw her?"

"No."

"We were told she was seen with your car on the Rewa road about a fortnight ago."

"Your spy is a liar."

"I don't doubt that he is—in some respects," replied Spearpoint, "but he did tell some such yarn, didn't he, Sharpe?"

Thus appealed to, Sharpe replied cautiously, "If I remember rightly, sir, what I saw was a girl whom I thought was Netta Maul standing a few yards from the Rewa Hotel talking to a man in a car which I thought was Mr. Camelback's."

"There's a damned sight too much thinking about what you say you thought you saw," retorted Mr. Camelback, angrily. Turning to Spearpoint, he demanded, "What right have your men to be spying on law-abiding citizens? Have you ever had anything against me?"

"Now, don't get excited," soothed the Inspector. "Mr. Sharpe here has not been spying on you, nor has anyone else, to my knowledge. In a place like Fiji it's impossible for a man to have a private life, as he may have in London or Sydney. You can't deny that your car is often seen parked in quiet places by the roadside."

"That's no business for the police, if it is," expostulated Camelback, sulkily. "Besides, I often lend my car to some of the youngsters at the bach."

"We know you do," agreed Spearpoint. "And this was not reported to the police in the usual way. Mr. Sharpe would never have mentioned seeing Netta Maul near your car if we were not investigating the circumstances of her death."

"I tell you I know nothing of the circumstances of her death. She hasn't spoken to me for twelve months."

"Then it wasn't you talking to her at Rewa?"

"Certainly not."

"Did you speak to her last night?"

"I did not."

"Did you see her at all last night?"

"No."

"You see," pursued Spearpoint, calmly, "I was driving down Waimanu Road last night at a quarter to ten. Just before the hospital your car overtook me. Just past the hospital I overtook Netta Maul on foot. You must have passed her—or was it someone else driving your car?"

JIM CAMELBACK, THE DEFIANT MAN 73

Camelback answered, without any show of embarrassment, "Now you come to mention it, I did pass her."

"And as I passed the end of Browne Street," continued
Spearpoint, "I glanced up it, and saw your car parked
under Dr. Halibut's hedge."

"Damned good eyesight you've got," sneered Camelback, "to recognise my car in the shade, when you're
steering a car round a curve in the other direction."

"It was your car?"

"It was."

There was a silence; Spearpoint waited for an explanation, which Camelback refused to volunteer. At last,
Spearpoint ventured, "I concluded you were waiting to
speak to Netta Maul."

"You were wrong," retorted Camelback, rudely. Then
he added, "As a matter of fact, I went to visit Dr. Halibut."

"And how long did you stay there?"

"About five minutes. I called to give him a lift to the
Club."

"And then you drove him down Amy Street and
Holland Street to the Club?"

"Yes."

Sharpe made as if to speak, but Spearpoint gestured
to him to be silent. Camelback observed the gesture and
amended his confession. "I drove myself that way.
Halibut was out. I went on down to the Royal Palm
and had a yarn with a chap and didn't go to the Club
at all. I got home about 11.15."

"Do you remember the last occasion on which you
spoke to Netta Maul?" asked Spearpoint smoothly, trying
to conceal the fact that he had noticed Camelback's
attempted lie. It was a very clumsy lie, anyway, since
one simple question to Halibut would have exposed it.

"As a matter of fact, I do."

"A year ago?"

"Yes."

There was another silence. Sharpe interrupted it, in

some excitement. "It's just a year since I landed, and I went to a dance at the G.P.H., my first night, and saw Netta Maul there. She was such a stunning beauty, although she was so fat, that I naturally asked who she was. And two days later I saw her walking along Victoria Parade with the biggest black eye I ever saw in my life."

"I remember that black eye she had," remarked Spearpoint, looking hard at Camelback. "She told some yarn about having fallen downstairs, didn't she?"

"She did fall downstairs," confirmed Camelback, staring at the inkpot.

"Was it about that time you spoke to her last?" enquired Spearpoint. "But that was a month or more after you had finally quarrelled with her?"

"Oh, yes," agreed Camelback, with an assumption of carelessness, "more than a month." Then he apparently decided to be more communicative. "You see, she tried to blackmail me. She wrote me a letter asking for money; stupid thing to do. I met her, and obtained from her the evidence she had against me—and that was the last time we spoke. It was the day before she got that black eye."

"How did you get the evidence from her?"

"I don't see that has any bearing on the matter. This happened a year ago. In any case, it was not a legal matter. If she had handed the evidence to you, you could not have done anything to me with it."

"I wasn't thinking of that aspect of the matter. I was wondering how you persuaded her to part with her weapon. I suppose you gave her in exchange the evidence you held that she was a blackmailer?"

Camelback smiled at that, and answered grimly, "What do you think?"

Spearpoint smiled also, and also grimly. Then he asked, "As a matter of mere human curiosity, and not at all in connection with this enquiry, did you give her any money?"

Camelback, apparently quite at his ease, laughed out-right, and chortled, "Did I hell?" Then he added, in the most friendly tone he used during the interview, "Of course, I spent quids and quids on her at one time. And, by George, she was worth it, while it lasted."

Spearpoint, who had been looking at his notes, and not fully attending to this last remark, glanced up and said, "Well, I can take it, then, that you passed her at a quarter to ten last night, stopped outside Dr. Halibut's, called for him, found he was out, got back into your car, and drove to the Royal Palm via Amy Street and Holland Street?"

"Yes, you can take that, old chap."

"You didn't see Netta Maul when you came out of Dr. Halibut's?"

"No."

"You didn't pass her in Amy Street?"

"No."

"There are just another couple of questions, I think," Spearpoint continued. "What time do you reckon you arrived at the Royal Palm?"

"About ten o'clock. As a matter of fact it was exactly ten o'clock. I went up to Malleable's for a wad, and he happened to ask me the time, and it was exactly ten."

"That's good," Spearpoint said, making a note; "exact evidence is what we want."

"Well, old chap, I can give you some more exact evidence, if you like. I left the Royal Palm exactly at eleven. I know that because young Bob Eachway came into the room, and I drove him back to the bach; and he and I and two of the other fellows sat up till all hours playing poker."

"All hours being?"

"Oh, I don't know; between one and two."

"Do you happen to remember if, when you passed Netta Maul, she had her silver handbag with her?"

Camelback considered and finally said, "I don't remember seeing it. I was going pretty fast, you know."

Then, the visitor having scornfully denied all knowledge

of the button, the torch and the lipstick, Spearpoint stood up, saying, "Well, Camelback, I'm afraid you're not much help to us. We'll have to make other enquiries. I suppose you wouldn't mind giving evidence, if necessary?"

"All I could say was that I saw her last night. I don't mind saying that. Sorry I can't help you any more, Spearo." Camelback rose also. "But I've had nothing to do with her for a year. Cheerio," and he put on his topee, and walked out of the office.

"What do you think, sir?" asked Sharpe, when they had watched him drive past the window.

"It's only a guess, mind," said Spearpoint, slowly, "but I don't think she fell downstairs. I didn't think so at the time. I believe he blacked her eye; there were bruises on her wrists, you know. I believe he double-crossed her; got the compromising document from her; refused to return her letter; knocked her about and dared her to charge him with assault." Spearpoint smiled grimly, and continued, "Furthermore, I believe he did try to speak to her last night; and we'll ask young Bellamy if he heard any of the conversation. But there is one thing: how does he know that Halibut was out last night? If he didn't call at the Club, how does he know that Halibut was there? It seems as if he did call for Halibut, at least, whether or no he also spoke to Netta Maul."

CHAPTER SEVEN

BOB BELLAMY, THE NERVOUS MAN

(Friday: 10.50–11.15 a.m.)

"I SUPPOSE WE'D BETTER ask Bellamy's boss if he can spare his stock-clerk for a quarter of an hour," Spearpoint continued, lifting the telephone receiver.

"—Mr. Cutt, please.—There's no sense in annoying the old devil.—Oh, good morning, Mr. Cutt. This is Spearpoint. . . . We're sorry to trouble you, but would it be possible for us to have an interview with your man, Bellamy?"

"What you want him for, eh?" growled the redoubtable Willy Cutt.

"We're making enquiries on a very important and urgent case, and he has some evidence bearing on it."

"Can't you wait till to-night, eh?"

"I'm afraid not, Mr. Cutt."

"He'd have more time to-night, eh. You could talk to him all night, for all I care."

"Oh, no, we wanted to speak to him this morning, at once."

"Won't it wait? We're very busy, eh. There's a mail in and a mail out, eh. Can't the police manage their own business and leave us to manage ours, eh? What's the hurry?"

"We want to question him before the news gets all over the town."

"What's he been up to, eh?"

"Nothing that we know of. But we believe he may be able to give evidence. We are making enquiries concerning a certain person, and we understand that your man Bellamy saw that person at a time when his movements were vital. We want to find if Bellamy can corroborate his story or not. And we must see Bellamy at once before he——"

Mr. Cutt evidently realised that he was really too busy to argue, and that if he didn't prevent him the Inspector would make a speech—and a speech was the thing Mr. Cutt dreaded more than anything, more even than a slump in the copra market.

"Well, if you must have him, you must, eh," he growled. "You can come in and ask him, but don't delay him more than a minute or two, eh."

"We wanted him to come round to us, Mr. Cutt. We have to ask some private questions, and we can't very well interview him in your main office."

"All right, you can have him."

"Would you mind telling him to come round here, then, Mr. Cutt?"

The listening Sharpe laughed outright in admiration of his chief's doggedness.

"You interrupt my work to help you with yours, Mr. Spearpoint. All right. I'll send him, eh. But don't ask for him again on a mail day."

Spearpoint hung up the receiver and made a grimace at the instrument. Mr. Cutt was simultaneously doing likewise. Each thought, "What a pig-headed cuss that man is!"

"Congratulations, sir," smiled Sharpe. No one would have dared to congratulate Cutt, whatever triumph he achieved.

"Now I've got another job for you, Sharpe," said the Inspector, as they waited for Bellamy. "Take this razor to the three barbers and ask them if they recognise it. Don't tell 'em how you came by it, but try to find out the owner. Tell 'em you think it belongs to a white man. Say it's been found and you want to trace the owner. Say it's important. They'll probably think it's part of some Indian's thievings. I expect, if any of the barbers do recognise it, it will be Stakes, and we'll have to send to Auckland to ask him; but you may have a stroke of luck with the others. Come in when you've finished."

Sharpe went, and Spearpoint occupied the few remaining minutes before the arrival of Bellamy in elaborating the notes he had taken during the interview with Camelback.

Bellamy was short, slight and fair, with an undecided chin, a weak mouth, and a hesitant manner. His shyness occasionally exploded in bursts of over-confident volubility. He perched on the edge of his chair, and seemed

far more nervous than the occasion warranted; although
he certainly looked the Inspector more squarely in the
eye than had any other of the men interviewed so far in
the case, he blushed unaccountably at some of the questions,
and stammered in many of his answers.

"We're investigating a crime that took place last night,"
began Spearpoint, looking keenly at his victim, "and we
believe you can give us some helpful information."

Bellamy looked puzzled, frowned, blushed and finally
stammered, "I-I-I as-assure you, I don't know of any
crime."

"Possibly not. But we have reason to believe you were
on or near the spot. We should like to ask you a few
questions about your movements last night."

A flicker of fear passed across Bellamy's face, and he
turned pale, muttering, "I don't know anything about
any crime." Then he pulled himself together with an
effort, and added, "Of course, I'll answer any questions
you like. Am I to assume that anything I say will be
used in evidence against me?"

"That's almost a confession," thought the Inspector,
in surprise. Aloud he corrected the phrase: "It may be
used in evidence, not necessarily against you. If your
evidence is of any use, we may ask you to give us a written
statement later."

"I'd prefer that, if you'd give me time to think what
to write. But—you know—I haven't the faintest idea what
you're talking about."

"You soon will," replied Spearpoint, grimly. "Last
night, about a quarter to ten, you were walking along
Waimanu Road, towards the town, and were just passing
the hospital. Correct?"

"More or less," agreed Bellamy. "I can't say to
five minutes. I passed the hospital, certainly, in both
directions."

"I'm talking about the return journey. You were
following Netta Maul. Correct?"

Bellamy flushed crimson at the mention of the murdered girl, and retorted, with an unexpected show of spirit, "No, I was not following her."

"Are you positive of that?"

"Certainly I am."

"Well, I saw you both!" snapped Spearpoint, leaning forward, and trumping his opponent's ace.

Bellamy stared at him in astonishment—or confusion. He opened his mouth to speak, and shut it again. Finally he managed to gasp. "You—say—you—saw—me—following—Nett——her?"

Spearpoint nodded grimly. "I did."

Bellamy pinched his ear, looked down at the floor, wondering what to say, and finally glanced up with a smile and said wonderingly, "But would you repeat that before witnesses? It's libel, isn't it?"

It was the Inspector's turn to gasp.

"Libel?" he repeated, bewildered.

"Yes, of course. It's not true, you know. You couldn't have seen me following her. You can't produce any witnesses to say I spoke to her, or she to me."

"I didn't say you did speak to her. What I said was that I drove past you walking towards the town, and a hundred yards or so ahead I drove past her walking towards the town. How can you deny that?"

"Oh, I don't deny that," exclaimed Bellamy, with obvious relief. "That was very likely. You mean that we both happened to be walking along the road about the same time?"

"Of course. That was what I said."

"You said I was following her," protested Bellamy. "I thought you meant I was *following* her."

"Well, so I did. You were following her."

"No, I wasn't. There's a difference between following anyone and *following* them," argued Bellamy, stressing the repetition of the participle.

"Damned if I see it," growled Spearpoint. "Anyway, does it matter?"

"Well, it does to me. I was not following her——"

"——Oh, Lord——"

"——deliberately. I may have been walking behind her by chance. You see," Bellamy continued, subsiding into his usual apologetic manner once he had insisted on his mysteriously important distinction, "I was just out for a walk. We—er—I go out every evening when it's fine. Just as far as the golf course and back."

"I know," interrupted Spearpoint, impatiently.

"You know?" asked Bellamy, startled. "How on earth do you know that?"

"Do you think I go about the place with my bally eyes shut? Because I often see you, of course. I know your wife is in Australia because I saw her go off on the *Aorangi*. And I know you were in Waimanu Road last night because I saw you there with my own eyes, following Netta Maul."

"Excuse me," returned Bellamy, flushing but persistent. "Not following—walking at least a hundred yards behind. I didn't know she was there—not until I got to the corner of Browne Street. Why should I be following her?"

"Other young men," thought Spearpoint, "even married ones, have been known to follow her. He's so touchy about it that I almost wonder whether he really was tracking her." Aloud he said, "Let's calm down a bit. Don't be so touchy. You did see her later, then?"

Bellamy instantly accepted the olive branch.

"I'm sorry," he apologised. "I'm a bit upset. I'm afraid I'm having a bit of a strain just now. I suppose you know why I'm worried. And I'm all excited this morning; a great pile of urgent work came in by the mail. And I'm not used to being questioned by the police." A thought struck him, and he added, looking scared, "Am I being accused of anything? Because, if so, I ought to consult a lawyer before answering anything, oughtn't I?"

"No, we're not accusing you of anything," said Spear-point, still wondering whether he soon would be. "We're enquiring into the movements of Netta Maul."

Looking more frightened than ever, Bellamy asked anxiously, "Has she done anything?"

Spearpoint, realising that his witness needed nursing, decided to discard his fiercer manner, and said, "No, we don't think so. You'll know all about it later. Just now, we want you to tell us exactly what happened from the moment you saw her. Fire away. We won't keep you away from your work long."

Bellamy winced at the mention of the murdered girl, almost as if, thought Spearpoint, it conjured up in his mind the sight of her mutilated countenance, but he obediently began, "Well, it's not much of a story, anyway. I'm afraid I can't help you much. I was just going home after the stroll, and as I was turning from Waimanu Road into Browne Street—I live in Amy Street, you know——"

Spearpoint nodded, thinking savagely, "Get on with the story, man."

"Well, there was a car drawn up under the hedge of Dr. Halibut's, and a man standing beside it, and Netta Maul. That's all," he concluded, smiling, a little lamely.

"That's all, eh? And what did you do?"

"I just walked past."

"Did you speak?"

"No, of course not."

"Why 'of course not'?"

Bellamy flushed and muttered, "Well, I didn't."

Spearpoint was puzzled. Bellamy was apparently hiding something. He changed the subject. "Who was the man?"

"I couldn't see him properly. He was in the shade, with his back partly to me. I thought he was——" He hesitated. "I'd rather not say, I think; at least, not if it's important. You see, I'd be prepared to go into the witness-box and swear that it was Netta Maul, because I saw her quite plainly. She was looking towards me.

And I'd be prepared to swear that it was a man talking
to her; but I wouldn't be prepared to swear who he was.
I can describe him—vaguely, though. He wore white
coat and trousers, and no hat. He was fairly short and
broad, and with a bit of a—rather plump, that is." He
gestured to indicate a bulging tummy, and then blushed
as he realised that the man he was talking to was probably
sensitive on that subject.

"Whose car was it?"

"I don't know. Just a closed car. I'm—I'm not interested
much in cars. . . . It was an ordinary sedan Gawd, I
think," he added, with hesitation.

"Come," coaxed Spearpoint. "We know who the man
was. I'll write his name on this pad. I think you're pretty
sure who he was, even if you won't swear to him. Tell
me who you think it was, and I'll show you what I've
written."

"Well, I won't swear to it, mind, and I don't know
him at all well; but I thought it was Mr. Camelback."

Spearpoint displayed the paper on which he had
written that name, and continued, "His back was towards
you, and she was facing you. Were they close together?"

"Oh, no. A foot or so apart."

"Did they look at you when you came?"

"She did. He didn't. You see, I don't suppose he knew
I was there. I was wearing plimsolls. I didn't make any
noise."

"Your stick?"

"I may have been carrying it by the middle, or under
my arm. I often do—I suppose you know that, also?"

"Quite. But she saw you? Didn't she make any sign
—speak, or smile, or nod of recognition—which would
show him there was someone else there?"

Bellamy flushed and answered shortly, "No."

"She saw you?"

"Yes, I suppose she did."

"She saw you, and took no notice of you at all?"

Bellamy nodded.

"And you saw her and took no notice of her?"

Bellamy nodded again. He seemed too agitated to speak.

"That's strange," thought Spearpoint. "He's one of the politest people in town. It's difficult to believe he would walk past an acquaintance without any sign of recognition." Aloud he said, "You're one of her customers, aren't you?"

"No. I don't smoke, now. I expect you know that—you seem to know so much about me."

"Well, I thought you didn't smoke—or drink, either," agreed Spearpoint. "But I happened to see you coming out of her shop only yesterday——"

"Oh, yes, of course," Bellamy interrupted, eagerly; "but I wasn't buying anything. Mr. Cutt had sent me to collect her account. And I had some business there in connection with the stock. She gets her stuff from Marryam & Cutt, you know."

"Of course, I'd forgotten that. Did you collect anything, by the way?"

Bellamy smiled ruefully. "I'm afraid I'm not much good as a debt collector," he said, and then he stopped suddenly, realising that he had been in danger of revealing his employer's business.

Spearpoint considered a moment, and began again. "When you saw Netta Maul last night, did you notice if she was carrying her silver handbag?"

Bellamy pondered. "I'm sorry. I can't remember."

Another idea struck the Inspector. "Exactly where were they standing?"

As Bellamy considered, he prompted, "For example, on the grass? In the gutter? Just in front of Dr. Halibut's steps?"

Bellamy, expressing some doubt, decided that she had been standing just in front of the concrete steps leading to the doctor's front gate. Camelback had been facing her.

"And after you had walked on, did Camelback drive past?"

"No. Of course, it's only a couple of minutes to my house."

"You went straight indoors?"

"Yes."

"And after you got in, did you hear anyone drive past?"

"I can't tell. I couldn't remember if I did; so many cars pass. The Indian buses go through Toorak, you know."

Spearpoint left this matter for further consideration, and continued, "You say that Camelback and Netta Maul were talking: did you hear what they said?"

"Only a word or two." Bellamy spoke reluctantly.

"Can you remember any of it?"

"It wasn't intended for my ears.—Oh, well, he was saying, 'Yes, but, my dear——', or something like that. Protesting, but in a wheedling sort of voice. It was so different from the voice in which he grumbles about his account that it didn't seem like him. That's partly why I'm not sure it was him."

"And did she say anything?"

"She answered, and she saw me as she spoke, and then he answered her. I heard him say, 'Netta, my dear, you can't——'; and then I was out of earshot. I wasn't trying to overhear them. He seemed to be pleading with her."

"She was repulsing him?"

"Yes."

"You heard what she said?"

"Well—yes." Bellamy flushed, hesitated, and went on only under the compulsion of Spearpoint's eye.

"What she said was—and you realise that she was looking at me as she said it, and for the moment I thought she meant it for me—what she said was, 'You bloody swine! I'll get you this time.'"

"Why should you think she was speaking to you? You've had a quarrel with her, eh?"

"She hasn't spoken to me for over a year—nor I to her, for that matter."

"But you've only been in Suva about eighteen months. You've only known her that long. Besides, how do you mean, not speak to her? How do you collect her account?"

Bellamy was agitated, and he spoke with an effort. "I'd better tell you the story, I suppose. I came round to Suva from Malua a little under eighteen months ago, and, of course, I didn't know anyone in Suva. Of course, I'd heard of her, but I didn't take any particular notice of bach gossip. Well, one of the first jobs I got put on to was to go round and collect several outstanding accounts. I'm not much good at that sort of thing, you know, and I got more promises than cheques. She was one of those who only promised. She was very nice and charming and made me believe that she really would pay something next week. So when I came back and reported to Mr. Cutt, I said she'd promised something on account next week, and that I believed she intended to keep the promise, and he said—well, it doesn't matter exactly what he said——"

"You remember what he said? More than a year ago?"

"Well, as a matter of fact, I do," admitted Bellamy.

Spearpoint laughed outright, and commented, "Yes; I suppose there are plenty of people in Fiji who can remember things Cutt said to them longer ago than a year."

Bellamy flashed a rueful smile at him, and proceeded: "Well, the gist of it was that I was to go back and tell her that he was tired of her promises and that she'd got to pay ten pounds at once. He said I was to stay in the shop until she paid."

"How is it you're not still there, then?" asked Spearpoint, as Bellamy paused in an effort to bring his voice under proper control. ("Jolly him along, that's the idea," thought the Inspector.)

Bellamy managed to smile again, but the memory of the incident plainly agitated him. "I went back and I put it as nicely as I could, and sympathised with her, and tried to be polite as well as firm. And she was quite nice at first, and told me a whole rigmarole about how bad trade was—and, incidentally, she sold me a couple of tins of cigarettes, although I don't smoke—and showed me how much she'd got in the till. And, anyway, in the end I went back and told Mr. Cutt she'd promised five pounds for to-morrow. She seemed to me at the time to be quite honest and straightforward, and she absolutely convinced me she hadn't got the money, and I told Mr. Cutt so. And he said that if she could pay five pounds to-morrow, she could pay it to-day; and he told me to go back again and tell her that she'd promised to pay five pounds every Friday, but hadn't paid anything for three weeks; and that if she didn't pay ten pounds within half an hour, he'd seize her stock and her private property and sell her up, and turn her out of her shop. M. & C.'s were her land-lords, as well as her suppliers, you know, and they hold security over all her property."

"Quite. What happened then?"

"Well, when I told her that—and I tried to put it as nicely as I could—she turned really nasty. I wouldn't have thought it possible a girl who could be so pleasant, and—and charming, could turn round and be so bitter. She abused me for five minutes on end, in front of customers. A couple of chaps came in to buy some cigarettes, and she told them what a—well, she called me names, and told them all about how Mr. Cutt was plotting against her, and trying to put her out of business, and said a lot of nasty things about me; and she tried to hustle me out of the shop. But I wouldn't go; and those fellows just laughed, half in sympathy with her and half in sympathy with me. In the end, she took eight pounds out of her purse and gave it to me; but she let me see she'd got a lot more there, and I stuck out for ten, and got it in the end. And she's never said a word to me since."

Bellamy stopped abruptly and shuddered, and put his hands over his face; and then looked up defiantly, and muttered, "It wasn't fair. I was only doing my job. It was only what I had been told to do. She had the money all the time. It wasn't my fault Mr. Cutt sent me to collect it. She owed it. It wasn't fair."

"No, old chap, apparently it wasn't. But you still go to her shop?"

"Well, I have to. The trouble was that when I came back with the ten pounds, Mr. Cutt was astounded. He said he'd never thought I'd have got it. And so he kept on sending me to collect. I used to go in and say, 'Good morning, Miss Maul; Mr. Cutt has sent me to ask you if you would kindly let us have another ten pounds,' and she'd ignore me. She'd pretend I wasn't there. And I would sit on the stool until she got fed up with my presence, and then she'd put the money on the table and snatch the receipt out of my hand; and I'd take it back to Mr. Cutt, and he'd make jokes about her being my sweetheart and advise me of nice things to say to her during the hours I spent in her shop. That was at first; later, he began to get impatient and to ask why it took so long to get the money. It was intolerable. After she found ignoring me wasn't any good, she started other tricks. She put the spittoon on the floor by the stool and when I came in she'd turn her back on me and throw her cigarette ends, or lighted matches, over her shoulder at the spittoon, or rather, at me. But she got tired of that, and took to coming in and paying the cashier. But she fell behind again; and a couple of months ago, Mr. Cutt decided to have the stock taken twice a week, and to make her pay each time on account of her sales—and he made me take the stock and calculate the amounts." The wretched boy looked piteously at Spearpoint and appealed, "Can you imagine what a hell it is arguing over calculations with an angry girl who can't add correctly and who won't speak to you?"

Spearpoint grinned in sympathy and asked, "You mean she never said a word?"

"No; she might have been dumb for all she ever said to me. Of course, I heard her say plenty of things about me."

"Did you ever complain of her conduct to Cutt?"

Bellamy shrugged his shoulders. "What's the good? He'd only laugh and ask if I was afraid of a silly girl. Besides, he has no control over her conduct. And, it is ridiculous, anyway, that I should be so upset by it. But you just imagine!" he went on, in a torrent. "Just imagine living in a small town like this, where you can't go out of the door without meeting a score of people you know, where everyone is always meeting everyone else—just imagine constantly running up against someone you've done no harm to, who persists in regarding you as an enemy, and cutting you publicly and pointedly! Just imagine it!" He almost collapsed into tears; but recovered and muttered, "I'm sorry if I let myself get carried away. It's been a terrible worry to me, these eighteen months. And I'm very worried just now—about other things."

"Well," said Spearpoint, looking at him closely, "she won't worry you any more, if that's any comfort to you."

"Not any more?" cried Bellamy, looking up startled. "You mean—she's—she's done something? You've arrested her? She'll go to prison? Oh! I—I'm sorry. Of course, I've no cause to like her, but I wouldn't wish her that."

"No, it's not that," returned the Inspector, quietly, wondering whether Bellamy's conjectures were counterfeit or genuine.

Bellamy stared at him open-mouthed, a wild surmise working in his brain. "You mean," he jerked out, at last, "you mean—she's—murdered Mr. Camelback? She'll be hanged? My evidence—my evidence will hang her? Oh, my God! I can't give evidence like that! My God! Fancy hanging her!" And he pulled his handkerchief out of his hip-pocket and burst into tears.

Whilst Spearpoint was wondering what to say next, Sharpe knocked on the door, and walked in briskly. Seeing Bellamy huddled on the chair before him, he leapt to the obvious conclusion, and burst out inconsiderately, "My Sunday hat! Did *he* do it?"

Spearpoint shrugged his shoulders, to indicate doubt. They gazed at Bellamy; and then Spearpoint, catching sight of Sharpe's puzzled face, felt an insane desire to laugh. Presently the sense of Sharpe's remark penetrated to Bellamy's consciousness, and he looked up, calmer. "Me do it?" he asked, brokenly. "What do you mean? Why should I murder Mr. Camelback?"

"Jim Camelback?" echoed (more or less) Sharpe, surprised in his turn. "Has he been murdered?"

"Didn't you say so?" Bellamy enquired of Spearpoint.

"No. Now pull yourself together, old chap. Camelback is all right. So far as we know, Netta Maul has not murdered anyone. She is in no danger from the police. No evidence you can give will do her any harm. She is beyond our reach and your reach. In fact, she is dead."

"Dead?" exclaimed her enemy, incredulous. "But I saw her alive only last night!"

"And I saw her dead an hour ago. There's her body on the other side of the passage.—Like to see it?" and the Inspector moved towards the door.

Bellamy hastily made a gesture of refusal. "Oh, no, no. I don't want to see it. Then," it suddenly dawned on him, "then she has been murdered?"

"Apparently."

"Then who did it? Mr. Camel——?"

"That's what we're trying to find out. Now, sit down again. Perhaps you can tell us a few more things. Do you recognise this button?"

Bellamy regarded the object curiously, and shook his head.

"Or this?" and he held up the torch.

"I've got a torch something like that," assented Bellamy, "but mine has my initials scratched on the side. This isn't mine."

"Or this?"

"What is it?"

"It's a lipstick. Don't you know a lipstick when you see one?"

"I don't think I've ever seen one before," Bellamy considered. "Well, I've seen girls putting it on, but not closely. You see—well, as I suppose you know, as you seem to know so much about us, my wife doesn't use lipstick."

"I suppose she doesn't. But Netta Maul did. You don't happen to know if this was hers?"

"Not the least idea. I know she used lipstick, of course."

"Let's see, now," mused Spearpoint; having drawn blanks with the three objects, he consulted his notes for other questions. Without looking up, he asked, "Can you drive a car?"

"No"; turning to Sharpe: "you know I haven't a licence."

Sharpe nodded; he was wondering whether or no to produce the razor from his pocket.

Spearpoint asked, "What sort of razor do you use?"

Bellamy, mystified, named a much-advertised safety, and was about to add something when the Inspector brought out his final trump and cut him short. "There's one last thing that puzzles me rather," said Spearpoint, standing up: "Why, when I saw you last night, were you wearing gloves?"

Bellamy sat up sharply, blushing furiously. Was it surprise—consternation—guilt?

"Wearing what?" he exclaimed.

"Gloves."

"But I wasn't wearing gloves," he protested. "Gloves in this weather? Why, I haven't got any gloves—at least, only an old pair I sometimes wear when hacking down weeds in the garden. What makes you think I was wearing gloves?"

"Your hands looked so dark. Perhaps it was only a trick of the lighting.—Well, Mr. Bellamy, that's all for the present. If your evidence is likely to be of any use, I'll get you to write out and sign exactly what you saw and heard; and you may have to give evidence. Keep it all to yourself, so far. By the way, did anyone else see Netta Maul with Camelback?"

"Not so far as I know."

"Good morning, then."

"Good morning, Mr. Spearpoint. Of course, I'd like to be of any use I can, you know—I mean, I don't want to help to hang anyone, but I suppose I've got to do what I can, so if I can be of any use——" and nodding to Sharpe, the young man went.

CHAPTER EIGHT

STANLEY PENCARBON, THE JAUNTY MAN

(Friday: 11.15–11.45 a.m.)

"Was he wearing gloves, sir?" asked Sharpe.

"Oh, no, I don't think so; but I wondered what he'd say. Funny kid. He had a row with Netta Maul over a year ago when Cutt sent him to collect her account, and she hasn't spoken to him since. Cut him every time they met. Absolutely got him down, it has. He seems to have plenty of motive for murdering her. He says he saw Jim Camelback talking to her. He was pleading with her and she was threatening him. One of the two is lying point blank; and they've both got motives."

"I'd lay my Sunday shirt it was Jim Camelback rather than this kid," Sharpe objected.

Spearpoint shrugged his shoulders. "It seems fairly plain that whatever passed between him and Netta Maul, she had driven him nearly frantic. We'd better take a very careful check on his movements."

"For a start then, sir, we'll bag his fingerprints from the door-handle," and Sharpe proceeded to carry out his suggestion.

Presently he looked up, brush in hand, and asked anxiously, "Did you want Bellamy to see this razor, sir?"

"No, I don't think there's any point in that," answered the Inspector, busy with his notes. "Whoever it was tied her up slipped the razor inside her frock and must know that as we've found her, we've found the razor. So if he did it, and we showed him the razor, he'd deny it. The other objects are different. They were found in the car, and may have nothing to do with the murder. If we can establish the ownership of them they may help to establish whether the car was connected with the murder. Did you have any luck with the razor?"

"Not a smell. Old Gussy says he hasn't seen a cut-throat razor in ten years—incidentally, he's got four on the shelf in front of his nose, but you know what he means; and the other bloke doesn't know this one. It's an English razor, of course; he says he doesn't think any of the local merchants stock this make. But he's only been in Fiji a few months. He says the firm that made 'em went bung. Of course, sir, it's an old and well-worn razor."

"Well, we'd better send it to the Auckland police, and ask them to get in touch with Stakes, and see if he can identify it. Luckily, the *Niagara's* going south to-day; we'll be able to catch her mail this afternoon, and get a reply in four days, if Stakes can be found."

"I've got his address, sir," proclaimed Sharpe, proud

of this feat of detective work. He put his hand in his pocket, drew out his pocket-book, searched it in vain, slapped and emptied his side pockets, felt in his trouser pockets, and finally produced the address, scrawled on a portion of cardboard cigarette box. "And by the way, sir," he added, "I knew there was something I wanted to tell you: the news is out."

"Out? What do you mean?" Spearpoint looked up impatiently from the draft of the letter to the Auckland police.

"The murder. It's all over the town, sir. All the barbers said, as soon as I produced the razor, 'Is that what Netta Maul was cut up with?' I had a crowd of Fijians and Indian boys following me round, as admiring as if I'd done it myself."

"Blast it! And what did you say?"

"I said I'd come to obtain information, not to give it. I say, sir, how could it have leaked out? Who do you think would split?"

"Plenty of people must know officially by now. There's the arrangements for the inquest and the funeral. And she wasn't in her room last night. Nor at her shop this morning. Blast! I suppose Pencarbon knows, and I wanted to tell him myself, and see how he took it. But it can't be helped." And Spearpoint asked the telephone operator to get Pencarbon on the line for him, deeming it unnecessary to consult Pencarbon's employers. As soon as he had asked the young man to come round at once, he was rung up by Bellamy's employer.

"What's this I hear about Netta Maul, eh?"

"How do we know what you hear?" retorted Spearpoint, nettled by the peremptory demand.

"I see you've got a man guarding her shop, eh," continued Mr. Cutt, in more amicable tones. "What's up, eh?"

"She's not there, is she?" returned Spearpoint, playing for time while he decided how much information to impart.

"No. The place is locked. Do you know anything about it, eh? I'm told she's been found with her head cut off. Well, we're very interested in her business affairs, you know."

"Well, Mr. Cutt, we don't mind telling you that she is dead, and was apparently murdered. But it's an exaggeration to say her head was chopped off."

"So it is true, eh?" said Mr. Cutt, unperturbed. "First bit of scandal I've ever heard in this burg that was true. Well, we hold a Bill of Sale over all her stock and assets, including all her silverware, eh. Is any of that missing?"

"Not so far as we can make out, Mr. Cutt. At least, a good deal of it is still there. We'll have to check it with the insurance policy."

"We hold that, of course. We'll send a man along to check it, if you like, eh?"

"I don't think you need do that. We want to check it ourselves. If you'd like to let us have the list—— We want to make a thorough examination of her room and shop later to-day, and we don't want anyone to disturb them meanwhile. We've got a man on guard at her room also."

"Anything we can do to help, of course, we'll be ready to do—I mean, in investigating her assets and taking stock, and so on, eh. It's your job to find the murderer, eh. We're not interested in that."

"Quite," returned Spearpoint, drily. The last remark was supererogatory. In all the years he had known Willy Cutt, Spearpoint had never heard of his expressing interest in any matter unconnected with the affairs of Marryam & Cutt, Ltd., except for his two hobbies, bridge and fishing. The murder of Netta Maul meant nothing to him but the opportunity to obtain payment of an unproductive debt authorised by the kind-hearted Mr. Marryam during Mr. Cutt's last absence abroad. "If you let us have the policy, we'll check her property. And perhaps you could lend us a man later to take stock after we've examined her shop."

"Certainly. You can have Bellamy, eh. He knows more about her business than she did herself." Then Mr. Cutt permitted himself one of his rare chuckles. "I say, Spearpoint, did Bellamy murder her? Is that what you wanted to see him about, eh? Should I write to Auckland by this mail for another stock-clerk?"

"That would be premature, Mr. Cutt. We've no reason to suppose he had anything to do with it. He happened to see her last night, and was able to give us some information concerning her movements, that's all. When I say he saw her, I mean he walked past her in the street, and so could verify where she was at a certain time.—May we ask him to come and take stock when we're ready, without troubling you further?"

"That'll be all right. I'd like to know if her assets are intact, as soon as possible. We'll take the usual steps to protect ourselves, of course."

"Quite. Good-bye," and Spearpoint rang off abruptly as Pencarbon, unannounced, barged into the office.

The word for Stanley Pencarbon was jaunty. Of all the persons questioned by Spearpoint and Sharpe during this enquiry, none, not even Willy Cutt, showed more self-possession than did this lanky young Australian haberdasher's assistant. He bustled into the D.I.'s office with a hearty, "Good morning, boys! Bloody good morning to you;" took off his not-recently-whitened topee, handed it casually to Sharpe, snatched it back with a start of surprise and a "Sorry, ole mal; mistook you for the bloody butler," and hung it on a non-existent peg on the wall, whence it fell, bounced, and rolled upside down into a corner. Without waiting for the invitation, he settled himself in the visitor's chair, tilted it on its two back legs, and clasped his hands behind his head. Almost throughout the interview, he preserved the manner of an interested participant in the discussion-room of the Daisy Club; Sharpe felt that at any moment he might clap his hands and shout, "Tolo mai! Three bloody beers!"

"And what can little Stanley do for you, ole mal?" he enquired of Spearpoint.

"It's about Netta Maul——" began the Inspector, glancing at the notes he had prepared for the conversation.

"On the job already, eh? Smart work, boys, smart work!" broke in the Australian. "And I can tell you a thing or two about her, just quietly. I can give you the good oil on her. Too bloody true I can!"

"We don't doubt that," retorted Spearpoint, firmly; "but, firstly, we want to know when you saw her last."

"When I saw her last?" reflected Pencarbon, letting the chair down on its four legs. "When I saw her last? I don't know, ole mal. I don't bloody well know. To tell you the bloody truth, I never knew she had a last. And," he added, tilting his chair again, "I thought I'd seen everything she'd got."

"When did you last see her?" amended Spearpoint, impatiently, eyeing him narrowly, trying to judge if he was playing for time, and wondering whether it was wiser to ignore this quibbling or to reprimand him for it.

"Well, it wasn't last night, anyway," Pencarbon answered. "Don't see her every night, you know. Leave some for the other beggars! That's little Stanley. None of the dog in the bloody manger about him.—Do you mean, when did I actually see her last, or—or hold converse with her?"

"Both."

"Well, ole mal, the last bloody time I spoke to the sheila was at breakfast time yesterday. Yes, ole mal, breakfast time yesterday. She'd just taken a slice of paw-paw, so I passed her the bloody lemon and said, 'How would you like a little squeeze, dearie?' and she said, 'Not to-day, thank you,' or words to that effect. That's it, ole mal, bloody breakfast-time yesterday."

"And when did you last see her?"

"Ah, that's a different pair of bloody strides, as the bishop said to the barmaid. The last time I saw Netta

Maul was at half-past five yester-bloody-afternoon. She was standing on Victoria Parade outside Marryam & Cutt's and I was toddling along on the other side like the adjectival good Samaritan. She gave me a sweet bloody smile, and I raised my bloody hat. Always the little gentleman, Stanley Pencarbon. That's it, ole mal. That's about the bloody strength of it."

"You're sure you didn't see her later in the evening?"

"Ah, no," responded Pencarbon, sagely wagging his finger at the Inspector. "Never see Netta Maul late in the evening. That's a bad habit. Take my tip, ole mal. Take my bloody tip." He brought his chair to earth with a crash. "Say, you boys ever heard my imitation of a man without a roof to his mouth reciting 'The Death of Nelson on the Field of Bakerloo'?"

"No, and we don't want to!" retorted Spearpoint, firmly. "What we want is an account of your proceedings last night."

"Why, I went to old Joe Nomore's to give my bloody recitation. Bloody good, you know! Lelsol said to Welliltol, 'Welliltol, ole mal——'"

"We don't want to hear it. What time did you go to Nomore's?"

"What time? Oh, about half-past nine. About half-past bloody nine, ole mal."

"Was that the time you arrived there?"

"No, ole mal. That was the time I left the Royal Palm, —more or less, you know, ole mal, more or bloody less. Don't make up a bloody time-sheet, you know, of my evenings. I just keep an account of the cost, not the bloody time. And they cost a bit, too, I don't mind telling you."

"What time do you estimate you arrived at Nomore's?"

"Let me see, now. Let me bloody well see. Any time from a quarter to ten to a quarter past—do you want to know exactly?"

"It's important to know your time of arrival as closely as possible. Would it be before or after ten, for example?"

"Beggared if I know, ole mal," said the Australian, reflectively. He took a silver cigarette case from his hip pocket, opened it, selected a cigarette and put one end to his lips; then he shut the case with a snap, opened it again and offered it to the two policemen, who declined. Saying, "I can only think when I smoke. It lightens the bloody labour," he lit the cigarette and flipped the dead match at Sharpe. Then he shrugged his shoulders and repeated, "Beggared if I know. Round about ten, ole mal, it was."

"Ten o'clock's rather late to go paying calls, isn't it?"

"I was sitting up with a sick friend at the Melbourne Hotel," grinned Pencarbon. "At least, he was bloody sick later on. But, of course," he added, turning suddenly helpful. "Of course, I can tell you the exact bloody time I arrived. It was ten past ten. I went to old Joe's to listen in to the bloody wrestling from Sydney, and that started at ten-fifteen—eight-fifteen in Sydney, of course—dear old bloody Sydney. And I got in about five minutes before it started. Walked up Waimanu Road and nipped across the adjectival paddock. So that's about the strength of it, ole mal,—ten past bloody ten."

"I suppose you went over the soapstone and through Bellamy's garden?"

"Too right."

"And how long do you reckon it took you to cross the field?"

"Five minutes, ole mal, five minutes."

"I should say it was nearer fifteen."

"Oh, no, ole mal, wouldn't take fifteen bloody minutes to cross that bloody paddock.—Though, mind you, I did get bloody well bogged half way across and nearly lost a bloody shoe. Might have been ten minutes—not more."

"Well, that's near enough," conceded Spearpoint, making a note. "Did you happen," he added, looking up suddenly, "to hear a scream as you were crossing the field?"

Pencarbon leant forward with interest. "Why, was the gory deed done in that bloody paddock?"

"I'm asking you whether you heard a scream."

"No, ole mal, I didn't hear any bloody scream."

"Several, people round the field about ten o'clock did hear a scream, but it might have only been someone larking about," volunteered the Inspector.

"My oath it might!" agreed Pencarbon. "My bloody oath! If you boys knew what I know about that bloody paddock! But was that really where the poor kid was done in?" he asked, momentarily dropping his hard-boiled unconcern and revealing what appeared to be genuine fondness for the murdered girl.

Spearpoint made no answer, but continued to watch Pencarbon narrowly. The Australian looked at the ground, biting his lips. Then he muttered, "She wasn't a bad kid, you know, as sheilas go. Some good in her, I suppose." Turning to Sharpe, he exclaimed, "My oath! The begger that finished her off must have had it in for her! Too bloody right! They tell me she was cut into fourteen bloody pieces!"

Sharpe made to answer, but Spearpoint gestured to him to be silent, and said, "You can tell them, whoever they are, that they're wrong. She's all in one piece.— Would you like to see her?" he added, sharply.

Pencarbon laughed, quite at his ease. "Well, ole mal, I've got my share of bloody curiosity. If you've got any bloody corpses for view, trot 'em out, and I'll give 'em an eyeful for you."

"Sorry," said Spearpoint, convinced by the Australian's alacrity that the sight of the corpse would not lead to any display of incriminating emotion, "but it's too late now. The undertaker's got her." He glanced down at his notes. "What time did you leave Nomore's?"

"Not the faintest! Not the bloody faintest, ole mal! I was as shot as Chloe! Don't remember a bloody thing after kissing old Joe good night."

"Which way did you go home?"

"Search me!"

"Do you think you walked, or did someone drive you?"

"Beggared if I know! I was as shot as Chloe! And what a head I've got this morning! Take my bloody tip, boys, don't touch old Joe's home brew!"

"You mean that you don't remember anything until you woke up and found yourself in bed this morning?" persisted Spearpoint.

"My oath! I was as shot as Chloe!" repeated the Australian. "What a head, boys! What a bloody head!"

Deciding to have the story confirmed, Spearpoint abandoned his search for the truth, and produced in turn the torch, the trouser-button, the lipstick and an ebony ruler, handing each to Pencarbon and asking if any of them were his.

Pencarbon examined the torch with some care, unscrewing the two ends, taking out the battery and glancing at the label, and then refitting it and flashing on the current. Finally, he said, "I can't throw any bloody light on that, ole mal."

To the button he retorted instantly, "No, ole mal, no fly-buttons off me, as the bishop said to the barmaid."

And to the lipstick: "What do you take me for? A bloody hirumphrodite? What would little Stanley do with a bloody lipstick?"

He failed likewise to recognise the ruler, on which he conveniently left his fingerprints, and, then, frustrated again in his attempt to repeat the dialogue between 'Lelsol' and 'Welliltol, ole mal', retrieved his battered topee, and departed.

CHAPTER NINE

THE FIRST PAUSE
(Friday : 11.45 a.m.–2 p.m.)

"WELL, SHARPE, THAT'S all we can manage this morning," remarked Spearpoint, when the door had closed behind the Australian. "I can't say we've got much. We know that either Camelback or Bellamy is lying; and I suspect both Thomspon and Pencarbon are lying too. But there are a lot of things we must do yet before we can come to any sort of conclusion at all. However, I've got to go up and see about the inquest and all the legal rigmarole at twelve. I think you'd better make some more enquiries about that scream. And ask Williams if there've been any strangers round the Royal Palm this morning—I don't mean tourists in the bar, of course. You come and have lunch with me, will you, and we'll talk things over. Afterwards we'll examine that field. Then we'll do the room and the shop. By that time things may look a little clearer."

Sharpe took his khaki topee and went. Spearpoint picked up his pen and began to spoil a fresh sheet of Government foolscap. He was interrupted by a discreet double knock on the door-panel. In answer to his call, there entered Singh, his favourite Punjabi sergeant, who marched into the office stiffly, wheeled smartly in front of the Inspector's desk, clicked his heels, saluted with precision, and stood to attention until his superior officer's nod set in motion his organs of speech. He uttered his simple English phrases with an accent so thick that only Spearpoint could understand him.

"Sahib, I go to the creek, as you tell me, and I talk to the fishermens. I talk to twenty fishermens. They all say no boat not gone. Then one say boat gone. I say his boat gone? He say no, his boat not gone. Lum Chin, his boat gone. I say where Lum Chin? He say Lum Chin look for boat. I say where Lum Chin look for boat? He say Lum Chin just look. Lum Chin not know where look for boat. I look for Lum Chin. I see ten, twenty, thirty Chinamen. I say, you Lum Chin? They say no, me not Lum Chin. I look for Lum Chin long time, sahib. Then I find Lum Chin. 10.35 a.m. I find Lum Chin. Lum Chin on wharf. Lum Chin not find boat. Lum Chin bloody sad, sahib. I say, Lum Chin, where you leave boat? He say, what matter where leave boat? Boat gone now. Some bahstud take boat. I say, Lum Chin, tell me where you leave boat, Inspector Sahib find boat. He say Inspector Sahib not know what boat like. Lum Chin no find boat, Inspector Sahib no find boat. I say, Inspector Sahib no find boat, Inspector Sahib give Lum Chin new boat. I say Inspector Sahib missus always buy fish Lum Chin, no other damn Chinee. Lum Chin show me where he leave boat, sahib.''

The boat had been moored close to the Renwick Road bridge over the creek, opposite the timberyard, and in such a position that it could easily have been untied and pulled across to the spot where Mr. Thomspon's car had been parked. Singh then proceeded to relate how he and Lum Chin had borrowed a launch and set out on an exhaustive search, slurring over the detail of payment for the hire, in order to hurry on to his triumphant climax, the finding of the missing boat. It was in an improbable place, adrift among the mangroves and reeds of Walu Bay, the almost land-locked lake at the foot of the hospital cliff. They had taken it in tow, and, not without feats of crazy navigation among the fleet of pleasure craft moored inside the narrow entrance to the bay, had brought it back to its station in the creek, where Lum Chin had promised to stand guard pending its examination by the Inspector Sahib.

Spearpoint at once drove to the creek; but the boat gave him little information. It was quite in order, and its worn wood showed no suspicious markings. There was a little water in the bottom, but no trace of earth or sacking or bloodstains.

Singh's reward for his morning's work was a series of commissions to set about tracing all the Indians and natives Spearpoint had passed on his drive, and to organise a search for bloodstained garments among all the laundries of Suva.

For the remainder of the morning, Spearpoint was occupied either with routine matters or with legal formalities. He was irritated both by the necessity of deferring to his superiors and bargaining with his equals, and by the loss of the precious hour from the job in hand. But he succeeded in obtaining authority for all his proposed investigations, and sat down to lunch in no discontented mood.

Sharpe had spent a busy hour visiting all the residents of Waimanu Road between Dr. Halibut's and the Montgomery Thomspons', but his enquiries seemed to have produced little of value. Some families had been out all the evening; others had been at home but could say nothing. One had had the wireless on from eight till eleven and had heard nothing but atmospherics. Tom Humble, whose house was on the edge of the cliff overlooking Walu Bay, had been sleepless all night with prickly heat, and, hearing movements in the garden, had turned out of bed in time to flash his torch on a Punjabi Indian fumbling with the gate latch. He wondered bitterly why the police didn't do something to prevent his flower beds being used as a public lavatory. The mother of a half-caste family farther down the hill said she had been awakened by a piercing scream at five minutes past twelve; asked if she had looked at the clock to verify the time, she said, no, but she had thought it was about five past twelve. Her elder daughter said she had heard a succession of blood-curdling yells from the direction of the wharf at half-past two in the morning, adding that she had consulted her watch in order to note the exact time, because she was sure that someone was being murdered, and knew that the police would want the exact time. The younger daughter pointed out that her sister's watch was broken, and this led to an exchange of recriminations which the investigator found more amusing than helpful. Finally the father volunteered meekly that he had heard a single scream from somewhere up the road about ten o'clock; but the three women told Sharpe that he was always imagining things, and he needn't take any notice of father. At the last house, Sharpe had been detained an unconscionable time by a lady with a grievance against the Creator for having made chocolate-coloured people, and for having endowed them, when made, with the capacity for happiness and the voices wherewith to express that happiness. Every hour of her life in Fiji had been blasted by the shouts, the yells, the screams and the happy laughter of the non-European inhabitants of the Colony. Had she heard a scream last evening? Had she heard anything else? Her dinner had been rendered uneatable by the accompaniment of boisterous laughter from the road, her evening games of patience had been ruined by the yells of the blacks who dwelt in Toorak Road at the far side of the field, and she had been held sleepless all night by the steady drumming from the Indian lines.

Sharpe had also managed to interview the manager of the Royal Palm Hotel, who had said that the only non-resident and non-tourist who had been in that morning had been Mr. Cutt, who had been found trying the handle of Netta Maul's room, and asking impatiently where she was. He had evidently come up the back staircase, "as if," grumbled Williams, "he owned the bloody place." As a matter of fact, Marryam & Cutt, Ltd., held security over everything Williams possessed, and were his landlords as well as his importing agents, but that did not give Mr. Cutt the right, argued Williams, to walk into the female boarders' bedrooms. "Did he apologise? Did he hell? When I said I was beggared if I knew where she was, he just beggared off without another word."

"Well," commented Spearpoint, "that doesn't help as much as I had hoped it would. If we could establish that the scream I heard was Netta Maul's, we'd be getting somewhere. It would be most useful to establish the time of death. Halibut made it about eleven, perhaps as early as 10.30; and when I said she was alive at a quarter to ten, he said she must have died within the hour. Carnarvonshire, in his best dogmatic style, said she died at half-past ten. That's about as close as we're likely to get. It did occur to me that we could have had her cut open to see where her dinner had got to, but that wouldn't have timed it any closer than half an hour."

"Unless," Sharpe pointed out, "the doctor happens to know the exact gear she worked on."

Spearpoint related the conclusions he had reached from his reference to the tides, and then continued, "Here's my time-table. I left Karrkuss about nine forty-three and I drove very slowly—not above fifteen miles an hour. I've looked on the plan of Suva and I find his house is almost three-quarters of a mile from the corner of Browne Street. So I reached there about nine forty-six. Now, the natives I saw going uphill don't matter; only the people I saw going down. First there were two Indians, a man and a woman. Suppose I overtook them at nine forty-four and they were walking at three miles an hour—a mile in twenty minutes—half a mile in ten minutes; they'd get to Browne Street at nine fifty-four. Camelback was doing a good forty-five or more when he overtook me; and I reckon he'd get to the corner of Browne Street about nine forty-five and a half (in fact, just in time to get out of the car and come round to the back before I passed him at nine forty-six). I overtook Bellamy immediately afterwards, and if he was doing three miles an hour, he'd get to the corner of Browne Street about nine forty-seven and a half, and he'd be home by nine-fifty. Now, Netta Maul was about a hundred yards ahead of Bellamy, and as they were both walking about the same speed, she would be about a minute ahead of him. Then I overtook a laundryman; he doesn't matter much, because, although he must have seen Camelback, Camelback admits having pulled up in front of Halibut's. Then I passed Selkirk driving up.—Incidentally, I had a word with Selkirk this morning and he remembers passing me on the corner—at least, he remembers a Lostinit; but he doesn't remember noticing Camelback's car. That's not important, anyway. I reached the Montgomery Thomspons' house at nine forty-seven. That's a certain time. All the others are estimates from that. Now, there were two taxis going uphill, Nos. ST 17 and ST 35. I've got Singh tracing their drivers. I reckon they'd get to Browne Street about nine fifty-five, that is, about the same time as the Indian and his wife. It's most important to get them to corroborate either Bellamy's story or Camelback's. Did they see Netta Maul and Camelback together? That's the point. I saw some Fijians going up, but they'd arrive after the scream. We must trace them if we can, but I'm afraid that will be a devil of a job.

"Now, Pencarbon appeared on the scene about nine fifty-five or nine fifty-seven, and if he went straight across the field he would reach Joe Nomore's about five past ten. He says ten past, or rather 'just before a quarter past.' We must check that time with old Joe, though, if I know old Joe, he won't know. It will be difficult, but I think it's important, to discover exactly where Pencarbon was at nine fifty-nine."

"You mean," Sharpe broke in, "that Pencarbon could have arranged to meet Netta Maul in the field just before ten, have cut her throat and left her there, and then gone on to old Joe's to establish an alibi; and then disposed of her body on the way home? I've thought of how Conky's car could have been used for that, sir. Have you realised that there's a slope all the way from his house to the creek? Could the bloke have trussed Netta Maul up in the field, dumped her in the car, pushed the car into the road, with the bonnet turned downhill, given it a bit of a push, and then jumped in and just steered down the hill? The momentum would carry it over the bridge. That would account for the Thomspons hearing nothing and for no petrol being used. I say, if Pencarbon cut her throat and left her in the field while he made merry at old Joe's, he's got a nerve. Could he have done all that, do you think, sir?"

It was not at all what Spearpoint had meant. His intention had been to establish facts, and not to jump to conclusions about surmised facts. But as he visualised the lanky Australian carrying out this athletic feat of daring he had to admit that Sharpe had found a plausible explanation of some of the mysterious points in the case. Upper Waimanu Road runs along the top of an inland cliff, with the Suva golf course on the land side, and on the sea side a row of residences whose back gardens command wide distant views of the harbour, and the immediate prospect of that mangrove-bordered Walu Bay where Lum Chin's boat had been discovered. The Colonial War Memorial Hospital occupies a spectacular site at the end of the cliff, with the road cut out of the cliff side, dropping sharply beside it and below it, sweeping round in a generous double bend past Dr. Halibut's house. Middle Waimanu Road is residential, and slopes less steeply for a few hundred yards, but after passing the glory of the home of the Montgomery Thomspons it changes both its character and the angle of its contour; and lower Waimanu Road is the triumphant delight and unheeded death-trap of the free-wheeling Fijian cyclist, whose heart-stopping descents pass unenvied and unheeded by the industrious Buddha-posed cobblers, tread-ling Indian tailors, and calm-eyed Chinese storekeepers who earn their sparse livelihood in the wooden shops lining the road. At the foot of the hill is the hump-backed bridge over the creek, and immediately beyond it, on the left, the ungated timberyard, and, on the right, the large concrete department store of Morris, Hedstrom, Ltd., with its stone colonnade along the bank of the stream.

"It's possible," conceded Spearpoint, slowly. "At least, it's an idea we might bear in mind."

"And that explains why the car was left by the creek," broke in Sharpe; "the bloke didn't want to make a row driving it uphill again. He thought that if he left it by the creek, we should just assume that someone had borrowed it and been too lazy to put it back where they found it."

"Perhaps," assented Spearpoint, "but even if that is how the body was taken to the creek, it doesn't follow that Pencarbon did it. He must have known that he was observed to enter the field—he admits he did it, of course. No good denying that because, although he may not have recognised me in mufti and someone else's car, he would know there was someone in the car. And, for all he knew, Netta Maul was seen to enter the field also. We may get evidence of that later—but, to proceed. I heard the scream at nine fifty-nine. I am positive of that. I had my eye on the clock and it said ten-three. The evidence you have collected corroborates that so far as is necessary. Now, it was really at ten-three that someone drove Conky Thompson's car up Waimanu Road, and ten-four when Bellamy's light went on."

"Bellamy's light?"

"Yes. That might have something to do with the matter. If he'd continued walking at the pace he was walking, he'd have been home ten minutes before that. Suppose he's made up the story of the quarrel with

Camelback. Suppose he followed Netta Maul in the field
—remember how touchy he was at the suggestion that
he was following her?—I told you about that, didn't I?
—Well, suppose he was following her. Suppose he cut
her throat and nipped into the house for the cord and
the sack and so on. I don't think he's very likely, but the
fact that his light went on ten minutes after he should
have been indoors is rather suspicious.—To proceed:
Camelback says he got to the Royal Palm at exactly ten
o'clock. You'll note that he's exact about that time; and
he left exactly at eleven. To be so accurate is a bit fishy
in itself. Mind you, this doesn't contradict Bellamy's
story, because he could still have spoken to Netta Maul
and got to the Royal Palm at ten. But if he was at the
Royal Palm at ten, and did kill her before that, it follows
that it couldn't have been her that I heard scream at a
minute before ten. We must check his statements with
Malleable and Eachway. Certainly we must suspect Jim
Camelback for the present. Then Conky Thomspon: he
says he left the Club at ten-fifteen. Halibut corroborates
that. But Carnarvonshire makes it nearer ten-twenty, and
Bettina Bloggins makes it nearly ten-thirty. I suppose
it's two minutes from the Club to where they met, allowing for starting the car and turning in the road. The discrepancy doesn't matter much, because, as I said just now,
people don't notice the time very exactly. I mean the
discrepancy doesn't necessarily indicate that some of
these people are not telling the truth. But we ought to
try and find out the exact time Conky left the Club
because we ought to know whether it would have been
possible for his car to have been where I saw it at three
minutes past ten, and back where Conky parked it by
the time he left the Club. If, for example, he did leave
the Club at ten-fifteen, and the car was not there, and
he had to wait, say, five minutes for it to be returned,
then it might well be, say, about twenty-five past when
he picked up Bettina. That presupposes, of course, that

he knows (even if he did not know before ten-fifteen) that his car was borrowed, and naturally he knows who borrowed it. It suggests vistas that we mustn't attempt to explore until we have ascertained the facts. Whoever took Conky's car could have gone from where he passed me, up Browne Street, along Amy Street and Holland Street, and have left the car outside the Club, by ten past ten—provided he continued at the pace he was doing when I saw him, and provided he did not stop anywhere. But if he did stop for as much as five minutes, then the car could hardly have been back before a quarter past."

"But all this was after the scream," objected Sharpe, who had been following this involved argument with painfully knitted brows.

"I know, but there's something fishy about the car. Besides, we don't know for certain that the scream had anything to do with Netta Maul."

"Well, sir, the car couldn't have been driven by any of the suspects, could it?—Or could it?"

Spearpoint shrugged his shoulders. "It was someone fairly big. That's all I can say. One thing we may take as fairly certain: she was killed soon after I saw her. If she was killed when I heard the scream, and if she was taken to the creek in Thomspon's car, then her body must have lain somewhere in the field until eleven-thirty at the earliest (assuming that Conky's car was parked when he says it was), and probably until much later. We must go over that field with a toothcomb. Finished?"

"Well, sir," commented Sharpe, as they stood up. "There's another man who ought to be questioned pretty closely about this business, since he evidently saw her very soon before she was done in."

Spearpoint stopped with a jerk. What could he have overlooked? "Who do you mean?" he demanded.

"Inspector Spearpoint, sir."

"Rubbish! Besides, Mrs. Montgomery Thomspon will

give me an alibi for ten o'clock; and, incidentally, where were you at ten o'clock last night?"

"Me?" replied Sharpe, with dignity. "I have a cast-iron alibi. All the leading citizens of Suva can testify to me. I was in the bar at the Daisy Club."

Spearpoint chuckled, for the Daisy Club had been closed five years earlier.

CHAPTER TEN

THE PADDOCK AND THE PRINTS
(*Friday: 2–4 p.m.*)

"NOW YOU'D BETTER get to work and develop your photographs," suggested Spearpoint. "Then we'll have some idea of these chaps' fingerprints. I'll get off this letter to the Auckland police, and one or two other things, and then we'll go up and study the field."

As soon as Sharpe had left, Spearpoint telephoned to Mr. Montgomery Thomspon and summoned him to his office. He had determined to test Sharpe's theory of the free-wheeling car without the knowledge or assistance of that carefree youth. If anyone was to steer madly down Waimanu Road in the cause of detective science, it would not be Sub-Inspector Sharpe with his superior officer as passenger. Moreover, the post-luncheon drowsiness which Spearpoint had as yet found no means of overcoming could be more successfully fought by physical than by intellectual labour.

When Mr. Montgomery Thomspon appeared, he had recovered a good deal of his normal scanty stock of self-confidence, but he was plainly wondering anxiously why he had been called to this second interview. Relief appeared on his countenance as soon as he learned that he was not to be questioned, but was merely required to indicate exactly where his car had been parked. As they spluttered furiously up the steep incline between the Indian and Chinese balconied shops, the little man became garrulous, complaining of the delay in the construction of his new house. "When we sold our old house and went Home on holiday, we expected the new one would be ready when we got back, and here we've been renting this inconvenient place for nearly six months. It hasn't even got a garage."

Spearpoint knew that the delay was solely due to Mrs. Thompson's refusal to make up her mind concerning many details of decoration and lay-out. She liked the Waimanu Road house because it was conveniently close to her sister, who lived opposite, in the home where both had spent their childhood. The Fiji-born mingle reluctantly with the transient English.

Thomspon brought the car to rest, bonnet inwards, at the entrance to the cul-de-sac, just beyond the line of the front fence.

"Was this where you left it? You usually take it another dozen yards further in, level with the house, don't you?"

"Sometimes. But last night I left it here."

They got out.

"Now, do you think," suggested Spearpoint, "it would be possible to push the car backwards, over the rise there, and into the road, so that it would run downhill without needing to start the engine? Even from here you'd have heard it being started up in the middle of the night."

Little Thomspon pushed hard and vainly. The car, with its wheels planted on pebbles and weeds, would do no more than rock. Then the burly Inspector had a go. He put his hands on the radiator, and heaved. The car moved. It ran gently backwards, over the slight bulge of the road junction, and came to rest against the opposite kerb. He pushed the car back into position, and tried again, this time with the mystified owner sitting in the back seat.

To the alarm of that owner, he arrested the backward slide, ran quickly to the wheel, and twisted it so that the car pointed downhill. Holding it back with an effort, he wrenched open the door, clambered in, and steered triumphantly if breathlessly downhill, without starting the engine, gaining sufficient impetus to breast the hump-backed bridge, and turn with a dangerous lurch into the timberyard, coming to a standstill within a couple of yards of the spot where the car had been found that morning. It was a crazy and a reckless drive, but it did demonstrate that Sharpe's theory was tenable.

Even the meek Mr. Montgomery Thomspon was moved to protest. "What was the idea of that?" he enquired, as the colour returned to his cheeks. "You near as a toucher ran headlong into that lorry." He prudently refrained from mentioning the high-wheeled Indian trap he had almost sideswiped as it had emerged from All Nations' Street, and the Punjabi policeman who had leapt for his life so promptly that he had forgotten to salute first.

"I wanted to see if it was possible to get this car from where you parked it to where it was found, without running the engine," Spearpoint explained, casually. "It is possible. Now I'll drive you up to the Club and you can show me exactly where you parked it while you were inside."

The little man looked somewhat apprehensive at the prospect of being the Inspector's passenger for the drive up the opposite side of the valley, and presumably back again, but he acquiesced perforce, and Spearpoint was able to ascertain that the car had been left in a place where it was hidden from the Club, with the result that it would have been possible for it to have been borrowed and returned without the knowledge of its owner. His first experience of emulating midnight feats in the traffic of midday led him to postpone, at least until the night, if not indefinitely, any attempt to find out how long it would take to circle the town by the route Sharpe had suggested. Unless he knew for a fact that the car had made the trip, there was no point in knowing how long such a trip would take, he decided. Evidence discovered during the afternoon might make the venture unnecessary.

He drove Mr. Thomspon sedately to the Police Station, handed back the car to him, and, collecting Sharpe from the darkroom, drove back up the hill in his own car to the spot where he had last seen Netta Maul.

The path to the field, along which it was presumed that Netta Maul had gone, was bounded on one side by the hedge of Dr. Halibut's garden, and on the other by the paling fence of a family named Paul, who were on holiday in New Zealand. Spearpoint drew up in front of the vacant house, and the two policemen got out. First they examined the spot in Browne Street where Jim Camelback's car had stood. There were tyre marks in the mud at the side, but they were not distinctive. None of them were recognisable as the marks of Thomspon's tyres. The steps leading to Dr. Halibut's garden and the path leading to his house were of concrete. The concrete kerb and the gutter of Waimanu Road ended at his steps; beyond, in Browne Street, where the car had stood, was no kerb and no gutter, merely a depression which drained into the first gulley outside Paul's house. There was no pavement inside the kerb, a mown grassy verge serving instead. Paul kept this verge neatly cut outside his house; but lower down the road, where there were no houses, the grass grew irregularly and the soapstone below it protruded in places.

"I wonder," mused Spearpoint, "if Paul left his garage door unlocked. We might pop our car in there and prevent a crowd collecting." He strolled across the grass to the garage, but stopped at a bare patch immediately in front of the doors.

"No trace of a car," he said, "but what about these footprints?"

They were the impressions of a large pair of rubber soles, evidently made by a heavy man.

"Bellamy was wearing plimsolls, you said, sir," Sharpe pointed out eagerly.

"But his feet wouldn't be as big as these," objected his superior.

"A Fijian, I should think, then, sir," was Sharpe's next suggestion. "Some feet, eh! Look, they're as big as mine. And Fijians always wear plimsolls, if they wear shoes at all. All these little raised squares come from plimsolls, don't they? Never knew a rubber sole like that to a leather shoe."

"Plimsolls all right," agreed Spearpoint, who had been measuring the length of the stride, and finding it rather greater than his own. "They may or may not mean anything. But it's fairly clear those marks were made within the last twenty-four hours. There was that heavy shower yesterday afternoon which would have affected them. These are pretty sharp impressions; recent, if you ask me."

He called over his barefoot Fijian sentry and asked him in Fijian whether anyone had walked in the mud-patch that day. The native shook his fuzzy head vigorously and said, "Singeye, saka," meaning "No, sir," and repeated the negative emphatically twice, evidently going on the principle that whatever he said three times was true.

Spearpoint indicated the footprints and asked if he could explain them.

The Fijian shook his head even more emphatically than before, and said, "Singeye, saka! Singeye! Singeye!" Then he looked down at the prints, placing his own flat, splay-toed pedal organ alongside one, and exclaimed in wonder, "Sa levu! Sa lev'!" ("What a size!")

Spearpoint dismissed him, and turned to the garage. The double doors were normally fastened with a hasp and staple holding a padlock; but the padlock was missing and the hasp and staple were rusty. The hasp swung

off the staple readily enough, and both doors folded
outwards without the slightest creak of the hinge. Instantly
sunlight flooded the shed, revealing the beaten earth
floor, the pile of sacks in the far corner, a couple of old
petrol tins; and more of the marks of the plimsolled feet.
He decided to examine the garage before making use of
it. This did not take long, but it yielded important results.
The car tracks inside were obviously old; and there was
nothing suspicious about the petrol tins, but the sacks,
which were similar to the one the corpse had been tied
in, had the appearance of having been recently disturbed.
Spearpoint and Sharpe shifted the pile, examining each
sack superficially; but the lower ones had evidently been
in position for a long time and were creased and flattened
by their undisturbed rest. The top two or three, however,
had undoubtedly been handled recently—unfolded, re-
folded and replaced without much care. These were all
in poor condition, with holes or large patches of oil stain.

"It looks to me," exclaimed Spearpoint, "as if the
sack came from this pile. He rejected these top ones
because they weren't in good enough condition. They're
just like the sack she was dumped in."

"Yes, sir. We're on the track here, all right."

"And why did he lack a sack on the floor?" asked
Spearpoint, indicating a dirty sack stretched on the
ground at the back of the shed. Superficially it gave the
appearance of having been there a long time, but, after
examination of its turned-up edges and slightly-billowing
inside, the policemen decided that it had been placed
there only recently. Spearpoint lifted it gingerly. Underneath was a patch of earth damper than the surrounding
earth; the patch corresponded to a stain on that part
of the sack which had been immediately above it. Had
the garage been occupied by a car within the last few
days, both policemen would have assumed that oil had
dropped on the patch, and soaked into the sack carelessly
thrown on top of the puddle. On the instant, Spearpoint

did indeed suspect that a car had been garaged there last night; but then he remembered the age of the tyre marks on the floor; and immediately afterwards the exciting discovery of some long black hairs both on the underside of the sack and adhering to the ground on and around the damp patch suggested a more gruesome idea. This dampness was blood and this was the place where Netta Maul had been killed. Regarding this as the most important discovery they had yet made, Spearpoint sent his native constable for a spade and a clean pail, and told Sharpe to examine the door for fingermarks.

"No go, sir," reported Sharpe, presently. "The rusty iron of this hasp and staple won't show marks, nor will this woodwork.—If old Paul had had the place decently painted, now——" he added, regretfully.

The garage possessed a small back door bolted on the outside. Approaching the shed through Paul's front garden, Spearpoint found that a narrow brick path led from the front door of the house to the back door of the garage. Sharpe pointed out one more plimsoll mark between the front gate and the brick path; any other marks there may have been were masked by the grass. More important than this, however, was a series of incomplete marks, some very clear, forming a trail from the back door of the garage to a gap in the side fence. In the path outside were other footmarks, but they were fainter and more confused, and in one or two instances the plimsolls had stepped above them. The policemen followed the path for the whole thirty yards of its length, finding sufficient plimsoll marks to indicate that their wearer had walked right along it, except for that part between the roadway and the gap in the fence. They saw no marks of the girl's shoes at all in this part of the path; but from a bramble in the hedge Spearpoint detached a scrap of blue material, without doubt torn from the dress of the murdered girl.

In that part of the path between the road and the

gap, where the garage wall served in lieu of a fence, were the footprints of a man's large leather boot, and a few marks of a girl's shoe. The man had gone in both directions, but the girl had come out only.

"We can't be certain these are Netta Maul's," decided Spearpoint. "The shoes would make a different impression when walking; but this ridiculous little heel is very like the shape of the impression—so square in front and round at the back."

"Half the girls in Suva wear little high heels, though, sir," suggested Sharpe; "especially the kind who might have come along here last night,—Bettina, for instance."

Before exploring the field, they trespassed in Dr. Halibut's garden, but his concrete path revealed nothing and his flowerbeds bore the marks of no feet but bare ones, presumably those of his Indian cookboy-houseboy-gardener. Certainly these footprints were large ones, but then Dr. Halibut's boy was exceptionally tall for a Hindoo.

As they returned to the roadway, Spearpoint explained a theory he had been considering for some hours. "Netta Maul, as I think I told you, was bruised in rather a funny place—apart from the whacking great bruise on the temple, I mean. Dr. Halibut said the blow on the temple probably killed her. There's not much doubt it would have knocked her out. Well, I've never seen anybody killed by a blow on the temple, but I've seen men knocked out. Their knees give and they collapse. Now, suppose, Netta Maul had been standing in front of these steps, where Bellamy says she was standing, and Jim Camelback had given her a hard drive on the temple, she'd have sat down on these steps with a hell of a bump. And I reckon that's how she might have got her other bruises."

"You mean, sir, that the bruises prove that Jim Camelback killed her?"

"Not necessarily. Bellamy might have hit her—not with his fist, of course, but with the knob at the end of his stick."

"Or Pencarbon," suggested Sharpe. "Suppose these prints are Pencarbon's. He came out by the path, found her waiting here, dotted her one, dragged her into the garage, cut her throat——"

"But Pencarbon wasn't wearing plimsolls—at least, I don't think he was. Besides, Plimsolls didn't come out by the path. He was only in that part of it between the gap in the fence and the field. Mind you, I don't say that that is what happened. I'm only suggesting that as a possible explanation of what seems to me rather a mystery. We'd better examine the field before we theorise any more."

The field was a depressing one, as lumpy as the surface of an insomniac's bed, and as dirty as the play of a visiting football team. It lay in the wedge-shaped hollow between the two soapstone ridges on which stood the houses in Amy Street and the houses in Waimanu Road. The back gardens of Amy Street sloped towards the field and drained into it; but the Waimanu Road gardens were on the broad cliff which bore the houses also. The result was that the Amy Street side was a bank of mud, whilst on the Waimanu Road side grass grew. It was tussocky, tangled stuff, overgrown with patches of prickly sensitive-grass, and more than sufficient to hide all trace of footprints or of the recent presence of humanity. From it protruded a score or so of misshapen coconut palms and two or three large mango trees. The entire surface was pitted with the hoofmarks and dotted with the leavings of the half-dozen horses that pastured there. The far end of the field was its lowest level, and this was swampy all the year round. Partly by cliff, and partly by swamp, therefore, the field was guarded by natural frontiers which would be crossed only by people who were at the same time both in a hurry and heedless of mucky shoes. Only at Bellamy's garden did the soapstone jut through the mud, forming the natural causeway which Pencarbon had used for his approach to Joe Nomore's.

Cursing the sensitive-grass, the two policemen muddied their shoes, their ankles and the turn-ups of their trousers conscientiously and bravely, but they found nothing so exciting as the damp patch in the garage. If Plimsolls had crossed the field, he had left no traces beyond the end of the path. And although there were occasional marks made by the shoes of both sexes, and various other evidences of human visits, there was nothing that seemed recent or to have any bearing on the murder of Netta Maul, with the possible exception of the occasional trail in both directions of a man with rubber heels. This trail was recent and led fairly straight from a gap in the fence at the end of Mr. Montgomery Thomspon's cul-de-sac to the soapstone at Bellamy's house; but in the other direction it wandered, and the many marks by the fence suggested that the wearer had had some difficulty in finding the gap. Spearpoint sketched the pattern of the heels and measured the prints, thinking it likely that the owner would be proved to be Pencarbon.

Both the roadway and the pathways of the cul-de-sac were stony and overgrown with weeds, but on an oily patch on the side where Mr. Montgomery Thomspon usually parked his car, was a confused mark which might have been made by Plimsolls. But identification of the print was impossible. They took a few measurements and photographs, but they did not expect them to be of much value.

Returning to their car, they appropriated the stained sack, and dug some samples of earth from the garage floor; Sharpe hurried these to the Government Chemist for analysis whilst Spearpoint returned to his office in the hope of a further report from Singh. The fierce-faced sergeant was awaiting him, having traced the laundry-man on the bicycle: he had remembered Camelback's car because he had nearly run into it; but he had not recognised Camelback. He had noticed a white man getting out, but he had not seen his face. He would have been able to recognise Camelback, who was a well-known resident.

The night watchman on the wharf, protesting that he had been patrolling all night, had seen no one, with or without a large sack, on his territory. He had observed various light craft moving on the water, but had no evidence to offer concerning Lum Chin's boat.

Singh had not yet traced the Indian who had been walking with his wife behind Bellamy and Netta Maul, but enquiries were proceeding.

All this he reported in the five minutes during which Spearpoint drove him to the bridge over the entrance to Walu Bay. Here they transferred to a waiting launch and chugged into the reedy expanse which had been the hiding place of Lum Chin's boat. They observed nothing unusual. The entrance to Walu Bay is narrow, and within are kept many small pleasure craft. None of these had the appearance of having been recently fouled by a drifting fisherboat, and Spearpoint judged that it would have been impossible for Lum Chin's boat to have drifted to the position in which it had been found. It had plainly been either rowed in or towed in behind a launch—in either case, by someone familiar with the bay. But if it had been rowed in, there was nothing to show how the rower had disembarked; and if it had been towed in, why?

Spearpoint calculated that the state of the tide at his visit was about the same as when, according to Dr. Carnarvonshire's calculation, Netta Maul's body had entered the water, some twelve and a half hours earlier. But this designed coincidence gave him no inspiration, and he determined to explore more thoroughly another day, the heavy shower which invariably falls on mailboat days reinforcing his decision that for the moment his time would be better spent in the town.

He returned to the Police Station to find Sharpe ready with a sheaf of damp photographs.

"Firstly, sir, I should say," began the fingerprint

wallah, "that I've gone all over her clothes and the jewellery she was wearing, and I can't find a suspicious mark on anything. I thought I'd found something on a couple of her bracelets, but they were her own marks. Of course, her clothes were crumpled, but I couldn't find any recognisable mark on them, and I venture to agree with your theory that there was no struggle. The jewellery is tarnished from the water, but it isn't marked at all. I'm told she used to sit on the verandah at the Royal Palm every night before dinner and polish her jewellery and silver, so I reckon it was all freshly polished at the time she was done in. So I think," he concluded, regretfully, "that the murderer must have worn gloves."

"But her clothes would hardly retain fingermarks after being in the water all night, would they?"

"Not very likely, sir—not very likely to retain them at all, any time. Depends on how they were made. Of course, in London or Paris they could bring out marks on fabrics. I know how it's done, and I've seen it done; but I haven't got the stuff here to do it. I was thinking of a bloodstained thumbmark or something like that. And then there were the silver buckles of her belt and all these silver buttons; they might retain impressions. The bloke could hardly have avoided touching her bracelets, at least, when he was tying her up."

"So we've drawn blank there. What have we got?"

They examined the prints, finding sufficient evidence that both razor and shoes had been handled by both Halibut and Spearpoint. Netta Maul's own mark was on one shoe, and on the razor was a faint blurred edge, heavily overlaid by the doctor's thumb, that might have been Bellamy—or someone else not in the gallery. But Bellamy was plainly on the torch, and so was Pencarbon; they had both handled it in Spearpoint's presence. They were on the lipstick as well, and so was Bettina. Mr. Montgomery Thomspon and Bettina had both been in the front of the car; and on various parts of the car were marks which were assumed were made by his wife and daughter. The only exciting discovery was the certainty that Stanley Pencarbon had grasped both the inner and the outer handles of the back door. It was evident that he had got into and out of the rear of the car. There was no trace of Camelback.

As they walked to the Royal Palm to examine the dead girl's room, Spearpoint remarked, "You know, none of the jewellery she was wearing was stolen—at least, she was wearing as much as any girl could have room for; and all the silver in her room seemed to be there. But her handbag was missing. What do you make of that?"

"Money, sir? The chap would know he couldn't dispose of the jewellery and silver, and it would be too risky to have it in his possession."

"You may be right," conceded Spearpoint, theorising for a moment, "but I think the bag was taken because it contained her keys. I think there was something in her room or her shop that the murderer wanted. I shouldn't be surprised if we found her bag somewhere in her room, left as if she had left it there herself; but I'm sure she had it with her when I saw her last night."

CHAPTER ELEVEN

NETTA MAUL AT WORK AND PLAY

(*Friday : 4–6 p.m.*)

A HIGH PROPORTION OF the white or near-white residents of Suva live in hotels and boarding-houses, and Netta Maul (who had had no relatives closer than a reputed aunt and cousins) had boarded at the Royal Palm Hotel, a rambling old wooden public-house on Victoria Parade, facing Suva harbour. Her room was on the upper floor, the end one of a row of five, each of which had a door leading to the interior passage and french windows giving access to the verandah. The passage was reached, not only by a staircase from the ground floor, but also by an exterior flight at the back of the building. For four-fifths of its length the verandah was unobstructed and was used as the common lounge of the occupants of the four rooms; but the portion in front of Netta Maul's room had been partitioned off many years before in order to afford some measure of privacy to the star boarder of those days. Although Netta Maul could hardly have been described as the star boarder, the landlord had found it convenient to bestow on her certain unusual privileges without extra payment, including the considerable advantages of the end room. Netta Maul could have lain abed in the sunny morning, listening to the chatter of the minahs in the gutter outside, or the soft cooing of doves, and looking between the palm trees to the dusty-olive slopes across the harbour and the scarred peak of the unclimbable Joske's Thumb. It is more likely, however, that she lay and contemplated the many silver-framed photographs of herself which decorated her walls.

She had a passion for silver, had Netta Maul; Inspector Spearpoint had long ago decided that it was the only thing she really cared for. Her room gleamed with the precious metal. Her trinket set was silver, and silver of considerable solidity. The top of her chest of drawers bore a glittering array of silver ornaments—candlesticks, statuettes and an enormous rose-bowl; a shelf above the door held more. On the verandah was her lazyboy chair and her low silver-inlaid coffee-table. It was here that she spent her leisure hours, polishing and caressing the gifts of her admirers. This wealth was familiar to Spearpoint, who had twice secured convictions against attempting burglars. It had been on his advice (but he knew not at whose expense) that the edge of the verandah screen had been tipped with iron spikes. The door to the passage fastened with a spring lock, to which Netta Maul had held what she had believed to be the only key; but Spearpoint was aware that the landlord kept a duplicate. It had been with the aid of this duplicate (which he had commandeered) that he had obtained entrance in the morning and had assured himself that, superficially at least, the room was in order.

Her silver apart, Netta Maul's room had considerably more individuality than most boarding-house bedrooms in Suva. As all the cleaning was done under her own imperious eye, no corner was ever neglected or scamped. The mats were shaken daily. None of the furniture was in the least degree shabby or rickety. There were no beer-glass stains on the table-top, and no unauthorised holes in the mosquito net. The expensively-embroidered silk counterpane and the curtains matching it were obviously her own property. So was the massive cabin trunk, of thick hide, with silver plates and fittings, which served as a stand for three large and untidy piles of American film magazines. For the rest, there was a single wooden bedstead; a dressing-table, a chest of drawers, two small chairs, a bedside table and a large curtained recess for wardrobe.

Spearpoint led, up the stairs and along the passage, a small procession consisting of Williams the landlord, Matilda the Samoan housemaid, and Sub-Inspector Sharpe. Unlocking and opening the door, he called his sentry from the verandah, and, on receiving the expected report that the afternoon had been uneventful, sent him off duty.

Before entering, he asked Williams to examine both room and verandah, but not to move or touch objects, and to give his opinion as to whether it was as Netta Maul had left it. Protesting that he hardly ever saw the room, and had not been in it since Christmas Eve, the landlord said that as far as he could see, no one could have been there since Netta Maul had gone out at 7.30 the previous evening. He recommended Matilda as a more expert witness and withdrew, obviously wishing to be as little involved in the business as possible, although, perhaps, not dreading the extra temporary patronage the murder would bring to his bar.

Matilda was then sent into the room, and Sharpe was enabled to have his first glimpse of it, over the shoulder of his superior.

"'Struth!" he exclaimed, as the gleaming silver struck his eye; and then he stared wide-eyed, unable to find words to express his astonishment.

Matilda occupied longer than her employer had in the survey. She looked carefully at each silver ornament, standing with her head on one side, and her brow corrugated in thought; she fingered the curtains and the counterpane, and even peeped under the bed. Finally she said, "I not think anything stolen. The silver, it is all where Miss Maul kept it. The curtains, it is all here. But I think something happen. Something. I do not know what. The books—" and she pointed to the piles of American film magazines on the cabin trunk, "Miss Maul, she always say, 'Keep them in neat pile.' She always put them in neat pile. These all over place. Miss Maul, she not leave the books like that. Not Miss Maul. She always say, 'Put them in neat pile.' That what she always say, 'Matilda, put them——'"

"Yes, that's all right, Matilda, we understand," broke in Spearpoint; "thank you very much. Now you run along and get on with your work, and Mr. Sharpe and I will have a look round."

Matilda went, a little regretfully, doubtless wondering whether she had made clear Netta Maul's instructions concerning the magazines; and the two policemen were left alone in the room of the murdered girl.

"Before we start, sir," pleaded Sharpe, "let's see how many photographs there are—seventeen, if you count these three snapshots in the looking-glass. Yes, and three mirrors, too. She had a poor opinion of her looks, don't you think, sir?—always wanting to reassure herself. And, do you notice, sir, these are all portraits of herself—not one of any man? What do you make of that, sir?"

"I suppose she never cared for any man," answered Spearpoint, carelessly. He had given no more than a cursory glance to the portraits, and was examining, without touching it, the heavy leather trunk at the foot of the bed.

"Never cared for any man, sir?"

"There were too many men in her life for her to entertain any feeling towards them except the determination to get as much as she could out of each one."

"Do you think she ever got any money out of any of them, sir?"

"I've never had any evidence that she did. But she got expensive presents, and clothes—and excitement. Here, what do you make of this mark?"

They knelt side by side, peering closely at the lock of the trunk.

"It's a fingermark, all right," pronounced Sharpe. "But it's probably hers. Almost certainly not a man's."

"So I thought," agreed Spearpoint, as Sharpe got to work with his fingerprint powder; "but we'd better make sure. I think someone had her keys last night. Bellamy couldn't remember whether she had her handbag or not, but I'm pretty sure she had. She nearly always carried that silver handbag young Rogers gave her. Ever see her without it?"

"Len Rogers? That poor cow that cut his throat?" asked Sharpe, shocked. "He gave her that, and she still carried it about?"

"Well, in the note he left, he didn't mention her, of course. He said he was putting himself out because of the two hundred pounds he'd pinched from Yourran, Other's. Of course, everyone knew he'd spent it on Netta Maul—nearly forty quid went in aeroplane trips, you know. And he'd confessed—and Halibut had paid back the two hundred. It was only when he heard she'd thrown him over that he killed himself. He'd got the idea that when he came out of prison she'd marry him. It was a terrible blow to poor old Halibut—his favourite nephew turning out a nogooder."

Sharpe shrugged his shoulders. Embezzlement is the commonest crime among the Europeans of Fiji; one case is much like another, and you cannot feel much interest in an embezzler who was dead before you ever heard of him. "I suppose, sir," he remarked, "this room is full of mementoes of her admirers. She didn't need their ugly faces when she had their beautiful presents to remember them by. Who gave her this trunk, sir?"

"That must be the one Jim Camelback brought back from Home, and had such a row with the Customs over. That silver dressing-set was before your time, too; that was a youthful indiscretion of a young fool of a cadet who's now a magistrate in Central Africa somewhere."

"Well, there's something here that was honestly earned, anyway," suggested Sharpe, pointing to two swimming trophies on the display shelf. "Whatever else she was, she was a swimmer."

"Well, I wouldn't say anything she got was dishonestly earned," dissented Spearpoint. "It depends on how you look at it. This mark's pretty good, isn't it?" He took out the photographs and compared each with the impression now showing so plainly on the lock. There was no doubt that it was from Netta Maul's own finger.

"That's a blow!" exclaimed Sharpe, hastily. "That means she came back here——"

"Of course it doesn't mean anything of the sort," contradicted Spearpoint, squatting down in front of the trunk and fingering the locks. "After all, it's her own fingermark you'd expect to find on her lock.—I wonder how we can get a look at the inside of this trunk. It's a pretty strong and solid object."

"Is it a fact that she was never out of Fiji, sir?"

"Yes, I believe so. She never wanted to travel—I suppose she couldn't bear to be parted from her treasures."

"Then what did she want with such a posh cabin trunk, sir?"

"Just what I've often wondered. Hullo, it's not locked"; and he slipped back the catch and opened the trunk.

An unexpected sight met their gaze. Instead of the neatly-folded exquisite lingerie they had been prepared for, they found that the whole interior was filled with brown-paper bundles, tied with coloured ribbon. These bundles bore slight traces of having been piled in a semblance of order, but they were now higgledy-piggledy. Spearpoint picked one up. On it was written in Netta Maul's elaborately ornamental handwriting, "Mr. Montgomery Thomspon."

"These must be her love-letters," he exclaimed, and eagerly read the names on other parcels—names he knew or had known, of some twenty men, at one time, or still resident in Fiji. There was a slender packet, labelled 'Stanley Pencarbon'; but there were two significant omissions: Camelback and Bellamy. Spearpoint opened one at random and confirmed his surmise that it contained correspondence. One of the others had been left untied and carelessly wrapped, as if it had been hurriedly opened and searched. On the outside was written, "Mr. Cutt." It contained nothing but business letters, on the headed letter-paper of his company, and, so far as could be ascertained at a cursory examination, dealt solely with Netta Maul's debt to Marryam & Cutt, Ltd. It was impossible to tell whether the person who had disturbed this packet had abstracted anything.

The only other item in the trunk was a cardboard box with a gaily decorated lid, the sort of box in which handkerchiefs are packed for presentation. This contained several small notebooks; but Spearpoint did not stop to scrutinise them, for, underneath the box, was the missing handbag. He lifted this gingerly, inspecting it for fingerprints. Even without treatment, two sets were evident; and these were presently established as those of Jim

Camelback and Netta Maul. Moreover, one of Camelback's marks overlay one of hers.

"It seems plain to me, sir," burst out Sharpe, "that Jim Camelback took her bag, came here, got into the room with her key, opened this trunk, took out of it the bundle with his own name on it—and perhaps Bellamy's too—and hopped it."

"It's a possibility," conceded Spearpoint. "Anyway, here are her keys all right. And there's money here also. We'll take all these papers and examine them at our leisure. In fact, I think we'll take the whole trunk.—That theory of yours is all right," he continued, reflectively, "but it's so obvious that I almost wonder if it wasn't meant to be obvious. It's difficult to imagine Bellamy and Camelback murdering her in collaboration. And when did Camelback come in here? We'll have to check his times pretty closely. However, we shall see."

They then checked the silverware with the insurance policy, and found it was all present; the articles were easy to identify as the redoubtable Mr. Cutt had insisted on photographs being attached to the policy. But even he, apparently, had not been able to obtain a complete list of her assets, for the shelf held two large rose-bowls and a statuette of the Prince of Wales which were not mentioned in the instrument.

Further examination of the room showed nothing suspicious, but the Inspector was not satisfied. "This is as much as we need do now," he said, "but we've got to be very careful about this room. To-morrow morning you'd better come up here and go over it with a fine— with very great care. Go and fetch Beni and Tomasi and have this trunk taken down to the car while I have a chat with Williams. Ask him to come up, as you go down."

The landlord managed to hide his reluctance to be absent from the bar at the time the workers of Suva knocked off for the day, but he made no attempt to be helpful.

"Well, I did make a few enquiries," he admitted, in

answer to Spearpoint's question, "and as far as I can make out, no one saw her after dinner last night. She got up from the table and walked straight out on to the Parade, and that's the last anyone here saw of her."

"What time was that?"

"About ha'past seven."

"Was she alone?"

"Far as I could see."

"Did she have her silver handbag with her?"

"Never saw her without it."

"Yes, I know she usually carried it, but did she have it with her last night?"

"Can't say's I noticed. That handbag was a part of her, as much as her hair was. Took it everywhere with her. Used to sleep with it under her pillow—or so the boys say. I wouldn't know." The landlord winked. "At mealtimes she'd keep it on the table beside her plate. Why, she even used to take it to the bathroom with her. She had a little mackintosh cover to keep it from getting tarnished while she had her morning shower."

Spearpoint persisted. "Then you can't remember if she took it out last night? You saw her go?"

"Sure I saw her go. I don't remember seeing the bag; but I'd bet she had it."

"Did everyone else in the hotel come home last night?"

"What do you mean—come home?"

"Well, Netta Maul didn't. Anyone else didn't sleep in their beds?"

"Do you think I go round and tuck all my clients in and kiss them good night?" retorted the hotel-keeper.

"But surely you know whether they stay out all night?"

"Maybe I do," Williams grudgingly admitted.

"Well, did anyone stay out all night last night?"

The publican laughed as he retorted, "Netta Maul did for one."

"And for two?"

"Sometimes one of the boys will stay out all night. I

don't particularly notice. None of my business," parried Williams.

"Evidently," observed Spearpoint, "one of them stayed out all night last night. And I know who it was. But I want to confirm what I know. Who was it? If you won't tell me now, you'll have to tell it in the witness-box."

"Well, as a matter of fact, since you insist, young Stanley Pencarbon was out all last night. Not for the first bloody time, either—nor the last. He'd been out on the jag and must have slept in a ditch somewhere, judging from his trousers—but that doesn't prove that he had anything to do with your business."

"Not necessarily," conceded the Inspector; "I know a good deal about Master Pencarbon's movements last night. I just wanted to confirm that he didn't come home to bed. Anyone else?"

"No one else," announced the publican, readily.

"Was Jim Camelback here last night?" pursued Spearpoint.

"Yes. So I'm told. Came in the back way and sat yarning in Malleable's room half the evening."

At this point, Sharpe entered with two sturdy Fijian constables, who bore away Netta Maul's trunk. Spearpoint told him to lock it up safely and return, and then asked Williams if he had seen Camelback come or go.

"Saw him go. Eleven sharp, with Bob Eachway. Didn't see him come. He came in the back way—at least, he didn't come in the front way, or I'd have seen him."

"Any idea what time he came?"

"Not the slightest. But you can ask Malleable. He'll be in in ten minutes."

"Thanks. I will. Now, I'll thank you not to give Pencarbon the tip that I know he was out all last night. Will you promise that?"

"O.K., Chief."

They went into the corridor, and Spearpoint took care that the door had locked before he looked into each of the other rooms in turn. All the occupants were out, for it was only just on five. Netta Maul's two nearer neighbours were girls. Next came Malleable, and last Pencarbon.

Malleable arrived as they reached the end of the passage. He was spectacled, with Crookes medium-tinted lenses, pale of face and surly of manner. His hobbies were two: beer for the first half of the month, and books for the second. Payday was almost a week off, and he was growing querulous, bored with both Tolstoi and Balzac, his usual stand-bys during his periods of enforced comparative temperance.

"That's all right, Williams," said Spearpoint, dismissing the publican, who went eagerly enough. "I say, Malleable, I'd like to have a couple of words with you."

"Downstairs, eh?" suggested Malleable, hopefully.

"No, thanks. Your room will do. I understand you were in here all last evening?"

"What of it?" As he spoke, Malleable placed his spectacles on the dressing-table and began taking the links out of his cuffs and unbuttoning his cricket shirt.

"Well, were you?" Spearpoint insisted.

"Yes, I was," Malleable retorted, pulling his shirt over his head and flinging it on to the bed. A few undried drops of sweat glistened on his narrow, hairless chest, and his smooth-skinned, rounded shoulders.

"Reading?"

"What the hell else is there to do in this damned hole?" He was tugging off his shoes as he spoke.

"Did you happen to hear anyone unlock the door of Netta Maul's room, go in, and come out again?"

"Did I hell? Who the hell do you think I am?" A pair of white socks followed the cricket shirt. "Think I've got ears like Shakespeare's Bottom?"

"Well, did you hear?" persisted the Inspector, marvelling at the capacity of his questionees to evade simple questions.

"I did not hear," Malleable conceded, stepping out of his drill trousers stark naked. "Any other tomfool questions you'd like to ask before I have my shower?" And he reached for his bath towel and draped it round his middle parts.

"Yes, a few," answered Spearpoint, estimating his weight at one hundred and twenty pounds and his chest expansion at half an inch.

"Well, hurry up; all the other cows will be in soon, and they'll beat me to it."

"Did you have Jim Camelback in here last night?"

"I did. Any law against it?"

"What time did he arrive?"

"You've come to the wrong bloody shop. I never know the time. My watch has never gone since the time some bloody fool pushed me into the baths with all my clothes on." He spoke with an extra petulance which was perhaps excusable since the bloody fool in question had just opened the door and peeped in.

"Ah, come in, Sharpe," said his superior.

"Think this is your bloody room?" snarled the lawful tenant. "Inviting all the silly asses in town in? Well, you're welcome to it. I'm going to have my shower before the other cows get here"; and he made a half-hearted attempt to push past. Sharpe replied with a grin.

"Now, look here, Malleable," announced Spearpoint, firmly, barring his way. "You're going to give me proper answers to my questions, and you're going to answer them here and now, or you'll spend the night in a police cell, and that's flat."

Malleable promptly suggested another, and less possible use for all the police cells in Suva. (You are not afraid of even a District Inspector of Constabulary when your brother-in-law happens to be his boss.) However, he followed the obvious retort with a grudging, "What do you want to know, then?"

"We want to know what time Camelback arrived in this room, what time he left, and whether he stayed here all the time," said Spearpoint, ignoring the insult.

"He came in at ten, he went out at eleven, and he stayed here gassing the whole bloody time."

"How is it you're so sure of the times?"

"Because when he'd been here a minute or two he looked at his watch and said, 'Ten o'clock, old boy; time for a snorter,' and took his flask out of his pocket."

"Easy to remember that, then," laughed Sharpe.

"Did you see his watch?" Spearpoint questioned.

"Yes, I did."

"It said ten o'clock?"

"As near as dammit."

"Sounds pretty fishy to me. Did he know you hadn't got a watch or a clock?"

"I dare say he did. Anyway, his watch said ten o'clock, and I saw no reason to dispute it.—And I know it was eleven when he went out because young Bob Eachway came up, and said there was just time for a quick one before the bar closed. So we all went down and I saw the clock."

"Through the bottom of the glass, I bet," suggested Sharpe.

"And if you want me to bloody well prove he was in here," continued Malleable, making a face at Sharpe, "here's the bloody torch he left behind him." And he pointed to a powerful electric torch on the chair.

"Thanks, I'll borrow that," accepted Spearpoint. "Did he forget it?"

"Do you think he left it behind on bloody purpose?"

"Well, that's all for the present, thanks. Go for your life, and you'll just get the shower first," and Spearpoint stood aside. Malleable hurried out with the air of a man who doesn't care if a hundred policemen ransack his room, and by the time they had followed him into the corridor, he was out of sight.

"I want to have a look round Pencarbon's room," whispered Spearpoint. "Stay at the top of the stairs, Sharpe, and keep him talking if he comes before I've done." He slipped into the Australian's room, and surveyed it carefully. His eyes travelled along the horizontal wooden studding which formed a convenient shelf for small objects, and which did carry ashtrays, matches, two beer-glass trays on edge, bottle-openers, and a couple of pipes. He examined the top of the dressing-table, which had been carefully patterned with ring-marks from wet tumblers, and he took the liberty of looking into all the drawers, one of which was stuck and opened only with difficulty. He pulled aside the corner curtain which formed the wardrobe and glanced at the clothes hung behind. He opened the two empty suitcases under the bed. In short, he studied Pencarbon's worldly possessions sufficiently closely to assure himself, firstly, that his electric torch was not in the room, secondly, that none of the clothes in his dirty-clothes bag were bloodstained, thirdly, that the only dark suit he possessed was his dress-suit, which had all its buttons intact, and fourthly, that the room contained no shoes with rubber heels similar to those which had left the impression in the field.

Rejoining Sharpe, he drove with that youth the couple of hundred yards to Netta Maul's shop, which was part of a wooden one-story building on Victoria Parade. Unlike most of Marryam & Cutt's properties, which were kept in the worst state of repair consistent with the extraction of rent from the grumbling tenants, Netta Maul's shop was well preserved and gaily painted. Mr. Cutt had not expressed the least objection to the frequent repainting of either the exterior or the interior, provided it had been carried out at no expense to his company. and without causing any diminution of the repayments of the tenant's debt. The necessary labour had been contributed by various half-caste acquaintances of Netta Maul, probably in return for a few cigarettes. Inspector Spearpoint had noticed that each repainting had been done by a different man. One of these, a painter by trade, had used his employer's materials on the job, and had subsequently spent six months painting Government buildings under

the supervision of a warder. Another, whose residence had
adjoined a builder's yard, had suddenly left the Colony,
half-way through the contract, as a stoker on a sugarboat
bound for Vancouver. Netta Maul, of course, had had not
the slightest suspicion that these men who had undertaken
to redecorate her shop had not purchased the materials
in the normal way, and she had been shocked whenever
she had heard to the contrary.

The small window was neatly but sparsely dressed with
tobacconists' dummies. The display was always attractive
because the owner discarded the cardboard articles as
soon as they became warped or faded by the sunlight;
and the native curios which formed her lucrative sideline
were sold from the window before they had time to become
shop-soiled. Behind the window was a net curtain which
prevented passers-by seeing into the shop, but which
allowed those inside to see out. When passenger vessels
were in port, however, the curtain was drawn back to
induce tourists to glance at the enticing interior, with its
brightly-painted wicker-work, tortoise-shell-inlaid arm-
chairs and tables (an extravagance deplored, too late, by
Mr. Cutt), its decorations of native mats and fans, and
(more particularly) its two charming half-caste attendants.
Although Netta Maul had never been out of the Colony,
she was an earnest student of American fashion books, and
indented many of her clothes direct from abroad, through
the agency of Stanley Pencarbon's employer. The wife of
more than one high Government official, returning from
a trip Home, and intending to create a sensation in Suva
with the latest Parisian or New York fashions, had been
disgusted to find herself forestalled by Netta Maul. But,
on boat-days, Netta Maul dressed to attract custom, and
made the utmost use of her half-caste beauty. On such
occasions, she and Cecilia Snitch (her distant relative and
protégé) attired themselves in low-cut bodices and reed
skirts, decked their flowing black hair with scarlet hibiscus
blossoms, and affected a childish ignorance of European

ways. They even went to the artistic extreme of working barelegged and barefoot, with their shins closely shaved and their toe-nails polished a not very unnatural pink.

The shop possessed no counter, the stock being ranged on shelves and in cupboards, and the till protected by a screen hinged to the wall. On boat-days, Cecilia Snitch, who was good-looking enough to act as a partner to her more glamorous cousin, but, in the metaphorical sense, dumb, took the money, whilst Netta hooked the poor fish. But on ordinary days, Netta preferred to be alone—a preference expressed by a certain more-famous glamorous person—and Cecilia was free to spend the waking hours dozing in a deck chair under the palm trees at Suva Point —the occupation in life which gave her most pleasure.

Spearpoint and Sharpe examined the shop with care. Everything appeared to be in order, and they found no traces of any unauthorised visitor. There were a few obvious fingermarks, either Netta Maul's own, or too vague to be deciphered without materials. Sharpe considered that none of them would prove to have been made by either Camelback or Pencarbon. Netta had left a good thumbprint on the door-handle, and Bellamy had apparently handled some of the stock, but presumably in the course of his business.

Behind the shop was a small room, ostensibly a stockroom; but the door was always kept shut and even Spearpoint had no idea what it had been used for. The key was on the occupier's bunch, and the two policemen were able to satisfy their curiosity. The room, although clean and as well-painted as the shop, was almost bare. On one wall hung the 'native' costumes used on boat-days, and some European garments, including a couple of raincoats. On a shelf were some piles of American film magazines and some fashion publications, all neatly arranged and in date order; on another shelf, a silver-handled umbrella. In a cupboard below the shelves were some tobacconists' dummies and showcards, a half-filled can of kerosene, a primus stove and the materials for making tea. There was no stock; all this was kept in the shop—presumably to prevent Bellamy from entering the back room. The only furniture consisted of a wicker-work chair and a low table, on which stood an oil lamp. Along one wall lay a pile of native-made pandanus mats, a couple of dozen of them, ranged in size, with their edges of coloured wool over-hanging each other; on top of the pile, a couple of silk cushions.

Sharpe fingered the delicate texture of the topmost mat and observed, with a whistle, "Had another bed in here, eh? What ho, she bumps!"

Spearpoint shrugged his shoulders. "She might have used it for a couch, of course. Or, more likely, Cecilia Snitch did—she's the laziest girl in the Colony. But these mats are stock-in-trade, you know."

"You bet they are, sir," agreed Sharpe, "but this solves one problem."

"What?"

"Why, sir, one of the great mysteries of Suva was where she—well, where did she?—you know, sir."

"I don't think we're justified in concluding that," Spearpoint reproved. "There has never been any evidence that her life was not strictly moral."

"No evidence?" gasped Sharpe.

"No. Have you ever heard any man say that he'd ever slept with her? You've heard several fellows who've been reputed to have done so, deny it. Camelback always denied emphatically that he had. He dared the Colonial Secretary to prove it; and, of course, he couldn't. Of course, Camelback took her about everywhere, and spent pots of money on her, and gave the gossips plenty to talk about, but nothing was ever proved. And the same with all the others. They gave her those solid silver trinkets, and took her to every social affair her colour didn't bar her from, and made the most complete asses of themselves over her; and she sucked them dry, one after another, and never gave anything in return."

Sharpe whistled. "Do you believe that, sir?"

Spearpoint shrugged his shoulders. "It's our job to believe proved facts, Sharpe—not conjecture. And, in this case, the fact is—and every medical student up at the hospital has had the opportunity of verifying the matter for himself —the fact is that Netta Maul died a virgin."

"A virgin?" Sharpe gasped, his eyebrows almost disappearing into the forest of his hair.

Spearpoint nodded, enjoying the spectacle of his assistant's astonishment. "There's no doubt about that. I sent her up to the hospital so that they could see if she was going to have a baby, and old Halibut used her as the subject-matter of a lecture on anatomy. So there are about forty witnesses."

"Yes—but—but, all the men——How did she make them give her those presents?"

"How did she attract men? Personality. She didn't hold any of them for long, though. Either their money gave out and she chucked them, or they discovered there was nothing doing and chucked her."

"You mean they gave her presents for nothing?"

"Well, not exactly. Perhaps they were trying to prime the pump. Of course, they had the pleasure of her company, the anticipation of a pleasure that didn't actually materialise, the thrill of thinking they would succeed where other men had failed. It tickled a certain kind of man's vanity to be thought the lover of Netta Maul."

Sharpe considered this novel idea for a moment, and then remarked, "Jim Camelback kept on with her for a long time—on and off."

"On and off," agreed Spearpoint. "Yes. I think he liked her for herself—and I think he was one of the few men she liked. And yet—they were always quarrelling. It's hard to say whether they were friends or foes, really.— However, we can't discuss that. It's no business of ours. To-morrow, you'd better go over this place carefully, and study all the fingermarks you can find."

CHAPTER TWELVE

STANLEY PENCARBON'S ALIBI
(*Friday : 6–8 p.m.*)

As a little time still remained before dinner, Spear-point despatched Sharpe to interview Bob Eachway, who was, to some extent, a friend of the lanky Sub-Inspector, and went himself to visit Joe Nomore, who was by no means a friend of his own. He drove up Waimanu Road, and via Browne Street into Amy Street, and rapped on the glass of the drapery salesman's front door. The door was opened cautiously by one of the cross-eyed twin daughters, clad in a nightdress, and with her hair in curl-papers. The other cross-eyed twin daughter, judging from the noises which the opening of the door magnified, was apparently being spanked by its cross-eyed mother.

"Hallo, Polly, is your father in?" asked the Inspector, at random.

"I'm not Polly. I'm Lizzie. Polly is a naughty girl. Lizzie is a good girl. Mummie says so," returned the child, pertly, without giving way or opening the door wider.

"Well, then, Lizzie, go on being a good girl and tell your father that Inspector Spearpoint wants to have a chat with him."

Lizzie slammed the door abruptly, but through the open window came the sound of her shrill voice calling, "Daddy! Daddy! Here's the fat policeman to see you!"

Spearpoint hastily remembered the advice given by Mr. Hornibrook in the treatise quoted earlier in this book: "For example, a man may be standing waiting for a bus for a few moments. Instead of wasting that time, perhaps fretting and fuming over the delay, he can . . . quite imperceptibly retract and release his abdominal wall in such a way as effectively to stir up the abdominal contents, and thus help to prevent sagging and stagnation."

As he stood thus retracting and releasing his abdominal wall, the Inspector heard the fine fruity voice of a Nomore calling to its mate, "Put that beer back on the ice, quick!"; and then the door was reopened, and the two men met abdomen to abdomen.

"Come in, digger, and take a pew," invited the host, switching on the light. "Sorry we can't offer you anything to pour down your throat. End of the month, you know, end of the month.—Here, you kids, clear out!" This last was addressed to the two cross-eyed faces, stretched, one above the other, round the open doorway of the twins' bedroom. The faces wavered a little, but did not disappear, their eyes continuing to gaze intently at the two men, who had taken seats at opposite sides of the room. Joe Nomore dismissed them by turning his back on pretence of lighting his pipe.

"I just wanted to confirm one or two facts," began the Inspector, "about last night."

"Stan Pencarbon tells me the sheila was done in out in the paddock there," returned old Joe. "Fancy that! Who did it?"

"I'm afraid I can't tell you at the moment. What I want to know is: did you hear a scream about ten o'clock last night?"

Old Joe considered the matter, taking his pipe out of his mouth and rubbing his chin with the stem. Finally he said, slowly, "I don't know what we were doing last night. We might have gone to the pictures. I know there was some talk of going to the pictures" Then an expression of relief stole over his blank countenance and he took the course of the wise married man and announced, "I'll ask the wife. She'll know."

He struggled to his feet and ambled out to the kitchen, leaving the Inspector sitting self-consciously listening to whisperings of:

"He's fatter than Daddy."

"He isn't."

"He is."

"Isn't."

"Is."

"Isn't."

"Is."

"Anyway, Polly is a naughty girl and Lizzie is——"

"Lizzie is a little liar. Who stole the jam tarts?"

Then there was a sound of heads being smacked, an unimpassioned, "Go to sleep, you little bahstuds," and a wail of, "We were only saying the fat policeman was fatter than you, Daddy"; and then old Joe reappeared by way of the children's room, shutting the door behind him.

"The wife says we didn't go to the pictures last night," he announced, triumphantly, reseating himself. "We stayed at home. It was last week we went to the pictures," and he sat smoking placidly, as if assured that the Inspector's curiosity had been finally satisfied.

"Did you have any visitors last night?"

"Visitors?" repeated old Joe, apparently wondering what queer fowl they might be. "Really, I can't remember. I'd better ask the wife. She'd know." He got to his feet again, a little unwillingly, and made for the kitchen. A thought struck him and he turned to say, "We do have a cobber or so in of an evening, you know, sometimes, to listen to the wireless, or yarn. Passes the time, you know."

"Perhaps it would be as well if you asked Mrs. Nomore to come out here," suggested Spearpoint, impatiently. Joe Nomore had never been one of his favourite entertainments.

"Oh, couldn't do that, you know, digger, couldn't do that," reproved old Joe. "Cooking, you know, cooking. When a woman's cooking, you can't ask her out to answer questions, you know."

He ambled back a few moments later, however, followed

by his cross-eyed wife, who, having wiped her hands on her apron, offered one to Inspector Spearpoint and then flopped into a chair, saying in her complaining voice, "Isn't this a dreadful business, Mr. Spearpoint? Dreadful. I do hope you catch the man that did it, though, of course, it wasn't as if she was a white girl, now, was it? But I suppose these half-castes have their feelings, in a way, and, of course, murder is wicked, though, what I say is, with some people, they're better out of the way, but it isn't so much that as the fact that there is a man in our midst who can do a thing like that, isn't it? Really, until you catch him, we shan't any of us women sleep peacefully in our beds at night. With a man like that about there's no knowing who'll be the next." She paused for breath, fixing her baleful eye on the Inspector, who could not help remembering Sharpe's recent remark that he could never make up his mind who was more to be pitied, Mr. or Mrs. Nomore.

"I won't keep you long, Mrs. Nomore," he began. "I understand you're cooking, and I wouldn't like to interrupt you. But I just wanted to confirm one or two facts. Now, did you have any visitors last night?"

"We none of us went outside the house since Joe came home at half-past six," she retorted, almost angrily. "Besides, you've no call to go suspecting us of a thing like that." Her indignation surged up into a screech.

"Pardon me," said the Inspector, soothingly. "I do not suspect either of you in the least, and I never suggested that I did. But I have to check the movements of a number of people. Some people tell me one thing and some tell me another, so I come to you because I know I can rely on what you tell me."

"Of course you can rely on what we tell you," she said, still angry. "You can't rely on some folks, but what we tell you is gospel truth."

"Good. Then did you have any visitors last night?"

"What does it matter whether we had visitors or not?" she argued. "We didn't murder the girl."

"If you had visitors," explained Spearpoint, patiently, "they might have come along Amy Street, and so they might have met some of the people whose movements I'm enquiring into."

"Who are they?" she interjected, eagerly.

"I'm afraid I can't tell you that. But I want to know of all the people who walked along Amy Street last night."

"Well, the only visitor we had was Stanley Pencarbon," she rejoined, triumphantly, "and he didn't come along Amy Street; he came across the paddock."

"So he did," agreed old Joe, taking his pipe out of his mouth to corroborate his wife's evidence.

"Bringing his muddy footprints all over the house," complained Mrs. Nomore, bitterly. "So that's no use to you, Mr. Spearpoint."

"What time did he arrive?"

"What do you want to know that for?"

"I'm afraid I can't explain why I want to know all the things I ask, Mrs. Nomore; but, broadly, I have to check the movements of everybody who was in this part of town last night. Come, now, tell me what time he called."

"I don't know. About ten o'clock. He came to listen-in to the wrestling in Sydney."

"Wasn't that the night before?" suggested old Joe, taking a sudden interest in the conversation.

"Of course it wasn't," responded his spouse, scornfully. "The night before you were out yourself."

"Ah, that I was," agreed old Joe, winking at the Inspector. "I remember now. I was at the Daisy Club."

"The wrestling starts at 10.15, doesn't it?" asked Spearpoint. "Did Pencarbon get here much before it started?"

"Only a minute or two. In fact, by the time Joe had tuned in, it had already started."

Spearpoint pondered, while old Joe smoked contentedly, and Mrs. Nomore waited disdainfully. Then an idea struck him, and he asked, "Did you invite him to come and listen to the wrestling, or did he come of his own accord?"

Mrs. Nomore shrugged her shoulders, declining to answer so ridiculous a question; but Joe said, with unexpected presence of mind, "I didn't exactly invite him, you know; but he often drops in."

"Did you hear a scream a little before he came?"

"No," responded Mrs. Nomore, resentfully. "We don't spend our evenings listening to screams. I've got quite enough to do, looking after a house and a couple of kids."

"What time did Pencarbon go?"

"About half-past twelve."

"Is that the closest you can get?"

"Yes, it is."

"Do you know if your neighbour was home last night?" pursued the Inspector.

"I don't know anything about Mr. Bellamys," returned the mother of twins, giving the young man the plural form which some Suva residents habitually give to other people's names. "And he doesn't know anything about us," she added, unexpectedly, "so it's no good asking him what visitors we had, just to see whether we've been telling you the truth or not."

"I assure you I hadn't the slightest intention of doing that, Mrs. Nomore," said the Inspector, rising. "I fully accept all the information you have given me, which has been most helpful. Thank you for giving me a little of your valuable time to answer my questions."

Something of his irony was evidently apparent to her, for she answered as resentfully as ever, "If you saved your breath to catch the murderer instead of coming prying into the private lives of respectable people, you might be of more use to the Colony."

Joe smiled over his shoulder at Spearpoint, who took his leave readily enough. He got into his car, backed until a garage drive enabled him to turn, and drove up to the hospital, where he confirmed his surmise that Netta Maul had been visiting Cecilia Snitch the previous evening, and ascertained that she had left a little before a quarter to ten. The gravel on her shoes had evidently come from the hospital drive. Then he hurried home, to find Sharpe and dinner awaiting him.

"I saw Bob Eachway, sir, and he confirmed Jim Camelback's story. He says he raked him out of Malleable's room just before eleven, had a beer with him in the bar, and then Camelback drove him up to the bach and they sat up all hours playing poker—at least, they went to bed about one. Wills and Craven were there, too—playing poker, I mean, sir. I saw Wills by himself after, and he corroborated it. Craven was out. Incidentally, I asked Bob where Camelback's car was and he said in the shed in Carnarvon Street."

This was an official parking place for Government cars, in front of the Supreme Court building, and three or four minutes from the Royal Palm Hotel.

"I also had an eyeful of Camelback's room. It wouldn't be possible for him to go out at night without going along the verandah past several other chaps' rooms, and Tom Claypole sleeps on the verandah, anyway. I know that place fairly well, of course, and I don't see how he could have gone out after the game stopped, without the other fellows knowing. Tom Claypole's a light sleeper. I turned out Camelback's washing-bag, and found a suit for every day since Monday—the Chow tells me he only washes the clothes on Monday—and no blood on anything. In fact, Camelback seems pretty well cleared, sir. All his time is accounted for from ten o'clock onwards. Incidentally, sir, the Chow woke him up with the morning tea at seven this morning. All the chaps were pretty curious at my making enquiries about him, but they seemed to think it was only to be expected, seeing how thick he had been with Netta Maul."

"He went off on the *Whitman* all right?"

"No doubt of that, sir."

"And you told old Captain Stickithemud to keep an eye on him, to prevent him hearing any wireless news about the murder, and to bring him back to Suva? We may want him as a witness, if nothing else."

"I did, but he seems to me to be pretty well cleared, sir."

"Except," pointed out the Inspector, "for his finger-prints on the handbag, and the quarrel Bellamy overheard. Still, I think the next thing is to have another little talk with Pencarbon."

Taking the torch, they drove along Victoria Parade to the Royal Palm. Disregarding the curious glances aroused by their entry of the bar, Spearpoint curtly asked Williams if Pencarbon were in.

"Up in his room, I think."

"Right. We'll go up."

Sharpe winked at a couple of the patrons behind his superior's back, and followed him out of the bar and up the back stairs to Pencarbon's room. Spearpoint knocked and opened the door at once. The place was in darkness, but the lighted verandah suggested the tenant's probable whereabouts. He strode across and paused in the far doorway. Pencarbon sat in a deck-chair reading *Smith's Weekly* and sucking at a man-sized pipe. He looked up at the footsteps and recognised his visitors without the least sign of embarrassment.

"Why, hullo, chaps," he said, hospitably, taking the pipe out of his mouth; "come for a beer?"

"Not exactly. We wanted to ask you one or two more questions."

"Well, take a pew." Pencarbon flung the paper on the floor and yawned widely. "You're welcome to all I know, and that's bloody nothing."

Spearpoint, observing that the only available seat was a low-notched deck-chair, in which his dignity might be imperilled, elected to stand. Sharpe swung himself on to the verandah rail, and sat with his back to the harbour and his arm round a post. Pencarbon was thus between two fires, but, if he was conscious of this, he did not betray any apprehension. There was no one else on the verandah, and Malleable's room was dark.

"I'd like you to tell us a little more about last night," invited Spearpoint.

"Last night?" answered Pencarbon, casually. "Don't remember a bloody thing about last night. I was as shot as Chloe! And what a head I had this morning!"

"Where did you take the cargo aboard?"

"Part of it in the pub across the road," waving his hand towards the Melbourne Hotel on the opposite side of Hercules Street. "But most of it at old Joe's. Take my tip, boys, old Joe's is a bad imitation of home brew. Refuse all bloody imitations."

"No need to tell us that," retorted Sharpe. "You remember we refused to hear your imitation this morning."

Pencarbon grinned up at him without malice, and rejoined, "Your bloody loss, boy; not mine"; and yawned again.

"Roughly speaking, we want to know——" began Spearpoint, when the Australian interrupted.

"You don't want to speak roughly to little Stanley. We're all friends here, boy. I'll tell you any bloody thing you want to know, even if I don't know it myself."

"Firstly, we want to know what time you reached Joe Nomore's, and what time you left—and we don't want any back answers about it, either," added Spearpoint, impatiently.

"Well, I've told you before that I arrived about ten past ten," answered Pencarbon, as if explaining a simple matter to a not very bright child. "It was about five minutes before the wrestling started in Sydney and that started at fifteen minutes past bloody ten."

"Exactly ten past?"

"Well, it might have been nine or eleven minutes past. Think I time myself with a bloody stop-watch?"

"Would you agree that it was nearer fourteen minutes past?" persisted Spearpoint.

"No. Ten past, as near as dammit," persisted Pencarbon, likewise. "What the bloody hell does it matter, anyway? You can ask old Joe, if you like—but he wouldn't know."

"I did ask him, and he didn't know. But I asked Mrs. Nomore, and she says you got there only a minute or two before the wrestling came on."

"Well, she wasn't there when I arrived, so she wouldn't know. My God!" cried Pencarbon, turning to Sharpe, "fancy asking a cross-eyed old hen like that! What does it matter, anyway?"

"It's important to establish the exact time you took to cross that field," said Spearpoint, slowly. "You entered it between nine fifty-five and nine fifty-seven. You reached Joe Nomore's at ten fourteen. That is to say, you took from seventeen minutes to nineteen to cross the field, and it can be done easily in five."

"Oh, can it?" retorted the Australian. "I'll bet you couldn't cross it in five bloody minutes, not if you lost a bloody shoe in the bloody mud half way."

"You said this morning it wouldn't take more than five minutes."

"Well, anyway, I didn't take seventeen bloody minutes. I reached old Joe's at ten past. That makes your seventeen into bloody thirteen. Besides, how do you know what bloody time I went into the bloody paddock?"

"I saw you. I was sitting in my car outside Mrs. Montgomery Thompson's."

Pencarbon shrugged his shoulders. "Well, have it your own bloody way. I can't see that it matters a ruddy damn. It's not a crime to toddle across that bloody paddock at under twenty bloody miles an hour. But, I'll tell you what," he added, becoming suddenly helpful. "I'll tell you how you can bloody well prove what bloody time I reached old Joe's. Ask young Bellamys what time he went to see his aunt."

"You mean his wife's aunt?"

Pencarbon went into a great shout of laughter. "Have it your own way," he gurgled. "But what I mean is that when I got outside old Joe's there was the water rushing into Bellamy's tank like a bloody flood on the Murray River. He must have pulled the bloody chain just as I got into his garden. I came through his bloody garden, you know."

"Does Bellamy time himself with a stop-watch?" asked Sharpe, with mock interest.

Spearpoint waved the idea aside with, "Now, what time did you leave Nomore's?"

"Haven't the faintest. I was as shot as Chloe!"

"Well, what time did you get back here?"

Unblushingly, Pencarbon answered, "About seven o'clock this morning."

Evidently Williams had failed to keep his promise not to warn Pencarbon that the police were aware of his night out.

"Did you spend the night at Nomore's?"

"No, ole mal, I can tell you that all right, all right. Woke up this morning and found myself in some adjectival car down by the bloody creek. Don't remember getting into it. Must have been there half the bloody night, dead to the wide! Oh, boy, that was a night!"

"Whose car was it?"

"Beggared if I know. It was a Rattler; that's all I can tell you. When I woke up and found myself in the back seat of a bloody car, I wasn't worrying about whose bloody car it was. I just legged it back to the Royal Palm toot sweet."

"What time did you wake?"

"About half-past six, ole mal. Half-past bloody six. Daylight. Just gave me time to nip up here and have a bloody shower and put on a clean pair of bloody strides, and nip into bloody breakfast."

"I see. You say you woke up in the back seat of a car?"

"Too right!"

"Were the doors shut?"

"Don't remember, ole mal. Yes, they must have been. I opened one to get out."

STANLEY PENCARBON'S ALIBI   153

"Then you must have opened one to get in, or else shut it after you got in."

"My dear bloody Watson, you're a marvel."

"Which way was the car facing? Upstream or downstream?"

"Upstream, my dear Watson, upstream."

"Then this must be your torch, eh?" asked Spearpoint, quietly, producing it. "We found it in the car."

"Yes, ole mal, that's my bloody torch all right," admitted the Australian, without embarrassment. "When I got home this morning without it, I thought I must have dropped it somewhere and hadn't dared stoop to pick it up. I was so full of bloody beer last night that if I'd bent down I'd have spilt."

"But this morning you said it wasn't yours."

"No, ole mal, I didn't say it wasn't mine. I looked at the bloody battery to make sure it was mine. My bloody torch, all right."

"Well, it's a police exhibit now," retorted Spearpoint, putting it back in his pocket. "Now, this lipstick. Have you ever seen this before?"

"Only when you showed it to me this morning—if it's the same bloody one."

"Do you know who it belongs to?"

"I do not."

"Positive?"

"Abso-bloody-certain, ole mal."

"Why were you wearing your topee last night?"

Pencarbon grinned and answered casually, "Just happened to pick it up as I came out. No law against wearing a bloody sun-helmet by moonlight, is there?"

"You seemed to me to be keeping very much in the shadow as you walked up Waimanu Road," observed Spearpoint.

"Didn't want to get moonstruck," grinned the Australian. He volunteered no further explanation of his demeanour, and Spearpoint, thinking it over, came to the conclusion that the mere impression he had given of the desire to be inconspicuous could hardly be counted against him.

"Who's your laundryman?" Spearpoint asked next, deciding to investigate without concealment a matter that had been puzzling him since his previous visit to the room.

"What the bloody hell does it matter to you who my bloody laundryman is?"

"Now, look here, Pencarbon," rejoined the Inspector, firmly, "there's been murder committed in this town, and it's my job to find the murderer. And I'm going to find him. And it's your duty as a citizen to help me find him. You're known to have been a friend of the dead girl, and you were seen last night close to the spot where she was murdered. You can't give a satisfactory account of your movements last night, and you've already deceived us to-day on two essential points. I warn you that your actions have been highly suspicious, and that you had better do all you can to assist the police."

"All right, ole mal," conceded Pencarbon, without loss of composure. "Keep your bloody hair on. No need to go crook at little Stanley. What would I want to murder the sheila for?"

"I don't know. I'm asking questions, not you. Now, who's your laundryman?"

"My bloody laundryman is Sindbad."

"That's not a bloody laundryman; that's a bloody sailor," cut in Sharpe, in mockery.

"Bloody good laundryman, boy. Too right he is," demurred the Australian. "Bloody cheap, too."

"When did he last collect your laundry?"

"Monday."

"How often do you change?"

"Every bloody day, of course."

"So there should be four shirts and four pairs of trousers in your dirty clothes-bag at the moment?"

"That's right, ole mal. Four bloody shirts and four pairs of bloody strides."

"Monday, Tuesday, Wednesday, Thursday, and to-day's Friday. Been wearing these all day?"

"Look's like it, doesn't it?"

Spearpoint, surveying the creased drill trousers, the crumpled shirt with the sweat patch under the visible arm-pit, agreed that it did look like it.

"Did you change into clean clothes any evening?"

"I did not."

"But you put on clean ones every morning?"

"Of course. Got to look respectable in my bloody job. I'm not a bloody Sub-Inspector."

Sharpe blushed at this reference to an accident to his khaki uniform which had once (to the delight of Dame Rumour) earned him the censure of the Governor. Spearpoint ignored it, and asked, "Mind if we turn out your dirty-clothes bag?"

Pencarbon mentioned another article of furniture which they could turn out also, if they liked, but they confined themselves to the bag. It contained (as it had earlier) four pairs of white drill trousers, three white cricket shirts, four pairs of white socks and a handkerchief. None of the shirts bore the owner's name across the stiffening of the front opening; and, as Spearpoint had already ascertained, none of the garments bore bloodstains.

"Why are there only three shirts here?" asked Spearpoint suspiciously.

Pencarbon, who had lazily hoisted himself out of his chair, and was watching them with an amused smile, answered readily, "Oh, yesterday, I was wearing one of Malleable's. Sindbad mixed 'em up, and I didn't realise it wasn't mine till I got to work and noticed his bloody name across my bloody tummy. So when I took it off this morning I went in next door and put it in his bag."

"And how often does he put on clean clothes?"

"Every bloody day, of course."

"Then he ought to have four pairs of trousers and five shirts in his bag?"

"That's about the bloody strength of it, ole mal. But I wouldn't look, if I were you. He'd go crook if he knew you'd been at his bloody washing-bag in his absence."

Spearpoint ignored this advice and marched into the next room, with Sharpe and Pencarbon following. The bag did in fact contain four pairs of trousers and five shirts, all with the name marked across the front, and none with bloodstains. Four shirts had their sleeves unrolled, with cuff-link marks on the cuff-holes; the fifth had its sleeves rolled above the elbows, and no link-marks.

"That's the one I had on yesterday," Pencarbon explained, indicating the last. "I always roll my bloody sleeves above the elbows, and old Malleable wears bloody cuff-links,—bloody A.O.F.B. links, if you want to know." Then, as Sharpe, at a sign from Spearpoint, began to restore the garments to the bag, the Australian asked, with a suspicion of a sneer, "Satisfied, Mr. Inspector?"

"Now I want to have a look at your shoes," said Spearpoint. "Got a pair with rubber heels?"

For answer, the Australian flopped down on to the bed behind him and raised his feet in the air. He was wearing black shoes, heavily mud-splashed, with rubber heels similar to those that had been in the field.

"Those the shoes you had on last night?"

"The same bloody ones. Like 'em for the police museum?"

"No, thanks. I just wanted to make certain that the footmarks we found were yours and not someone else's," replied Spearpoint, enigmatically.

Pencarbon rolled to his feet, and asked again, "Satisfied, Mr. Inspector?"

Spearpoint shrugged his shoulders, non-committal, and asked, "Would you care to volunteer any further information concerning the events of last night?" He did not know what else to say, and still suspected that he had not been told the whole truth.

"I've told you all I know, ole mal," answered Pencarbon,

and yawned again. "You can't get much sleep in a bloody Rattler. I say, if you boys care to stay and make an evening of it, I'll send down for some——"

"No, thanks, we've got work to do."

"Asking more bloody questions, eh?"

"Yes," admitted Spearpoint, "and studying the bloody answers to find out how much truth there is in them."

"Oh, boy!" grinned Pencarbon, in appreciation of the sally. "I'll send that to *Smith's Weekly*. It's worth half a note. I say! there was a bloody funny joke about police-men in one of these——"

But they had gone before he could finish the sentence. As they got into their car, Sharpe remarked with a laugh, "Everything about him is bloody except the one thing we'd like to be bloody."

"What's that?"

"The shirt he wore last night."

CHAPTER THIRTEEN

JIM CAMELBACK'S ALIBI

(*Friday evening to Tuesday night*)

NEXT MORNING SPEARPOINT patiently and thoroughly examined the dead girl's effects and papers. He did not read every word of the many love-letters and other curiosities in her cabin trunk, but he read enough to satisfy himself that he missed nothing likely to shed light on his problem. It was obvious that some of the letters would have been invaluable to a blackmailer; the series from Mr. Montgomery Thompson, however, were all connected with business. For months past he had been arguing and bargaining with her on behalf of a client who was so close a personal friend that his relief at her death was sufficiently explained. (The friend, Spearpoint knew, was not in the Colony.) Spearpoint puzzled at first over the fact that she had received so many letters whilst living in a town where the writers saw her every day; but one passage in a characteristic note from Pencarbon suggested that her friends wrote to her because she insisted that they should. 'Why the hell do you want me to write to you,' he had asked, 'when we have breakfast together every morning, lunch every noon, and dinner every night, not to mention the frills after dinner?' If she had hoped to obtain from this astute youth any documentary evidence which he might later be extremely desirous of recovering from her, she had completely failed. His bundle was no more damaging to his reputation than was his ordinary conversation. But this was not so with many of her correspondents. Neither Camelback nor Bellamy was represented at all; and there were no half-castes.

Among other personal papers were a couple of cheap notebooks containing records which indicated that for some years past Netta Maul had been betting on horse racing in both Australia and New Zealand. She had evidently lost considerable sums, and latterly had gambled with increasing stakes. There was no record of the source from which she derived the money she lost.

In the afternoon, Spearpoint made a detailed examination of Camelback's possessions, searching, not only his room at the boarding-house, but his desk at the Audit Department. Although Sharpe had already turned out his washing-bag, Spearpoint turned it out again; indeed, he exceeded his authority so far as to examine the washing of his fellow boarders; but he found nothing suspicious. Camelback's size in shoes corresponded with the size of the prints, but he had left no plimsolls behind; and although he had a couple of dark suits, they both carried their full array of buttons, and, moreover, were so folded and packed that it was obvious they could not have been worn for some months.

But the Inspector did make one interesting discovery,

which Sharpe, despite his familiarity with the boarding-house, had carelessly overlooked. Strictly speaking, Camel-back's residence was not a boarding-house, but what is generally known in the Antipodes as a 'bach' (or a 'batch,' if you prefer to maintain fiercely that the word is derived, not from the first syllable of the word 'bachelor,' but from the idea of a number of similar things being grouped together). The establishment was the co-operative enter-prise of five bachelors, all Civil Servants, who rented a large house in Upper Waimanu Road, at the top of the cliff overlooking Walu Bay, and lived there without benefit of women, tended by a Chinese cook-boy-waiter and a Chinese laundryman-maid-of-all-work. 'Segai[1] Na Marama' (as the house had been christened, under the impression that this was the Fijian for 'without wives') was famous throughout the Colony (and was, in fact, pointed out by taxi-drivers to tourists) for its two unique features: the capacious ice-chest in every bedroom, and the notice above the gate, which said in large letters: 'Segai Na Marama. The Bachelors' Mess. Visitors only by invitation. No women admitted under any circum-stances.' The notice meant what it said. Overwhelming though its frequent hospitality might be (and no man could claim acquaintance with the life of the town unless he had slept at least once on the verandah of 'Segai Na Marama'), the bach received the uninvited guest with the reverse of courtesy, and if he should refuse to comply with the order to withdraw, was prepared to fling him out neck and crop. The bachelors valued their privacy; and the police were unimpressed by occasional protests from that section of the community known as the 'wowsers' that illegal orgies went on there. Nor were the bachelors misogynists. On the contrary. But, even at their parties, women did not enter the precincts. The opinion of the proprieties held by the Governor officially had to be respected by these Government employees.

[1] Pronounced Singeye.

Spearpoint, who, as he came armed with official authority, could not be flung out, examined the house and its surroundings with great care, and interrogated, not only Camelback's four bachmates, but also the two Chinese, both in their sketchy English and through an interpreter. The building was T-shaped; it contained five bedrooms, side by side, with a verandah in front, and, at one end, the T was crossed by the dining-room and the kitchen. The back verandah was a short one, and was reached from only the middle three rooms. Camelback's room was the furthest from the dining-room, and, although it contained two very large window openings, it had no means of exit except via the front verandah. The windows had no frames and no glass, being entirely covered with wire netting. The front verandah was boarded to waist height; above this were louvres, hinged at the top, and kept open by sticks resting against the horizontal member. It was certainly possible for any moderately active person to climb out of the verandah under one of these louvres, but it would have been a difficult feat to do so without disturbing the other occupants of the building, and to climb back from the ground, which was three feet below the level of the verandah floor, would have been impossible for a man of Camelback's height. There was, however, an alternative way out for Camelback, and that was through the room of his neighbour, Bob Eachway, who had doors opening on to both verandahs. The middle room was occupied by Craven, the next by Wills, and the one next the dining-room by Tom Claypole, the only one of the four who was Camelback's equal in rank. Tom Claypole was a first-class clerk in the Public Works Department, and he slept, not in his room, but on the front verandah itself, at the top of the steps. On the night of the murder he had attended a bridge party, in impeccable company, and had arrived home about two a.m. He had driven his car into the garage, where Camelback's already was. Although the garage could hold two cars comfortably, its shape was such that the second barred the exit of the first; it was thus clear, Claypole maintained, that Camelback's car could not have been used between two a.m. and seven-fifty, when they had both driven off to work. In any case, he added, if either Camelback's car or his own had been used, the noise of starting it up would have wakened him.

Claypole's narrative, however, gave Spearpoint the clue which Sharpe had missed. He said that as he had mounted the verandah steps, he had been called softly by Bob Eachway, who had then come out of his own room, and joined Tom in the kitchen, where they had sat for an hour or so more, talking, surprisingly enough, about work. Bob Eachway was an engineer in the Public Works Department, and they were both interested in plans for the coastal road. During this hour, Spearpoint realised, it would have been possible for Camelback to have escaped from the building via Eachway's room; but it did seem as if an hour would have been too short for all that he would have had to do, if he were the murderer. It was not half a mile from the bach to the garage where the bloodstains had been discovered; but the transportation of the body from the garage to the harbour was more than half an hour's work, and the return from the harbour to the bach, if done on foot, must have occupied twenty minutes, at the very least. Both Claypole and Eachway were positive that they had been abed by half past three, and had not been disturbed afterwards. The fact that Lum Chin's boat had been found in Walu Bay, immediately below 'Segai Na Marama' suggested that the murderer had climbed the cliff, a feat which Spearpoint had not previously considered possible. Certainly it could not be done without leaving traces on the clothes of the climber. There were no such traces on Camelback's clothes; but the garments he had worn last night might have been hidden, or disposed of.

Spearpoint had a further private talk with Bob Eachway,

asking him to repeat his story of calling at Malleable's for Camelback. It agreed with all previous evidence on the matter, but when Spearpoint asked further by which route they had driven home, a curious fact emerged. There were two routes, equally possible, one along Victoria Parade and straight up Waimanu Road, the other via Holland Street, Amy Street and Browne Street into Waimanu Road. Bob Eachway hesitated at first. He did not seem to be quite sure which route they had used. "We're always coming home from the Government offices," he explained, "and sometimes we come one way and sometimes the other. But—I remember now—we came by Holland Street that night, because that was the night we nearly ran over the mongoose."

"The mongoose?"

"Yes. One dashed right across the road. In fact, it came out so quickly I never saw it. And Jim didn't know what it was until he'd passed it. He jerked the wheel so suddenly we nearly went over the top. I can remember now: I'd just made a remark about his watch, and then he jerked the wheel, and——"

"What did you say about his watch?" asked Spearpoint, trying to hide his interest.

Eachway hesitated. He evidently realised that he had said too much. A bolder man might have lied his way out, but Eachway was an honest youngster, and he had no time to invent a story. "Oh, I don't know," he admitted, in response to Spearpoint's determined eyes. "I just mentioned his watch. It was on his wrist, you know."

"Yes, I suppose it was. But can't you remember what you said? It may be important—I can't tell; any little fact may be important. And if you withhold anything material it may be serious for you."

"Well, it was nothing much anyway," grumbled Eachway. "I just pointed out that his watch was slow."

"How slow?"

"Twenty minutes or so, I think."

"You mean," suggested Spearpoint, making a calculation, "it said a quarter to eleven instead of about five past?"

"Yes. At least, I thought it was. But then the mongoose
dashed out and in the excitement I forgot all about it.
But I remember that when we were playing later, I glanced
at his watch, and it was right. So I must have been mistaken in the car," he concluded, with obvious relief.

"Perhaps," agreed Spearpoint; "then you can't really
be sure that it was twenty minutes slow when you left
the Royal Palm?"

"Well, it couldn't have been. It was right at twelve
o'clock."

"But he could have put it right after you got out of
the car, before you started playing?"

"Yes, I suppose he could."

"You didn't notice it again while you were in the car?"

"No. I forgot all about it until we were playing, and
then I glanced at it and it was right; and I forgot about
the whole matter until this moment. It's nothing, is it?"

Eachway was attempting to minimise the incident, which
to Spearpoint's mind was one of the most vital discoveries
he had yet made. If Camelback's watch had been twenty
minutes slow, then when he had entered Malleable's room
and his watch had said ten it was really twenty past ten.
As he had suspected, the alibi had been faked. Camelback
could only just have reached the Royal Palm by ten if he
had stayed at Dr. Halibut's a minute or so after Spearpoint
had seen him outside the doctor's house. But in the extra
twenty minutes he would have had time to parley with
Netta Maul, kill her, hide her body in the garage, drive
to the Royal Palm, enter Netta Maul's room via the back
stairs, open her trunk, abstract the package bearing his
own name, alter his watch, and stroll into Malleable's
room to establish an alibi. The alibi would have failed
immediately if Malleable had had another visitor with a
watch, or had chanced to be aware of the exact time, but
this, apparently, had not been the case. Bob Eachway's

story of the slow watch corroborated Bob Bellamy's story of the quarrel; at least, it tended to corroborate it.

Spearpoint remarked guardedly that he had had reason to believe that Camelback's watch had been slow on Thursday evening, and enquired if he possessed a torch.

"Yes, a posh one. Ek dum tik wallah. But he never carried it about with him—just kept it in the pocket on the door of his car." This explained to the Inspector how he had come to forget the torch in Malleable's room; he had taken it to aid in his burglary, and left it behind because he was unused to carrying it.

All the facts so far discovered seemed to point to the guilt of Jim Camelback, but Spearpoint refused to believe that the crime had been solved until he had discovered exactly how and when the body had been thrown into the harbour. Plainly, this could not have been done before ten o'clock; and it appeared to be equally plain that it could not have been done by Camelback after—unless both Claypole and Eachway were lying. The most promising line of investigation, pending the evidence of the barber in Auckland, seemed to be Montgomery Thompson's car. Enquiries in Amy Street gave reasonable corroboration to Mrs. Nomore's statement that Pencarbon had left about twelve-thirty; two households had been disturbed by his eloquent farewells. From Joe Nomore's house to the timberyard by the creek was a walk of some ten minutes for a normally sober person. Stanley Pencarbon would probably have taken longer; his footprints in the field proved that his homeward route had been more divergent than his outward one. But he would not have taken much more than, say, twenty minutes. The effect of beer upon Stanley Pencarbon was not a subject concerning which no information existed; the many observers who had studied the subject more or less scientifically all concurred in the opinion that the stage of sound sleep followed the stage of joyful song within not more than thirty minutes. And when sleep came, it imprisoned him for hours. If Pencarbon had not reached the car by one o'clock, therefore, he would have slept in less comfortable quarters—under a tree in the field, or in the doorway of some Indian cobbler in Waimanu Road. The car must consequently have been in position before one o'clock; and if it had been used for the carriage of the corpse, that journey must have been accomplished during the time that Jim Camelback was allegedly playing poker with three other Government officials in 'Segai Na Marama.'

In an attempt to prove the truth of this reasoning, Spearpoint subjected his subordinates to a rigorous cross-examination on Sunday morning, and finally obtained evidence that the car had, in fact, been parked in the timberyard before one a.m. This information was dragged most unwillingly from Genghis, the rawest recruit on the Suva roll-call, and the most callow-looking Indian in a body of Indians who are apparently originally selected for their air of unchesty callowness. His unshaven face was a patchwork of sprouting tufts of delicate beard and areas of ivory smoothness, and his habitual expression wavered between the fierceness he considered essential in a police-man and the pride he could not dissemble in his khaki uniform and his clumping military boots.

Under the pressure of the District Inspector's stern gaze, he admitted that he had patrolled Waimanu Road and Renwick Road (which is its continuation on the far side of the bridge over the creek) between twelve-forty-five and one; and he stated that as he had come on to the hump of the bridge he had noticed the car in the timberyard, and had intended to investigate its presence there, but that his attention had been distracted by the sight of an old Punjabi lying asleep in Morris, Hedstrom's colonnade on the opposite side of the road. Genghis had kicked the Punjabi in the ribs and wakened him; and had been told a story of a late arrival in town by lorry bus and no other place to sleep. Impressed by this hard-luck story, Genghis had left the man there; but when he had returned half an hour later to ask his name and place of residence, the spot was empty. Fearing a reprimand for negligence, Genghis had decided not to report the incident. When he finally slunk away from his interview with the District Inspector, he realised that he would have been wiser to have reported it.

Spearpoint considered the possibility of the car having no connection with the murder, and resolved to explore the cliffs of Walu Bay; but Sunday was a torrent of tropical rain, Monday was even wetter, and Tuesday was nearly as unsuitable as Monday. He fretted through these three steamy, clammy days, extracting what consolation he could from the reflection that on Wednesday he might receive the cable from the Auckland police giving Stakes' verdict on the razor, which verdict might render the climb unnecessary.

Meanwhile, Sharpe devoted himself to scientific criminology. So industriously did he comb Netta Maul's room and shop for fingerprints that he exhausted his supply of powders, and wore out nearly all his camelhair brushes; but he made no discoveries of importance.

The zealous sergeant Singh tramped, in his waterproof cape, for miles around the environs of Suva, interviewing scores of Indians, Fijians and Chinese, and reporting at intervals in the thick, mispronounced, ungrammatical and incomprehensible English of which he was so proud. The evidence he unearthed was all useless, except that it tended to prove that Camelback had not reached the Royal Palm until at least 10.10; his car had been seen parked in the Government car-shed in Carnarvon Street at 10.15, but had not been there at 10.5.

Spearpoint made a number of fruitless enquiries among the whites and the near-whites; but all he learned was that the lipstick had been purchased on Wednesday by Mr. Montgomery Thomspon, who had hinted to the salesman that he desired the transaction kept secret.

It was Sunday evening before Dr. Halibut paid the visit which Spearpoint, knowing the acting P.M.O.'s insatiable curiosity, had expected. The Inspector had been smoking on the verandah, puzzling over his problem, trying to piece the known facts into a connected story, and making mental notes of the matters still to be examined; but he did not resent the intrusion because it afforded him the opportunity of making enquiries without formally seeking the doctor's aid.

The conversation stumbled over other matters for almost ten minutes before Halibut ventured to ask bluntly how the case was going.

"Can't see daylight yet," admitted the Inspector. "We've ascertained a mass of facts, and heard a good deal of rumour, but there are still some missing links."

"You've got some pieces of chain, then?"

Spearpoint shrugged his shoulders. "If you had a jig-saw puzzle with a lot of extra pieces in the box you'd start by fitting bits together without knowing whether you wanted them or not. Most of the facts I've gathered probably have no bearing on the case at all, but I must go on finding facts until I get a complete chain."

"Do you suspect anyone?" asked the doctor, taking a liberty few would have dared.

"I suspect several people, of course. There are several who had either motive or opportunity—or both. I can't say that I have serious grounds for suspecting anyone."

"Do you think you'll find your man?"

"I'm sure I will."

"He must have been pretty smart to have eluded you so far, though."

"He's not smart enough to get away with it, all the same." Spearpoint dismissed that aspect of the matter, saying, "I've been looking up the subject of rigor mortis. I gather it's delayed in the Tropics?"

"Putrefaction sets in much quicker, though."

"You reckoned she'd been killed between ten-thirty and eleven, and was in the water six or seven hours. She was fished out about five, so, by your reckoning, she was put in between ten-thirty and eleven-thirty. In other words, she was tied up and put in the sea as soon as she was dead."

"It must have been done while she was still warm."

"I've got a medical dictionary here," persisted the Inspector. "It says:

'Rigidity begins at four to ten hours after death . . . and is complete a few hours later . . . if a joint be forcibly bent, rigidity does not return.'"

"Quite true," agreed Dr. Halibut.

"I deduce from that and the fact that she was rigid, that she must have been doubled up and tied before rigor set in."

"Definitely."

"But that could have been done safely at any time within the first four hours after death—or even later, as the Tropics delay rigor?"

"In theory, yes," conceded Halibut.

"In fact, assuming she was killed at ten, she need not have been tied up until, say, two—and if she was killed at eleven, she might not have been tied up till three, and, therefore, put in the water until, say, three-thirty?"

"In theory, yes; but that's not possible in this case. The state of the body proved definitely that it had been in the water several hours—six at the very least."

Since he was unable to retort that Dr. Carnarvonshire had stated as his opinion that the body had been in the water only two hours, Spearpoint let the matter drop, and turned to a point on which he had been speculating ever since the Government chemist had confirmed his suspicion that the earth of Paul's garage floor had been soaked in blood.

"You remember," he said, "that her throat was cut all on one side. I was wondering how to account for that."

Halibut shrugged his shoulders. "Pure ignorance, I should say."

"I was wondering," went on Spearpoint, slowly, "whether she could not have been held face downwards, half on her side, perhaps—I'm assuming she had been knocked unconscious by the blow—and cut with an upward movement. That would account for the cut being on one side, and also it would account for our not being able to find any bloodstained clothes."

Halibut puffed at his cigar before replying cautiously, "That's an idea, certainly. It might have been done like that. I must admit that I thought at the time it had been done with a downward stroke—the head pulled back. But, as you say, an upward stroke from below would account for those two points." Then he added, "But the fact that you haven't found any bloodstained clothes doesn't prove there are none."

"Quite," agreed the Inspector, gloomily; he had no more questions to ask, and consequently no more suggestions to impart. The talk wandered to other matters, and some half-hour later Dr. Halibut left, the major part of his curiosity unsatisfied.

Spearpoint immediately strolled up to Dr. Carnarvonshire's, and consulted him on the same two points. This second authority gave it as his opinion, first, that the body need not have been tied up until well after midnight, and second, that the wound in the throat might have been caused in the manner the Inspector suggested.

CHAPTER FOURTEEN

BOB BELLAMY'S ALIBI

(*Wednesday morning*)

WEDNESDAY MORNING BROUGHT a cable from the Auckland police which sent Spearpoint's thoughts into a different channel. It read simply: "Stakes says razor belongs Bellamy Cutt."

Spearpoint tossed the paper across the table to Sharpe, saying, "What do you make of that?"

Sharpe's eyebrows rose higher than ever, and he whistled excitedly. Then he remarked, "Bellamy or Cutt, eh? I suppose they've both got razors of that type, and Stakes doesn't know which. Well, it'll be easy enough to ask them to produce their razors.—And, sir, it looks as if it was Bellamy's print."

"Probably. I think we'll ask Bellamy first," decided Spearpoint. "I can't exactly see myself going to Willy Cutt and hinting that I think he killed Netta Maul. Now, let's consider Bellamy for a minute. . . . Where is this bally time-table? . . . Here, I saw him at nine-forty-five and I reckon he would have got home at nine-fifty; but he didn't turn on the light until ten-four. That's fourteen minutes. Hardly time for him to kill Netta Maul and tie her up in a sack."

"No, sir," agreed Sharpe. "But suppose Camelback did go to call for Dr. Halibut. Suppose Bellamy's story of the quarrel between him and Netta Maul was concocted by Bellamy. Suppose Bellamy came upon her and stunned her—you said he was carrying a heavy knobbed stick—and shoved her into the garage, and cut her throat, and then went home for the cord."

"You think he'd have the razor in his pocket?" queried Spearpoint, with a sarcasm his assistant ignored.

"Yes, sir, if he really was following her. You told me how touchy he was at your saying he was following her."

"You think he'd arranged to meet her?"

"Well, no—perhaps. I can't suggest the details," conceded Sharpe. "But he was carrying a stick that could have been used to stun her, and it was his razor, and there's those fourteen minutes to account for."

"Yes, it will be interesting to see how he accounts for them. But, of course, the razor may be Willy Cutt's. We don't know what his fingerprint is like, do we? Still, I think we'll try Bellamy first. That means another

argument with Cutt, I suppose." He picked up the
receiver and asked for that gentleman. "That point
about the stick is interesting," he said, as he waited.
"Halibut says the blow on the temple probably killed her.
Carnarvonshire says it was done before death. I've looked up
that point, and I find a corpse won't bruise after death.
So all the bruises must have been caused before death."

"Who'd want to hit a corpse, anyway?" asked Sharpe,
to corroborate his superior's reasoning.

"Who'd want to slash a corpse's face?" retorted
Spearpoint. "The cuts were made after death; they
hardly bled at all. I thought at first the bruises might
have come from the murderer dropping the body whilst
carrying it, but that's impossible.—I wish that girl would
hurry up and get my number.—Perhaps, while I'm talking to old Cutt, I might as well ask him a question or
two about his movements on Thursday night. We know
he was at the Fiji Club at ten o'clock, but we may as
well find out his later movements. We'd never have found
out about Camelback's watch if I hadn't asked Bob
Eachway which way he went home."

"Could Bellamy and Camelback be in league?" suggested Sharpe. "They're not the sort of fellows to act
together, though, even if they did both have cause to
hate Netta Maul."

The telephone bell rang before Spearpoint could reply,
and Mr. Cutt's less impatient tone (for the Inspector had
assisted, rather than impeded, Marryam & Cutt's claims
to Netta Maul's estate) asked, "What you want, eh?"

"I just wanted to check up on that bridge game last
Thursday, Mr. Cutt. I understand you were playing
with Carnarvonshire against Dummfish and Montgomery
Thomspon?"

"That's right."

"And it broke up at ten-thirty?"

"I can't remember the exact time, but it was a little
before that."

"And then Montgomery Thomspon went?"

"Yes."

"And did you go yourself then?"

"Yes." From the way he barked this affirmative it was evident that Mr. Cutt's benevolent attitude towards the police was vanishing.

"Home?"

"What the hell do you——?" began Willy Cutt, explosively. Then he chuckled, and resumed, cheerfully, "Oh, so you think I murdered the girl, eh?"

"Oh, no," Spearpoint promptly climbed down. "I was just wondering which way you went, in case you saw—anyone else."

"Well, I'll tell you which way I went," offered Willy Cutt, magnanimously. "I drove down Hercules Street, along Victoria Parade and Thomson Street, and along Rodwell Road to Walu Bay, eh. There I parked the car near the Vacuum Oil shed, got into my launch, and went fishing, eh. I came back about one, got into my car again, and drove home, eh. And I was alone all the time, eh. How's that, Mr. Spearpoint?" The voice at the other end of the line chuckled again, and Spearpoint did not know whether to believe it or not. Putting the statement aside for further consideration, he reverted to his real purpose. "Thank you," he said; "that doesn't seem to be much use. As a matter of fact, I had another purpose in ringing you; do you mind if I have another word with Bellamy?"

"Certainly. Do you want me to send him round?"

"If you don't mind, Mr. Cutt."

Whilst waiting for Bellamy, Spearpoint told his assistant what Mr. Cutt had said, and Sharpe dutifully acquiesced in the theory that the redoubtable little man had been leg-pulling. But his story was plausible; fishing was his chief hobby, he did keep his powerful petrol-launch moored in Walu Bay, and he did occasionally take midnight voyages in the harbour.

Bob Bellamy appeared more nervous, if possible, than ever.

He sat on the edge of the seat indicated, and looked unhappily from Spearpoint to Sharpe and back, rubbing his white-drill-clad knee with his right hand, and fidgeting the fingers of his left.

"When you were here last Friday," began Spearpoint, "you told me that you used a Royce razor."

"I do," agreed Bellamy, in some surprise.

"How long have you been using it?"

"About six weeks. My wife gave it to me for a present when she went away."

"What did you use before that?"

"A cut-throat——" Bellamy winced at his own word, coloured, and hastened to amend it to, "an ordinary razor, you know, open."

"Yes, I know," Spearpoint agreed, grimly. "Do you know where it is now?"

Bellamy hesitated, blushed deeper, and finally admitted, "No."

"Is this it?" asked Spearpoint, handing over the photographs of the murderer's weapon.

Bellamy studied them with care, and with some interest. Spearpoint wondered whether he was merely trying to gain time for thought. The paper shook in the young man's trembling hands. He looked up at last, and said, "It might be mine. That's the maker's name all right. Mine had a black handle; and the blade was very worn. —Was this the—the one?" His voice faltered.

"It was." Spearpoint spoke more grimly than ever, and Sharpe kept his gaze fastened on the wretched visitor's knees. "This is the razor that was found hidden in Netta Maul's clothes. Those patches on the blade and the handle are bloodstains. We sent the razor itself to the Auckland police, and asked them to show it to Stakes, who's in New Zealand on holiday, as I suppose you know, in order that he might identify it, if he could. We had a cable this morning saying he thought the razor was yours."

Bellamy, still looking at the photographs, but not with attention, muttered, "Then I suppose it is mine. He used to set it for me. He'd know it all right."

There was a silence. Spearpoint waited to see if Bellamy would volunteer anything further, and then said, sharply, "Well, can you explain how your razor came to be involved in the murder of Netta Maul?"

Bellamy sat up sharply and braced himself against this attack. His face was crimson and his mouth was working miserably. He managed to shrug his shoulders and utter the word, "No." Then he half turned towards Sharpe, who refused to meet his eyes.

"You must have some explanation to offer," Spearpoint argued. "You admit it is your razor. How did it get where I found it?"

"I don't know. I don't know at all," protested Bellamy, unsteadily. Then he asked, holding up the photograph, "Whose are all these fingerprints?"

"Chiefly——" began Spearpoint, and paused. He had been about to say, "Chiefly mine and Dr. Halibut's," but he amended this to, "Chiefly those of the people who found the razor; but there's one there that looks like yours."

"Like mine?" asked Bellamy, startled. "Where did you get my fingerprints?"

Sharpe, taking pity on him, decided to attract his attention and steady his nerve, and, not without professional pride, came over with another photograph, explaining, "You left them on the doorhandle. Look. These are yours. Now, this chap here, on the handle, overlain by this great thumb,—that looks like yours. Of course, there's not enough of it to be certain, but, as you see, it has these curves.—And, of course, we found your fingerprints all over Netta Maul's shop."

"All over her shop?" cried Bellamy, in horror. Then he recovered himself, and expostulated, "But, of course,

I had to take stock there. I was always touching the shelves and the stock. You can't hold that——"

"We know that," cut in Spearpoint. "We know you took stock there. Your fingerprints prove nothing. We know that. We're not worrying about them. What we want to know about is this razor. Now, what explanation can you offer?"

"I can't offer any explanation. I'm sorry."

"It's your razor. You admit that?"

"Well," began Bellamy, accenting the verb. "It *was* my razor—apparently. But I don't know who had it after me. You see, when I got my new razor, it—it was given away."

"Given away?"

"Yes."

"Who was it given to?" asked Spearpoint, forgetting the niceties of English in his excitement.

"I don't know," answered Bellamy, more at his ease now and smiling weakly.

"You don't know?"

"No."

"You don't know?" repeated Spearpoint, mystified. "You gave your razor away, and you don't know who you gave it to?"

"Well," admitted Bellamy, reluctantly, "it wasn't I who gave it away. I said I didn't want it any more, so —so it was given away," he concluded, lamely.

"Who gave it away?"

He did not answer.

"You mean your wife gave it away?"

Reluctantly, he nodded.

"Well, she'd know who she gave it to. We must ask her. What's her address?"

"Oh, no, please," Bellamy pleaded. "At least, can't you wait until next month? It—it should be over then. Don't worry her now."

"But, good God, man!" shouted Spearpoint, impatiently.

"That's absurd! Don't you realise this is a murder case?"
He calmed a little, and said, "It's urgent. It's a matter
of life and death."

"Yes, I realise that," conceded Bellamy, sadly. "But
my wife is involved in a matter of life and death, too."

Spearpoint softened. He had been a father, himself.
Indeed, he still was a father. In as kindly a tone as he
could muster, he said, "Look here, old chap, you don't
want to let that get you down. Your wife will be all right.
Why, when she went away last month, she was looking
fine. I've known her since she was a schoolgirl—in fact,
I've known Phyllis Booth far longer than you have, and
I've never seen her looking better than when she went
off on the *Aorangi*. So don't you worry. She'll be all right;
and they'll both come back bonny." Then he remembered that he was interrogating a suspected murderer;
and that if Bob Bellamy was a murderer he might never
see his child, and might see his wife again only to bid
her farewell for ever. He paused, and considered. If
Phyllis Bellamy had really given away her husband's
razor, it would be no strain on her to be asked, and to
tell, to whom she gave it. But if she had not given it away,
if Bellamy had really used it to murder Netta Maul and
was lying when he said his wife had disposed of it, then
the question would be incomprehensible, and therefore
distressing to her. The question must be asked, nevertheless; for, if Bellamy were guilty, he would, perhaps,
rather admit his guilt than subject his wife to questioning
at such a time. While it was true that she could not be
forced to give evidence against him, she could obviously give
evidence in his favour, and a refusal to give such evidence
would be tantamount to evidence against him. If Bellamy
were innocent, and his wife had disposed of the razor,
it would not be unduly inconsiderate to ask her to whom
she gave it; and Bellamy's objection to her being asked
could surely spring only from the fact that he knew she
could not answer. So Bellamy must be forced either to

give the address or to withdraw his explanation of the disappearance of the razor.

"Look here," Spearpoint resumed, "it'll be no hardship to her just to be asked what she did with your razor, will it? And, don't you see, until we know that, things look rather suspicious against you?"

"Yes, I suppose they do," Bellamy conceded. He thought a moment, and then said wearily, "All right. I'll give you her address. But—but may I ask her myself?"

"If you'll let me see what you say," agreed the Inspector, making a mental note to stop any other cable Bellamy might send to his wife. He offered pencil and paper. Bellamy pulled his chair up to the desk, considered for a moment, and then wrote, "Sorry to trouble you, but what happened to my old razor. Hope going on well. Love, Bob." Looking up, he said, half smiling, "I suppose I ought to pay for that—at least, half of it. And reply paid, too, I suppose. I'll have to get some money."

"We'll send it off right away, and see about the cost later," said Spearpoint, calling for a messenger. When he had issued instructions for the immediate despatch of the cable, he resumed, "Before you go, there's another thing or two I'd like to ask you about."

"All right." Bellamy had recovered his composure, and, with it, his air of honesty. Spearpoint thought that he did not look like a murderer, but, he reflected, he had never seen a European murderer, except in effigy in Madame Tussaud's, and so he did not know what one should look like.

"How long have you had that razor?"

"I've had it ever since I started to shave," Bellamy confessed, smiling and blushing at the admission of his youth, "about eight years. I brought it with me from Home."

"You remember last Thursday night?" Spearpoint continued, glancing at his notes. "You were foll— walking down Waimanu Road behind Netta Maul. You said you turned up Browne Street, overhearing a piece of dialogue between her and Camelback, turned into Amy Street, and so home."

"Yes; that is so."

"Now, I calculate that I passed you in front of the hospital at nine-forty-five; that you reached the corner of Browne Street at nine-forty-seven and a half, and that you would be home by nine-fifty. That's on the basis that you were doing three miles an hour. Here's a plan of the streets, with the distances marked. What do you think of those times?"

Bellamy examined the map, but took the distances for granted; he worked the times mentally, and agreed to them.

"In other words," he said, slowly, "you calculate that I reached home at ten to ten. Of course, I can't say that that was so; but these calculations prove that, near enough."

"What did you do when you went in?"

"I sat and read for half-an-hour or so, and then went to bed," answered Bellamy, after some thought. "That's what I usually do."

"Which room did you sit in?"

"The back room."

"Did you go in by the front door, or the back door?"

"The back door. I always use the back door, the lock's stronger. The front doors are pretty flimsy, and we always keep them bolted on the inside."

"The back door's really at the side, isn't it, opposite Joe Nomore's back door?"

"Yes."

"Well, I suppose the first thing you'd do when you got in would be to turn on the light?"

"Quite."

"So the time you turned on the light would be the time you got in?"

"I suppose it would—near enough." Bellamy seemed

a little doubtful of this, plainly wondering to what these questions tended.

"You see," explained Spearpoint, with an air of triumph, "I happen to know your light went on at exactly four minutes past ten."

Bellamy received this in astonished silence; he did not even enquire how the Inspector knew.

Spearpoint condescended to explain. "I was sitting in my car in Waimanu Road. I remembered that I'd passed you; the thought flashed through my mind that you lived in Amy Street; I looked across the field to your house, and it was all dark. That was certainly after ten to ten. Actually, the light went on at four minutes past ten. Can you explain what you were doing for those fourteen minutes, between the time you should have got home, and the time you did get home?"

"Good gracious!" exclaimed Bellamy, astonished. "You seem to have kept a pretty close watch on me."

"Apparently it was as well I did," retorted the Inspector, grimly. "Now, can you explain what you were doing for those fourteen minutes?"

Bellamy blushed, began to speak, hesitated, and finally said, "As a matter of fact, I can. Normally, I couldn't tell you exactly what I did on any evening—at least, a week after. But I can on that night, because, well, the circumstances were unusual. As I came along Amy Street, I was feeling—I wasn't feeling very well. So—so, as soon as I got in the back door, I turned on the light in the back hall—you couldn't see that from Waimanu Road, because there's a curtain over the doorway,—and then, then I went to the lavatory——"

Sharpe made as if to speak, but Spearpoint waved him into silence, and then said to the bewildered Bellamy, "Yes, we know you went to the lavatory——"

"You know?" cried Bellamy, jumping to his feet, and then sitting down again. "You're not going to tell me you saw that?"

"No, but we know, nevertheless. But what I disagree

is the time. Or did you spend fourteen minutes in the lavatory?"

"No, only two or three," protested Bellamy, blushing. He was in a thoroughly nervous and excited state. "As a matter of fact, though, I didn't actually go to the lavatory. I——"

"You said just now you did."

"Yes, I know, and so I did, in a sense, but, you see—— Well, I didn't actually go to the——"

"You've said that before," interrupted Spearpoint, impatiently. "Now, what do you mean? Did you go, or didn't you?"

"Well, yes, but——"

"Well, what do you want to say you didn't for?"

"Well, I didn't, actually."

Spearpoint scratched his head, and sighed, and looked despairingly at the grinning Sharpe. Bellamy, his face scarlet, continued, "What I've been trying to say is, that I was sick."

"Sick?"

"Yes, I only just got in in time. I'd been feeling sick all the way home, and as soon as I got in—well," he concluded, lamely, "I was sick."

Spearpoint, considering this, thought it very likely that if this nervy little fellow had killed Netta Maul, the sight of her dead face might well make him vomit, and asked, sharply, "What made you sick?"

Bellamy hung his head, and then explained, shame-faced, "As a matter of fact, I'd been smoking."

"Well?"

"Well, you see—I haven't smoked for years—and I never did smoke much—and it often used to make me feel a bit sick—when I did smoke; but they say smoking soothes you—when you're worried—and, and nervy—so I thought I'd try again—I've been very worried lately, you know—so I bought some cigarettes—and smoked two, well, nearly three—but they weren't a bit soothing— they only made me feel sick—so I went out to see if the air would make me feel better—but I felt worse—and I only just got home in time."

As Bellamy made this tragic confession with averted face, the two policemen were able to relieve their feelings by exchanging smiles without his observing them.

"And how long were you being sick? Fourteen minutes?"

"No, only two or three. I was all right as—as soon as I'd brought up my dinner."

There might be something in his story, thought Spearpoint, or there might not. The question is, how much of an actor is Bellamy? Is he a quite innocent and sincere young man, or is he a cunning criminal who can tell a ridiculous story such as he has just told against himself in the assured belief that no one will suspect of murder a man with so queasy a stomach? But, obviously, the will and the capacity to murder are not confined to those who are habituated to tobacco. He repeated, "Are you sure you were not in there for fourteen minutes?"

"No, only two or three," Bellamy reaffirmed, blushing. "Only two or three."

"Your claim is," suggested Spearpoint, "that you entered the house by the side door at ten to ten, turned on the light in the back hall, went into the lavatory—that leads out of the back hall, I suppose?—and came out again at, say, five to ten?"

"About that."

"That still leaves nine minutes to account for. I put it to you that you really came in at three minutes past ten, turned on the light in the back room, and then went to the lavatory, coming out at, say, seven minutes past ten." As he spoke, the thought flashed through his mind that perhaps the drain had been utilised for the disposal of some incriminating document connected with the murder, say, a paper stolen from Netta Maul's bag.

"I don't think so," Bellamy objected. "That's if your time is right—if you really overtook me at nine-forty-five.

I came straight home. I had to. You see, I—well, I wasn't feeling well. But, after I had—well, when I was all right again—I remember now: I went into the kitchen, and turned the light on there. The window's at one side, and it's got a dark blind, because it faces old Joe's window. I washed my hands in the kitchen, and then I got myself a lemon drink, out of the ice-chest—and that's in the back hall. And then, there was an old newspaper spread on the kitchen table. It was an English paper, with some football results in it, and I stood and read them for a few minutes while I had my drink; and then I went into the back room and turned on the light there. That might easily have been four minutes past ten. Of course, I can't say what time it was; but what I am quite certain of is, that I didn't do anything else when I got in. I went straight to the place. And I didn't turn the light on in the back room for at least ten minutes afterwards. The switch is on the far wall, you know. I had to walk right across the room to turn it on."

Spearpoint played another trump card. "If you were in the kitchen by five to ten," he asked, "how do you account for the fact that the water was still running into the cistern at ten past?"

"Was it?" asked Bellamy. "So that's how you knew? Well, it's a very unsatisfactory cistern, and it takes a long time to fill."

"A quarter of an hour?"

Bellamy shrugged his shoulders. "It might."

Spearpoint stood up. "Well, there's no time like the present. Can you lend us the key so that we can go up and test it?"

"Certainly," Bellamy agreed. "But I'd like to come too, if I may."

This was not to Spearpoint's liking. He preferred to search in the absence of the owner, but he could hardly object, so the three of them got into his car, and chugged up the hill to Amy Street.

"Now," said the Inspector, as they drew up outside Bellamy's house, a square, wooden bungalow, with corrugated iron roof, "you can show us exactly what you did when you came home last Thursday night."

Bellamy, politely holding the gate open for the policemen to pass through first, blushed, and said, "Well——"

"You go ahead," Spearpoint ordered, waving him on. "You went straight round to the side door?"

"Yes." Bellamy led the way along the front of the house, and round to the side door, which was set about a third of the way along, opposite Joe Nomore's side door. Bellamy produced the key from his trouser pocket, unlocked the door, stood aside again for his visitors to enter, and then, in response to Spearpoint's gesture, went in first. When they were all in the back hall, he said, "Well, the first thing I did was to switch on this light," and he indicated the switch behind the door. "Then I went in here"—pointing to a door in the wall immediately to the left of the back door. Beyond this door was a door, standing open, which gave access to the shower-bath. On the wall between the two doors was a second electric switch. "At least," Bellamy amended, "I turned the switch on first. You see, this one serves for both places." He hesitated.

"Right," agreed Spearpoint, noting the positions of the two doors and the switches; then he looked at the dark roller blind at the window, and the curtain separating the back hall from the back sitting-room.

"Was this blind down?"

"Oh, yes," affirmed Bellamy, positively, "and so was the one in the kitchen. We always pull them down as soon as we turn on the light. The windows face Nomore's, you know. Then," he continued with a rush, "I went into the kitchen and washed my hands under the tap, and, then I suppose I switched on the light there, and got a tumbler, and went to the ice-chest." He opened the top of the ice-chest, and pulled a bottle off the block of

ice therein. He hesitated slightly, and then said, apolo-
getically, "Would you chaps care for a drink? I'm sorry
it's only lemon."

It was a perfectly genuine hospitable offer, but Spearpoint rejected it, somewhat to Sharpe's regret, for the
day was warm, and even a lemon drink better than
nothing.

"Well," continued Bellamy, replacing the bottle, "then
I stood here drinking, and reading the newspaper," and
he indicated the newspapers spread on the kitchen table.
"I was interested. That might easily have taken ten
minutes. It's extraordinary what a close level of performance there is in the football leagues."

"How long does your tank take to refill?" asked
Spearpoint, dismissing the kitchen and the football leagues.

Bellamy shrugged his shoulders. "Goodness knows.
A long time. It's quite an efficient one, you know. It
works all right; but it's just a bit slow."

"We'll test it," announced the Inspector, and opening
the little door, he leaned forward and pulled the chain.
A protesting gurgle was the only result. He tugged at it
a second time, and nothing happened. Sharpe was so
misguided as to laugh.

"It is like that," said Bellamy, apologetic. "You sometimes have to pull it three or four times, but it works in
the end."

Spearpoint grasped the handle a third time, and jerked
it suddenly and viciously. A cupful of water came roaring
down, promising to deliver the goods, but the promise
was not fulfilled.

"It's easy enough to see what you were doing for those
fourteen minutes," grinned Sharpe, happy at being able
to point out a fact in favour of the boy's innocence. He
thought of Bellamy as a boy, though their ages were the
same.

"No," conceded Bellamy, honestly. "That wasn't it.
It always works first time with me. There's a sort of a

knack about it. All right when you know it." He obviously did not want to boast of his accomplishments, but at the same time he was unwilling to be exonerated unfairly. "Shall I have a go, Mr. Spearpoint?" he offered, humbly.

Spearpoint did not deign to reply. His back, which was all his companions could see of him, was the resolute back of a man who refused to admit that anyone could excel him at pulling a chain. If there was a knack in it, he would master that knack. His next attempt was a triumph for perseverance. The tank emptied itself with the fury and ebullience of the inevitable Falls of Lodore, and continued intermittently to transfer to the bowl the replacement that started to flow in. As soon as he was assured that he had done the trick, Spearpoint glanced at his watch, which showed seventeen minutes to eleven, and then stepped backwards into the hall to await the coming of silence.

Sharpe had perched himself comfortably on a low cupboard, and was smoking with an air of enjoyment, marred only by the sweat on his forehead. Bellamy was nervously transferring his weight from one foot to the other, not keeping still an instant. But, when Spearpoint emerged, he hastened into the kitchen to fetch the Inspector a chair. Spearpoint waved the chair aside, but, as the water continued to run noisily into the tank, and quickly out again into the bowl, he presently sat down with an abstracted air, and felt for his cigarette case. Sharpe's grin grew gradually broader and broader, but Bellamy displayed no awareness of his triumph. When the sounds died away with a final gurgle, the hands of the Inspector's watch pointed to five minutes to eleven.

"Well, that proves that," exclaimed Sharpe, jumping down from his perch, and stubbing out his second cigarette on the horizontal studding of the wall. The careful Bellamy hurried into the kitchen, and reappeared with a tin bowl, which he proffered as an ash-tray. Spearpoint dropped his butt into the receptacle, and stood up, thoughtfully.

"I think we ought to try it again," he announced, "and listen outside. After all, it was heard outside."

"And, of course," Bellamy pointed out, anxious not to allow any point in his favour to pass unchallenged, "this doesn't prove that I did pull it at five to ten; it merely proves that I didn't pull it before five to ten."

"Obviously," agreed Spearpoint, drily; and at his tone Bellamy's friendliness retreated. But he consented with alacrity to the Inspector's instructions to "Try it again"; and he did succeed, as he had claimed he would, in flushing the pan at his first attempt. The three of them then went into the garden, shutting the door behind them, and stood there, scanning the wide view across the field, over the houses in middle Waimanu Road, to the calm waters of the harbour, the green hills of the farther shore, the thin white line of the reef, and the blue ocean stretching to the dim horizon. Bellamy and Sharpe exchanged a few comments on the scene, both agreeing that they preferred the Strand, or even the Old Kent Road (Bellamy), or the Lea Bridge Road (Sharpe). But when Bellamy went so far as to suggest that even the suburban railway journey into Liverpool Street station was preferable to his ten-minute walk up Toorak Road, Sharpe ventured a doubt. Spearpoint stood grimly silent, wondering whether this slim, nervous, precise young man could possibly be a cunning murderer. The evidence of the razor was not in itself conclusive; Mrs. Bellamy might be able to explain that; but, even if she could not, there were many points which remained to be settled before guilt could be brought home to anyone.

This time eleven minutes passed before the complaining waters ceased; and Spearpoint was almost convinced; but —but the razor had not been explained yet. He decided that, whilst he was on the spot, he would search the house, and he announced his desire with such show of determination as was calculated to persuade Bellamy to submit without questioning his authority.

Bellamy shrugged his shoulders, and said, "You're welcome. There's nothing much here, you know—so long as you don't disturb my wife's things," he added, as an afterthought. He hovered round, either trying to assist, or attempting to divert attention from suspicious matters, Spearpoint was unable to decide which. He did not seem to mind what they examined so long as they did not disturb his bookcase; Spearpoint consequently decided to look behind the books, and had them all shifted out. But nothing at all incriminating was found. Bellamy's only dark suit, folded at the bottom of a camphor-wood box, had all its buttons intact. His torch was on a shelf in the kitchen. There was no cord anywhere similar to any of the pieces used to truss the corpse. His plimsolls, neither new enough nor old enough to suggest that he possessed a second pair hidden or disposed of, had soles of a different pattern from those worn by whoever had been in the garage; they were, moreover, much smaller. Everything in the house was tidily in its place and every room was swept and dusted. There was no other man in Suva, Spearpoint thought, who would live so neatly without a wife to tidy the home for him. The garden, it is true, was untidy; but Bellamy professed himself no gardener, and said that the only reason he ever went into it was to obtain some exercise by hacking down the waist-high weeds with a cane-knife. After looking under the house for traces of cord or sacks, and looking in vain for any evidence at all likely to incriminate the tenant, the two policemen retired, leaving Bellamy a little reproachfully tidying his books.

CHAPTER FIFTEEN

WILLY CUTT, THE FORMIDABLE MAN

(Wednesday: 12.30–1.30 p.m.)

"Where are we now, sir?" asked Sharpe, as they drove back to the Police Station. "Bellamy's cleared all right. I'm glad of that. He's a decent sort of chap."

"Maybe. But he's not cleared yet. He was quite right when he pointed out that all we have proved is that he might have been home by five to ten. He may not have got home until five past. And then there's the razor."

"Are we sure it's his razor?" queried Sharpe. "After all, it may be Willy Cutt's."

"Bellamy admitted to it. And then there's his finger-mark on it."

"It's a very doubtful mark, sir. It could be his, of course. But when you can only see a little bit of a mark, you can't be certain. Someone else may have a finger with those particular lines."

Spearpoint did not answer; he was engaged in dodging an Indian sulky coming over the Naboukulau bridge; and Sharpe relapsed into silence.

When they were back in the station, however, the irrepressible Sub-Inspector burst out with another idea.

"Look, sir, I've been thinking," and he continued without heeding the expression of surprise that came over his superior's face. "Suppose we've been barking up the wrong tree all this time. Suppose all our previous theories have been wrong."

"We haven't had any previous theories," Spearpoint contradicted, stressing the personal pronoun. "You have had a great many theories, and doubtless they've all been wrong. But I form no theory until I have discovered the facts."

"I mean, sir, the idea about Conky Thomspon's car. Suppose that's got no connection with the murder,—or that Chow's boat, either. Pencarbon may have gone home less drunk than we thought, and have taken the car for a lark."

"And Lum Chin's boat?"

"That need not have had anything to do with it. He may have tied it up carelessly, and it came adrift; or some of his pals may have borrowed it.—What I'm trying to suggest, sir, is that Netta Maul's body wasn't necessarily taken down to the creek in Conky Thomspon's car."

"You don't need to suggest that to me; I've had that in mind all along. It's a possibility that the car was used; but it may not have been. So far we've found no other form of conveyance."

"No, sir; but supposing she wasn't conveyed? Suppose she went to town of her own accord?"

"How so?"

"Suppose Bellamy was right in describing the quarrel between her and Camelback. But, remember, he didn't hear the end of the conversation, only a bit of it. Suppose Camelback succeeded in pacifying her. She may have got into his car and gone with him to the Royal Palm, gone up to her room, left her bag in the trunk——"

"It had his fingerprints on it."

"Yes——" Sharpe was momentarily nonplussed at that, but added, quickly, "He may have handed it to her when she got out of the car.—After that, she went out, met Cutt and went fishing with him, and he murdered her in his launch."

Spearpoint considered this for some moments, and then said, "That theory doesn't fit the known facts. How about the scrap from her frock, the shreds of sack in the car, the blood and the hairs in the garage? How about the fact that she never went anywhere without that precious bag of hers?"

"Yes, there do seem to be difficulties," conceded Sharpe, crestfallen. "But there was the bundle of letters with Cutt's name; and he was prowling round her door early the morning after she was murdered. Could he have had a private key, and got in to pinch the love-letters he'd written her?"

"And walked bang into Constable Maharaj! The idea of association between him and Netta Maul is fantastic."

"Well, sir, it did seem as if he disliked her. The way he pressed her to repay her debt, and so on. But might not that have been a blind? After all, we don't know the facts, do we?"

"We do know that a piece of her frock was found on a bramble of Dr. Halibut's hedge, and that her hairs and blood were found in Paul's garage. And that would seem to dispose of the suggestion that she could have been murdered in Willy Cutt's launch. Nevertheless, we've got to ask him about that razor. I wonder if we can induce him to come along here"; and he picked up the receiver. As soon as he announced himself, Willy Cutt enquired:

"Have you arrested my stock-clerk? I see he's not come back yet."

"No; we haven't arrested him. We left him at his house. It was after twelve, and I suppose that he thought it wasn't worth while coming down again before lunch. But I wanted to have a talk with you, Mr. Cutt, in private. Can you come round?"

"I'll call in on my way to lunch, eh," decided Mr. Cutt, refusing to make any concessions to the police, and they rang off.

The little man arrived, however, almost immediately. He had evidently not waited until the stroke of one released all the workers of Suva for that midday hour during which the whole town lunches. He had a bald head, mobile and bushy eyebrows, and piercing blue eyes; he carried a fat little abdomen which would have benefited considerably from Mr. Hornibrook's exercises, but he was otherwise as sprightly as any man of fifty-five can be who has spent thirty years on a South Sea island. His white ducks were creased and by no means immaculate, and his bow tie was a disgrace. Although only five foot four, he was the biggest man in Fiji, and, because of his single-minded concentration on his job, he deserved to be.

"Well, Spearpoint," he growled, taking the visitor's chair before it was offered, "are you going to arrest young Bellamy, eh?"

"We have no intention of doing so at the moment, Mr. Cutt."

"Be a damn fool if you arrest him at all, eh. He didn't do it."

Spearpoint, a little surprised at this positive assertion, could only answer, "Oh, do you know who did?"

"Do you think I'd tell you if I did know?"

"If you did know, Mr. Cutt, it would be your duty to tell me. Otherwise, you would be an accessory after—or, perhaps, before."

"Thank you for the information," growled Mr. Cutt. He stuck his thumbs between the buttonholes of his braces —for he was one of that minority of Fiji whites who find a belt intolerable—and patted the sides of his abdomen with loving solicitude. But, despite the comfort of this habitual gesture, he seemed slightly ill-at-ease. He was accustomed to sit in a low swivel chair behind a specially low desk. Here, he was in front of the desk, on a straight-backed chair which was of normal height, and which compelled his legs to dangle. He waited for the Inspector to speak.

"I suppose you know," began Spearpoint, slowly, "that Netta Maul was found in a sack in the harbour with her throat cut. A razor was found with her, tucked down in front of her frock. It was a cut-throat razor, rather worn. It had been ground and set many times; we asked all the local barbers if they recognised it, in case they had done the setting. None of them knew it, so we sent it to the Auckland police, and asked them to get in touch with Stakes, who does most of that sort of work in Suva. He's on holiday in New Zealand. The answer came this morning.

Here it is." He handed the cablegram to Sharpe, who passed it to Cutt.

The little man read the message without change of expression, and sat, with his head down, considering it for perhaps half a minute. Then he held it out to Sharpe, who replaced it on the desk.

"Bellamy's razor?" he remarked. "Well, I still maintain the boy didn't do it, eh. Could he account for his razor being down the front of the girl's frock?"

"As a matter of fact, he couldn't. He said his wife gave him a new razor when she went to Sydney, and that she gave away his old one—he doesn't know who to. We haven't got the actual razor, of course, but here are some photographs of it."

Cutt glanced in perfunctory fashion at the photographs, and handed them back to Sharpe; but Spearpoint gestured to Sharpe not to take them, and asked, "Do you recognise the pattern, Mr. Cutt?"

Mr. Cutt answered without looking at them, "We've never imported that brand, eh. Yourran, Other's used to. But even they gave 'em up. They're no good, eh."

"I mean," Spearpoint explained, "is your razor like that?"

"My razor?" asked Cutt; and he looked at the Inspector curiously. Spearpoint did not know how to read his expression, but he took it as a sign of confusion.

They stared at each other for a moment without speaking, and then Cutt said, "Oh, I see; Bellamy couldn't produce his razor, so you want to know if I can produce mine?"

"Exactly."

"Well," the little man went on, plainly thinking quickly, "I can't. If you got a search-warrant and went over my house with a fine tooth-comb"—Sharpe giggled, and Mr. Cutt glared at him in reproof—"you wouldn't find a razor like that one."

"Might I ask what you did with it? Did you give yours away, too?"

"You may ask, Mr. Spearpoint, but I'm not bound to

tell you, eh. I take it"—he continued, before Spearpoint could reply to that defiance—"I take it that your problem is that you know the girl was killed by one of two razors; and you can't find what either owner has done with his razor. If I could produce the fellow to the one you found, I take it I should be freed of all suspicion?"

"Exactly——" Spearpoint hastened to correct himself. "We have not intimated that you are the object of suspicion, Mr. Cutt."

"But you want me to produce my razor?"

"Only as a matter of form; we have to check all the information we receive."

"Well, Mr. Spearpoint, I ought not to be discussing this matter with you without consulting my solicitors. You know that, of course."

"Naturally." This remark seemed to Spearpoint to put an entirely different complexion on the matter. He had dismissed Sharpe's suspicion of Willy Cutt as too fantastic for consideration, and had regarded the production of his razor as merely a matter of form; but the little man's refusal to discuss the matter suggested that he considered it likely that a charge might be laid against him. It was almost a confession of guilt; and, certainly, his manner was suspiciously ill-at-ease.

"May I take it, then, Mr. Cutt, that you would prefer to adjourn this interview until you have had a chance to consult your solicitors?"

"I am prepared to hear what else you have to say," answered the little man, cautiously.

"Firstly, we must ask you to produce the razor."

"Well, Mr. Spearpoint, I can't do it. What next?"

"You admit that you were out in your launch on the harbour, alone, last Thursday night, from ten-thirty onwards?"

"Yes."

"Do you know anything about the murder of Netta Maul, other than the facts known to the general public?"

"No."

"Her body was found in the harbour on the morning after you had been cruising about alone late the previous night; and her throat had been cut with a razor of the same pattern as yours. You did not see anything suspicious on the water that night; and you cannot produce your razor?"

"What else, Mr. Spearpoint?"

"Well, Mr. Cutt, I'm bound to point out that the sack she was found in was branded with the initials of your company, the nail-bag her head was in came from a firm of manufacturers for whose products you hold the sole agency in the Colony, and the cord is similar to cord sold in your store."

"Every baker in Fiji uses our flour, eh. Our nails are the best and most popular on the market. Every one knows we have all the best agencies in the Colony. The cord might have come from anywhere and been bought by anyone. Think again, Mr. Inspector."

"Netta Maul kept in her room a cabin-trunk full of the love-letters she had received from various men, each in its brown-paper parcel, labelled with the name of the man. There was a parcel there with your name on it, but——"

At this Cutt looked genuinely astonished—or was it confused?—but he recovered himself speedily enough to interrupt with, "—but there were no love-letters in it?"

"No," conceded Spearpoint. "They were all business letters; but the parcel, unlike all the others, was untied. Someone had evidently ransacked the cabin-trunk during the night, and had opened your parcel."

"Doubtless looking for the material to blackmail me with," Cutt pointed out, calmly. "I have had no demands for money so far. When I do, I'll let you know."

"On the other hand, you yourself were outside her room at half-past nine the morning after she died—before anyone except the police and the people who found her knew of her death."

"Before I knew of it myself. You say I was outside her room. I tried the handle, and the door was locked.

Are you suggesting that I squirmed through the key-hole, Mr. Spearpoint?"

"I am not, but, since you say you cannot produce the razor, you force me to ask if you will explain your presence in the Royal Palm Hotel that morning."

"Of course I can explain it. Every morning at nine-fifteen I go along to Netta Maul's shop for a cup of kava. I went along that morning, and the shop was shut; and that was a mail-boat day, when she made most of her profits. I naturally went along a step farther to find why she wasn't on the job."

"You were not so busy yourself on a mail day that you could bother about her comparatively small account?" Spearpoint thought he had cornered Mr. Cutt, who would hate to admit that he devoted disproportionate attention to this debt because it was an indiscretion of Mr. Marryam's. But the little man merely said, "In business, no account is too small to worry about, eh. In detective work, you don't think any fact is too small to worry about, do you? I had time to spare, as the mail had not been delivered, eh. Think again, Mr. Inspector."

"Can you produce anyone to prove that you were out alone in your launch?"

"If you question my man, Williami, who prepared the launch, and had it waiting for me at the steps by the bridge, he'll tell you that I came alone as usual, and that I didn't have a flour sack and a nail-bag and several long pieces of cord with me, eh. Are you suggesting that the girl came out to me in a rowing-boat?"

"There was a rowing-boat found adrift next morning," broke in Sharpe, excited.

Cutt turned to Sharpe and growled sarcastically, "Are you suggesting that the girl came out to me in a rowing-boat and brought with her a flour sack and a nail-bag and several long pieces of cord, and asked me to truss her up, put her head in a bag, cut her throat, and heave her overboard, eh?"

Sharpe did not answer.

"Is that what you suggest?" Cutt repeated.

"No," Sharpe was forced to admit.

Mr. Cutt returned to Spearpoint. One of his rare chuckles escaped the throat of the redoubtable little man.

"Did you seriously ask me here to ask me about my razor?" he asked.

"That was the main reason."

"Read the cable again, eh," Mr. Cutt directed, with authority. "What does it say? 'Stakes says razor belongs Bellamy Cutt.' You took that to mean that both Bellamy and I have a razor of the same pattern?"

"Quite."

"Well, it means nothing of the sort. If it did mean that, it would be incorrect, eh. What can Stakes know about my razor? I never go into his shop, eh. He's no customer of ours. Yourran, Other's supply him. Besides, I use a Royce razor, eh. Always have done. Best razor on the market, eh. We have the agency. Do you think I'd use an inferior brand that was imported by Yourran, Other's?"

"Stakes must have made a mistake," conceded the unhappy Inspector.

"Stakes made no mistake. When he used my name he didn't mean me; he meant my company, eh. There are two Bellamys in Suva, aren't there? There's Bellamy of the P.W.D., eh. And there's Bellamy of Marryam & Cutt. The Auckland police abbreviated the name, eh. They ought to have remembered our cable address: Marryncutt —known all over the world, eh."

"You're probably right," agreed Spearpoint. It was obvious as soon as it was pointed out.

"Of course, I'm right," growled Cutt. "Besides, the razor proves nothing. There must be scores of these razors in Fiji. When Yourran, Others started to import them they went like hot cakes—grabbed eagerly at first because they were cheap, and then sold off at a knockout price later on because nobody wanted them. I dare say they went the same way in England; the manufacturers went bung, anyway. Bellamy probably brought his out from Home." He snorted, and added, "Fancy suspecting Bellamy! He's about the last person to suspect of this murder!"

"Why," asked Spearpoint, meekly, deciding to be revenged on the little man by picking his brains, if he could, "are you so confident that Bellamy didn't do it?"

"Because he could no more do it than I could," retorted Cutt. "That girl weighed eleven or twelve stone, eh. Could a shrimp like Bellamy have packed her in a sack, and lifted her into a boat, and tipped her into the harbour? If he'd tried to lift a lump of a girl like that, dead weight, out of a boat, he'd have capsized, eh. This crime must have been committed by a big, strong man—or by a syndicate, eh. Who else have you been suspecting?"

Spearpoint, finding Mr. Cutt willing, in his triumph, to be helpful, gave him a brief account of his discoveries to date, stressing the fact that his method was to discover all his facts before he built theories on them. Mr. Cutt listened with attention, making a number of pertinent comments, all of which the Inspector noted for consideration at his leisure. Finally he said, "It's all very well to rely on facts, Spearpoint, but you want to be sure your facts are right. I can tell you one fact of yours that isn't a fact, and though this hasn't any bearing on the matter, it might suggest that others of your so-called facts are worth re-examining, eh."

"I'd be grateful if you would."

"You say Halibut was reading on the Club verandah from nine o'clock until ten-fifteen. He was certainly there when I left, between ten-fifteen and ten-thirty, but he was not there at ten o'clock. I know, because I was dummy, and I strolled out to speak to him. I waited about for a minute or so, and then went back to the card room."

Spearpoint thought this over, and then said, "Can you remember when he paid you your share of the winnings?"

"How do you know he had to pay me?"

"Pretty obvious. He was playing with Conky Thomspon against you and Carnarvonshire, wasn't he? You were bound to win."

The little man nodded. "When Halibut got up, he was thirty shillings down, eh; and he said he'd pay whoever was up on balance at the end."

"And did he pay then?"

"Naturally. He came into the card room just before ten and asked how we were getting on. I said I'd be packing up in about a quarter of an hour, and he still owed me the thirty bob. Then he walked out."

"And he paid you in cash just before you went?"

"Naturally. I always play for cash. Everyone knows that."

"And when you went on to the verandah at ten o'clock to speak to him, where did you think he had gone?"

"Well, if a man goes out of the room for five minutes," retorted Mr. Cutt, scornfully, "where do you think he goes to? When I went back to the verandah ten minutes later, he was sitting there reading, just as he had been for the past hour. I suppose you're suspecting he chartered an aeroplane and flew over to Waimanu Road, and murdered the girl in that space of time, just because you saw her alive outside his house?"

"No," conceded Spearpoint, "but what exactly was the space of time? From some minutes before ten until ten-fifteen he was out of your sight. That's nearly twenty minutes, isn't it?"

"Yes; and if you think that even a hefty fellow like Halibut could cut that girl's throat, tie her up, and throw her into the harbour, and get from the Club to his house and back, and from his house to the harbour and back, all in twenty minutes, you've got a fine idea of his capacity."

"I don't suspect him in the least," replied Spearpoint, realising that his leg had been pulled, "but I do want to get at facts."

"You suspect too many impossible people, eh," growled Mr. Cutt, struggling to his feet. He turned to go, and then, with the door half-opened, he faced the two policemen, and shaking his head in mock reproof, jeered, "Fancy suspecting little Conky Thomspon! Why don't you suspect his wife?"

CHAPTER SIXTEEN

ALGERNON CHARLES, THE PASSIONATE MAN

(*Wednesday: 1.30–6 p.m.*)

SHARPE MOPPED HIS forehead with his khaki handkerchief, and blew out the air between pursed lips in admiration and relief. "Golly!" he exclaimed. "He was just leading us up the garden all the time!" Then, as Spearpoint remained mute, he asked anxiously, "You don't think he really did it, do you, sir?"

Spearpoint shook his head.

"And Mrs. Montgomery Thomspon, sir? Was that a hint?"

Spearpoint sighed deeply, and got up. "It's nonsense, Sharpe," he said, as he took his topee from the table. "I must admit she's my pet enemy. But that doesn't make her a murderer. She's not malicious or vindictive. She fights fair. She's not so bad." He shrugged his shoulders. "It's a leg-pull of Cutt's like the one about Dr. Halibut going outside for five minutes.—Well, one hour from now, we start to explore the cliffs."

Exactly to the minute, Spearpoint parked his car on the waste land by the Walu Bay bridge, and sent his native constable clambering down the steep banks to the dinghy someone had left invitingly tied there. Beni hauled the boat along to a more accessible spot and the two officers stepped in; then, not without difficulty, they

navigated through the maze of craft just inside the bay.
It was some minutes before Beni could row properly, and
even then, Spearpoint, more intent on scanning the cliff
face for signs of a path than on steering, almost rammed
Dr. Halibut's launch.

The edges of the landlocked bay were a tangle of reed
and mangrove swamp, and there was only a small stretch
of clear water in the centre. The cliff, irregular both in
height and in surface, and overgrown with grass and
bedraggled vegetation, did suggest to Spearpoint's eager
eyes that it might be climbable, provided there was a
landing place at the foot. He could discern ledges and
jutting-out points which would probably afford a foothold,
trees and shrubs which would bear a man's weight and
enable him to pull himself higher, and, in two places near
the top, overgrown gullies which promised well. These
two gullies, however, were far apart, and could not form
portions of the same track. The one on the right (which
suggested access close to that part of Waimanu Road
where Netta Maul had last been seen alive) appeared to
lead to a vertical rise of several feet, to the eye insur-
mountable. The one on the left, which presumably gave
access to the back garden of a house in Upper Waimanu
Road, appeared to run right to the top.

At last, some obstruction in the muddy bottom gripped
Beni's oar, and he would have been pulled overboard had
not Sharpe grabbed him in time. The boat rocked violently,
spun round, and wedged itself against a mangrove bush. In
the middle of the bush's many branches, sundering them,
was a fallen tree that looked rigid; a jutting stone beyond
suggested a further stepping-stone, and then, right at the
foot of the cliff, a low ledge, wet still and probably covered
at high tide, indicated the beginning of an upward path.
The cliff sloped at this point. There was plenty of foothold
and handhold. It seemed possible to clamber upwards and
sideways for twenty feet or more—at least as far as an
overhanging ledge which hid further view.

Warning Sharpe and Beni to hold the boat steady, the Inspector decided to trust his fourteen stone to the log. It gave immediately under pressure, squelched deeper into its bed, half turned over, and would have flung him into the water had he not leapt agilely to the left, getting one foot on the slippery stone and the other on the ledge, before he sprawled face foremost, his arms eagerly clasping the base of the cliff. He scrambled up hastily and glared round with suspicion. The ludicrous attempt Beni made to stifle his grin on catching his officer's eye caused that officer to laugh outright; and Beni gratefully responded with a succession of deep-throated chuckles which continued to burst from him long after Spearpoint had begun his climb. Sharpe remained impassive, sulking a little because he had been told to remain in the boat.

Spearpoint soon observed a tendency to work to the left, instead of to the right towards the ledge he had marked from below as his first goal. Progress to the left was much easier; but he determined to combat this tendency, and finally, with much panting, and marvelling not a little at his own agility, he hoisted himself on to the ledge. It was disappointing. It led nowhere, fading into nothing. He stood there for a few moments to recover his breath, and then started to return, proceeding, crablike, backwards. It was more difficult than going up, but he suddenly found himself on what almost amounted to a path, traversing the face of the cliff. He called to ask Sharpe if the path was visible from below; it was not. Spearpoint found that it was possible to walk upright, holding on to the cliff face or to bushes, along a track which hardly rose at all, and which bore slight traces of use. The surface was grassy, slippery from rain, and treacherous; but he decided that a man who was familiar with it could follow it at night, particularly if he had a torch and if (as had been the case on the night of the murder) there was no rain.

At last he came to a stop. The path ceased behind the

roots of a wild lemon tree. Looking about for its continuation, he observed two possibilities: a series of footholds to the right, up a slope that was not difficult; and a more precarious clamber to the left. He went to the right, and presently found himself in the gully he had discerned from the bay. He walked up this, and arrived at a dead end. He stood with a secure foothold almost at the top of the cliff; but before him was a smooth wall, and he could only just reach to the top. It was possible that his assistant, with another four and a half inches to spare, could reach far enough to scramble over the edge. Retracing his steps to the lemon tree, he beckoned to Sharpe to join him. Sharpe obeyed with alacrity, demonstrating the ease with which the lower part of the cliff could be negotiated by a man in good condition. At the top of the gully, he looked dubious, but he got his hands over the edge, and, scrabbling about for a grip there, encountered with his right a projection which he said felt like the stump of a small tree.

"If you give me a bunk up, sir, I think I could manage it," he suggested.

"We're assuming our man made the journey alone," Spearpoint pointed out, "but it may be that if you get up once you can see how to do it a second time without help." No sooner had Sharpe pushed his head above the level of the cliff than he gasped, "All right. Let me down again." When he was lowered, he explained, "There's a stone over there to the left. With one hand on that and the other on the root, I think I might be able to get up alone. Hold my helmet, if you don't mind, sir."

It was a fierce struggle, but Sharpe succeeded. After kicking his superior on the shoulder, and then narrowly missing his nose with the other boot, he heaved himself triumphantly out of sight. His flushed face reappeared a moment later, and he panted, "I'm right on top, sir; but I'm not sure where I am. I'll have a look and let you know in a minute."

He returned presently and reported that he was in Tom Humble's garden. Tom Humble's house was the last one in a grassy cul-de-sac that led off Waimanu Road. The cliff path had led the policemen to within a hundred yards of the garage where Netta Maul's body had lain.

"Shall I stay here?" enquired Sharpe. "I could pull you up, you know."

Spearpoint considered, eager to verify Sharpe's report for himself; but he realised that any attempt by Sharpe to drag his fourteen stone up over the cliff edge would probably result in his dragging Sharpe down instead, and decided that he had had enough rough stuff for one afternoon. "No; we'd better go back to Beni. Anyone seen you up there?"

"No; I don't think so. There's a hibiscus hedge and a fence. Tom Humble's taken care his kiddies don't fall over the top."

"Can you get back here all right?"

"Feet first, I think," and, suiting the action to the words, Sharpe lowered himself dustily beside his chief.

They returned to the lemon tree, where they decided to explore the other track. Sharpe led the way, and for some yards it was easy enough; then difficulties began. Sharpe had secure handhold, with both feet together on a projecting crag, and was doubtfully measuring the distance of the next possible step. Spearpoint, a yard or so behind, was waiting comfortably, when his eye caught a flutter of white in a hole above him, out of reach. It looked like a piece of rag. It might have been part of a bird's-nest, but it looked too clean, and too smooth. It was more like the side of a bundle; but who would thrust a white linen bundle into a hole in the cliff, fifty feet above Walu Bay? The Inspector became interested in the rag, and made several ineffectual attempts to grab it and pluck it from the hole. But however he shifted his footing and his hold, he failed by a good six inches.

Presently Sharpe came sidling carefully back to the

ledge where Spearpoint was. "Can't get any further," he announced, regretfully. "Not even a goat could get beyond."

"We'll have to go back then. But, before we go, see if you can get that bit of rag."

Sharpe dutifully took hold of a tuft of grass, which had been out of the Inspector's reach, tested his weight on it, braced his foot against a root, and, with his face close to the cliff, felt upwards with his right hand. He fumbled, a shade awkwardly, for some seconds; he could only just reach it; and then his arm came down, and Spearpoint saw that he held a white bundle, like a handkerchief tied by its four corners. Sharpe returned to a position of comparative equilibrium, and handed the bundle to his superior. As he did so, they both noticed some strands of black hair caught in the knot; and, so excited were they at the discovery, that their prize fell between them, hit the ledge they stood on, and sagged off. Even as they swore, and clutched vainly, they observed it had become caught in an overhanging bush. The only way to recover it was to retrace their steps and venture on a lower route, which they managed successfully, but not without taking more risks than in their former climbs.

The discovery proved worth taking risks for. It was a portion of a large white pillow case, devoid of embroidery or laundry mark; and it contained a mass of thick, luxuriant black hair. There was no doubt about it. It was Netta Maul's hair. Parts of it were matted and stained, presumably with blood, but it was still glorious.

"Now why on earth was it hidden in that hole?" asked Sharpe, in wonder.

"I suppose," answered Spearpoint, composedly, "because whoever put it there knew that no one but an extremely active and foolhardy man would ever clamber to this part of the cliff."

"He didn't bargain for the Fiji Constabulary being so active and foolhardy, did he, sir?" boasted Sharpe, gleefully, "Shall we get back to the boat now? What's that, sir?"

Spearpoint, who had been running his fingers through the tresses—it was the first opportunity he had ever had to do so, and he was marvelling at their fineness and glossiness—had found a piece of screwed-up paper embedded in them, and he now handed it to Sharpe whilst he retied the parcel. Sharpe unrolled the paper, and spread it out. It was a sheet of printed matter, and he studied both sides with a frown of more than usual bewilderment.

"It's poetry, sir," he exclaimed, evidently more astounded at that than at the finding of the hair; and he read aloud, in an uncomprehending voice, the half stanza:

"'From the midmost of Ida, from shady
    Recesses that murmur at morn,
They have brought and baptized her, Our Lady,
    A goddess new-born.'"

He read on to himself, and then burst out, "Golly! I say, sir, this is stuff!

'Old poets outsing and outlove us,
    And Cat—Catullus makes mouths at our speech.
Who shall kiss, in thy father's own city,
    With such lips as he sang with, again?'

Pretty hot, eh?"

"That doesn't seem to rhyme," criticised Spearpoint, busy with the knots.

"No; nor does it—and down here it says:

'She slays, and her hands are not bloody;
    She moves as a moon in the wane,
White-robed, and thy raiment is ruddy,
    Our Lady of Pain.'

That bit's underlined. Netta Maul's raiment was ruddy, not half. And there's some more——"

"Let's have a look." Spearpoint took the paper. It was a leaf from a book, pages 165 and 166, and both pages were headed 'Dolores,' which was the name either of the poem or of the book. The last four lines Sharpe had read aloud were underlined in pencil; and the next two stanzas were marked likewise:

'They shall pass and their places be taken,
    The gods and the priests that are pure.
They shall pass, and shalt thou not be shaken?
    They shall perish, and shalt thou endure?
Death laughs, breathing close and relentless
    In the nostrils and eyelids of lust,
With a pinch in his fingers of scentless
    And delicate dust.

'But the worm shall revive thee with kisses;
    Thou shalt change and transmute as a god,
As the rod to a serpent that hisses,
    As the serpent again to a rod.
Thy life shall not cease though thou doff it;
    Thou shalt live until evil be slain,
And good shall die first, said thy prophet,
    Our Lady of Pain.'

The two policemen puzzled over these flowery, incomprehensible and venomous lines, pondering the essential significance of two that were doubly underlined:

'They shall perish, and shalt thou endure?'
'Thou shalt live until evil be slain.'

"I wonder what book that came out of," mused the Inspector. "Recognise any of it, Sharpe?"

"Not me, sir. Wish I did. Pretty hot, eh?"

"I daresay there's someone in town who'll know," and Spearpoint put the page carefully in his pocket-book. "That chap Bellamy had a lot of books, hadn't he? We'll give him a call. Now—it looks to me as if we could get on a bit further. Perhaps we could reach that slope."

He pointed. Sharpe needed no further hint, and presently the two gained the slope, crawled up it, and lowered themselves into the left-hand gulley. Further progress was easy; and before they realised they had reached the top they found themselves peering side by side through a hibiscus hedge at a bungalow, twenty feet away. And there was no doubt what house it was. It was 'Segai Na Marama.'

Sharpe turned to the Inspector, and winked. Spearpoint put his finger to his lip to caution silence, and they returned to the patiently waiting Beni. It was a difficult and slippery descent, and they arrived dirty, hot and breathless; but triumphant. The tide was high, and the boat was floating within a step of the firm ground.

"It's almost five o'clock," announced Spearpoint; "we'll go home and have a shower and put on clean togs, and then meet at my house for a cold beer off the ice."

"Not half we won't," agreed Sharpe.

Spearpoint, however, did not await the coming of his assistant, but had his cold beer immediately on getting in; doubtless he would be capable of accompanying Sharpe in another presently; doubtless, also, Sharpe would be able to find one for himself at the barracks. In fact, Spearpoint, bathed and dressed, began to wonder whether Sharpe had not found himself a dozen; and, torn between the desire to have a second himself whilst waiting, and his curiosity concerning the poem, he decided to drive up the hill to make enquiries of Bellamy.

That young man, who was just settling down to a high tea of bread and butter and tinned corned beef and pickles, received his visitor with a mixture of alarm and friendliness.

"No, I won't be here a minute," Spearpoint began, declining a chair, "I just wanted to find out something, and I thought you might know."

"I'll tell you anything I can, of course," said Bellamy, nervously.

"Poetry. Do you know anything about poetry?"

Bellamy was astonished at this question; he blushed as furiously as if he were being accused of adultery, and admitted, "Er—yes, a little."

"Ever hear of a poem, or a book of poetry, called 'Dolores'?"

Bellamy considered. As soon as he realised that he was being consulted as a possible expert, he gained confidence, and Spearpoint's suspicion that his agitation had been caused by the fact that he himself had hidden the verses in the hair, disappeared.

"'Dolores?' Well, there's Swinburne's 'Dolores', of course."

"Swinburne wrote a book called 'Dolores'?"

"A poem. It's in his *Poems and Ballads*. It's a long poem."

"Would you recognise a bit of it if you saw it?"

"Very likely. If it was a whole verse. I'd recognise the metre, anyway. It's a long poem. I don't know it by heart.—I've got it here, if you want to see it."

Spearpoint signifying his desire to see the poem, Bellamy went to his bookshelf and, without hesitation, laid his hand on a slim volume which, the Inspector realised with delight, was about the size of the torn page in his pocket. The reader of poetry turned over the pages at random until he found the beginning of 'Dolores,' and then handed the book to Spearpoint.

"Page 154," remarked Spearpoint; "you're right to call it a long poem. What's it all about?" and he turned to pages 165 and 166, which, he observed with some regret, were intact. There must be two copies in the Colony.

"It's addressed to a lady that Swinburne had been in love with, saying she was cruel and deceitful and the reincarnation of all the vile and false lovely women in history," explained Bellamy, eloquently but nervously.

"A sort of hymn of hate, eh?" suggested the Inspector. His eye fell on the stanza:

> 'Thou wert fair in the fearless old fashion,
>   And thy limbs are as melodies yet,
> And move to the music of passion
>   With lithe and lascivious regret.'

and then slid lower to:

> 'Hair loosened and soiled in mid orgies
>   With kisses and wine.'

He read on uncomprehending until he came to the lines:

> 'On thy bosom though many a kiss be,
>   There are none such as knew it of old.'

when he found himself blushing and shut the book with a slam.

"I can't compliment you on your literary taste," he thought, but he realised that it was better to handle Bellamy gently, and commented aloud merely, "I've heard Swinburne was pretty hot, but I've never come across any of his stuff before. Is all his poetry like that?"

"More or less. He's a very musical poet."

"Musical?"

"Yes; his rhythms and rhymes and the use of vowels and consonants, and the way he balances words of similar sounds and repeats statements in slightly different ways, and so on—no poet has ever been quite such a craftsman."

Spearpoint grunted. He could not understand anyone reading stuff like that, but he dismissed the aesthetics of the matter, and asked abruptly, "Have you another copy of this book?"

"Oh, no," returned Bellamy; "but you can borrow this if you like. There are some good poems in it."

"I don't want to borrow it for myself," protested the Inspector. "I don't read poetry. This is what I'm after. I want to find the book this was torn out of." And he produced the crumpled page.

Bellamy looked at it, and then hastily examined his own book to make certain that it was intact. He compared the two. "It's from the same edition. It's the cheap edition, of course. I didn't know anyone else in Fiji had a Swinburne. But I suppose that's not unexpected. There must be a few people interested in books."

"You think anyone interested in books might have this?" asked the Inspector, incredulously.

"Interested in literature, I should say. Swinburne was one of the great poets."

"Any idea who might have a copy? Is there a literary circle in Suva where you sit round and read—poetry to each other?" After all, thought the Inspector, there are several circles in Suva where they sit round and drink beer and tell dirty stories, and it might be that the ones who don't drink beer prefer to obtain their satisfaction in rhythms and rhymes and the skilful arrangement of consonants and vowels. There is mutual contempt between the man who prefers beer and Mademoiselle from Armentières, and the man who prefers lemonade and Dolores; but the difference between them is one of palate, and not one of kind.

"No," answered Bellamy, regretfully, "I've never met anyone in Fiji who ever mentioned Swinburne. But, of course, I don't know many people."

It was plain he could give no further information, so Spearpoint thanked him and left, pondering the problem of how Jim Camelback could have had access to a copy of Algernon Charles Swinburne's *Poems and Ballads : First Series*, in the Golden Pine edition.

CHAPTER SEVENTEEN

THE CASE AGAINST JIM CAMELBACK

(*Wednesday evening*)

"Now," said spearpoint, when the two police-men had obtained the due reward for their afternoon's exertions, "let us set down the facts as we know them:

"First, Camelback was too friendly with Netta Maul for H.E.'s liking, and was told he must discontinue the association.

"Second, he did not discontinue it. You saw her by his car only last month.

"Third, they quarrelled last Thursday night. Bellamy saw and heard them. And, incidentally, that quarrel must have been the continuation of an earlier incident. They had had no time to develop a quarrel. He must have been pretty desperate to risk being seen talking to her in the street.

"Fourth, we suspect she was blackmailing him.

"Fifth, I heard the scream at nine-fifty-nine.

"Sixth, Camelback altered his watch to prove that he was in Malleable's room at ten, whereas we have ample evidence that his car was not in Carnarvon Street at five past ten; and his fingermarks on Netta Maul's bag suggest that he was in her room that night.

"Seventh, no one saw Netta Maul alive after Bellamy saw her talking to Jim Camelback. There was the torn scrap of her frock in the hedge nearby, and her hair and the blood and the sacks in Paul's garage. There can be no doubt that her body lay in that garage. I believe it was in the garage that her throat was cut.

"Eighth, Camelback could have got out of his room between two and three, which would have given him time to get to the garage, put the body in the sack, steer it down to the creek in Conky's car, row out to deep water in Lum Chin's boat, and get back to the bach via the cliffs before daylight. Whether his bachmates knew of his nocturnal prowl we don't know yet, but we may find that out in time.

"Ninth—answering the possible objection that he could not have had time to tie her up between the time I saw him and the time he entered Malleable's room—she need not have been tied up until four hours after death, that is, say, two p.m., as rigor doesn't set in for at least four hours. But we do know she was tied up by then.

"Tenth, and lastly, her hair was found on that cliff route, which was certainly not common knowledge. It is a route leading straight to 'Segai Na Marama,' and it is reasonable to assume that Camelback knew of it."

"That seems pretty conclusive, sir," exclaimed Sharpe. "You'll remember I gave him the shortest odds."

"But it's not a watertight case, by any means," objected Spearpoint. "It demonstrates that he might have done it. I believe he did do it. He had the opportunity. He had the motive. He was the last person to see her alive, so far as we know. But we want more facts still."

"I don't see what more facts we can get, sir."

Spearpoint pondered. "There are three facts we must have," he announced at length. "The first is the razor: did Camelback have such a razor? The second is his clothes: were they blood-stained, or muddy with climbing? I've asked about that once, and so have you; we must go into it again. The third is the poem: had he access to a copy of the book? If the answer to these three questions is yes, then he's our man."

"I think you're right, sir," agreed Sharpe.

"We'll go up to 'Segai Na Marama'," announced the Inspector, "and make a few enquiries."

"They won't welcome us," Sharpe pointed out. Although he was a frequent guest at the bach, he had uncomfortable recollections of a gate-crashing exploit a few weeks earlier.

"They've got no choice with us when we're on official business," returned Spearpoint, grimly.

The tropic night had already fallen when they pulled up outside the bach, but lights on the verandah indicated that the bachelors were at home. As soon as Spearpoint pushed open the gate, the famous warning-bell clanged, and four voices shouted as one: "Keep out. This means you." Then Wills, who had the loudest voice, called, "We've got bottles ready to throw if you come inside."

"This is Inspector Spearpoint, and I insist on being admitted," replied the Inspector. He had authority to enter at least Camelback's portion of the bungalow.

There was silence for a moment, and then Tom Claypole said, genially, "Come along up, Spearo. We've got a full bottle for you."

It was a warm evening, and Sharpe, in his uniform, envied these four fellows sprawling pyjama-clad in lazy-boy chairs, drinking cold beer and apparently yarning about nothing in particular. The policemen accepted chairs and drinks, Spearpoint judging he could obtain their assistance only by a show of friendliness. This was a policy which Sharpe warmly approved.

After a brief general conversation, Spearpoint came to his object with, "What I came for was to ask for some information on the subject of razors."

"Cut-throat razors?" the four chorused. It was as if they had practised the question; and, as a matter of fact, they had; they were planning a mock murder trial for their next party, a fact Spearpoint learned subsequently.

"Yes," he answered, unmoved; "do any of you chaps possess one?"

"Not guilty, my lord," replied Tom Claypole, solemnly, and he turned his head to Craven, on his left.

"Not guilty, my lord," said Craven, solemnly, and he turned his head to Bob Eachway, on his left.

"Not guilty, my lord," said Bob Eachway, solemnly, and he turned his head to Wills, on his left.

"Not guilty, my lord," said Wills, solemnly, and he turned his head, first to the left, and then to the front; whereupon they all turned to the front, and replied, solemnly, in unison, "Not guilty, my lord."

Craven then added in a more normal voice, "Actually, I have got a cut-throat, but I never use it."

"Can you produce it?" asked Spearpoint.

"Too right," and Craven heaved himself out of his chair and lounged along the verandah to his bedroom.

"What about Camelback?" was Spearpoint's next question.

"Safety," answered Claypole, briefly.

Wills named the brand, and Bob Eachway added, cheerfully, "Always bloody well going wrong," at which they all laughed reminiscently.

There was a pause, which Wills broke by addressing Sharpe. "It's a bit of a bloody coincidence you blokes coming along this evening, because we were just talking about the detection of murders. We were wondering how it was done. Perhaps you could give us a few tips."

Sharpe grinned a little sheepishly, and said, "I might be able to, and again I——"

"——might not be able to?" concluded Wills.

"The only bloody tip he could give anyone would be at the baths," explained Bob Eachway, who shared with Malleable a grievance over a certain incident at the Municipal Salt Water Baths some weeks earlier.

Nettled by this, Sharpe retorted, "It's jolly hard work, I don't mind telling you."

"Too hard for some people?" suggested Bob Eachway.

"Would you say it was mental work or physical work?" enquired Wills, with interest.

"A bit of both," parried the Sub-Inspector, cheerfully; and he winked at Spearpoint. They knew, did he and his boss; and there was an unpleasant surprise in store for these friends of Mr. James Camelback—that was what the wink conveyed; and it flashed across the Inspector's mind to wonder whether they were already aware that their bachmate had committed the crime.

"No; what we were wondering," put in Claypole, smoothly, "is how the police set to work on the job. Do they evolve theories, and look for facts to fit them, or do they look for facts, and evolve a theory that will fit them?"

"A little of both," began Sharpe. Spearpoint got up and strolled along the verandah to Craven's room; and Sharpe went on, as if he thought his chief was out of earshot. "My boss believes in accumulating facts. I'm no good at facts. So I jump to theories. Then the Inspector points out how my theories don't fit his facts, and that suggests extra facts to look for; and so on. That's why we work so well together."

"Yes, you've only been a whole bloody week trying to find out who killed Netta Maul," agreed Wills.

"A week, and a bloody sight more to come," Bob Eachway added.

"'The police are following up important clues, and an arrest is imminent'," quoted Wills. "I believe the *Fiji Times* has kept that set up all the week."

Spearpoint heard the banter, but he paid no attention to it. He was watching the puzzled Craven, who was flat on his front on the floor, fishing under the ice-chest with a golf club. He emerged flushed and disconcerted. "I'm afraid I can't find it," he confessed. "I keep it on the ledge here; but I haven't used it for some time. One of the boys may have moved it."

"When did you see it last?"

"I don't know.—Yes, I do. It was——" He hesitated, and made a calculation. "It was last Friday morning."

"You mean Thursday morning, don't you?"

"No. Friday morning. I'm sure it was Friday."

"How are you sure?" asked the Inspector, sternly. He believed Craven was lying.

"Because that was the day Jim went to Lau. It was the morning after the murder."

"Yes, it was," agreed Spearpoint, significantly. "Go on."

"Well, Jim was packing his suit-case, and came in to borrow a bottle-opener," began Craven, regaining his self-assurance, almost as if he had decided what lie to tell. "He'd lost his last one a couple of nights before, throwing it at a cat. And I keep my bottle-openers on the ledge here, next to the razor"—he indicated the four bottle-openers on the horizontal studding of the wall behind the ice-chest. "And I handed him a couple of openers and asked if he'd like the razor as well. His safety was always getting out of order, you know."

"And what did he say?"

"Oh, he just laughed, and said he didn't want to cut his bloody throat just yet.—But I suppose he must have taken it after all. I don't remember seeing it since."

"And you're quite sure this took place on Friday morning?"

"Positive."

"What time on Friday morning?"

"About half-past seven. Just after breakfast. Jim was packing up to go to Lau." He was unshakable, but Spearpoint did not believe him.

"What sort of a razor was it?"

"An ordinary cut-throat. Black handle. Rather worn blade. Pretty rusty round the thick edge; but the blade was all right. I never used it to shave with; but I kept it sharpened for cutting corks."

"What was the maker's name?"

"Beggared if I know."

Spearpoint decided to go a step further, and, producing the photographs of the razor found with Netta Maul's body, asked, "Was it anything like this?"

Craven seized the photographs eagerly, asking in his turn, "Was this what did the gory deed?"

"I'm asking you if it is anything like your razor."

"Something like," Craven admitted. "But it's not my razor, anyway. It couldn't be, because mine was on this ledge at half-past seven, and this one was tucked down Netta Maul's front hours before that."

"You seem to know a lot about it."

"Too right we do!" cried Craven. "We know more about it than the bloody police themselves!" he jeered. Then he broke off suddenly, realising that he had fallen into a trap. Spearpoint had not deliberately set the trap, and did not know whether the boast was an indiscreet statement of fact, or merely a taunt, but he seized on it at once.

"It is your duty to communicate to the police everything you know," he said, severely. "Otherwise you may be charged as an accessory after the fact. And an accessory after in a case of murder is in a very serious position indeed."

Craven retreated abjectly. "I'm sorry, Inspector. Of course, we don't know anything, really. That was only a bit of fun, you know. It was a silly thing to say. No; we don't know anything, really."

"It was a damned silly thing to say," corrected Spearpoint. "You'd better be very careful in future what you say to the police. Now, tell me, and be truthful about it: when did you last see your razor?"

Before Craven could reply, there came a burst of laughter from the verandah, and Wills admonished him over the Inspector's shoulder, "Speak up, little Lord Fauntleroy. When did you last see your father?"

Spearpoint did not take his eyes from Craven's face. That youth grinned, but sheepishly, and answered, "I told you—last Friday morning. That *was* true."

"You're sure it's true? You may have to swear to it in the witness-box."

"It's absolutely true, Inspector. Besides, Bob heard me offer it to Jim. He was here, too."

"That's right, Spearo. I heard him," Eachway corroborated.

"What did you hear?" asked Spearpoint, over his

shoulder, still keeping his eyes on Craven. He was not sure how long the others had been crowded round the doorway listening, and he wanted to ensure that Craven did not signal to his bachmates.

"Why," answered Bob Eachway, cheerfully, "I was in here watching old Craven tying what he thought was a bow, and Jim came in and asked for a bottle-opener. Craven said, 'Take a couple off the ledge; and you'd better take the razor as well, in case you should want to cut your bloody throat while you're away.'"

"And what did Camelback say?"

"No bloody fear, or words to that effect."

The two versions did not agree exactly, but the variations merely served to corroborate each other. Had both repeated identical accounts of this week-old scrap of banter, the story would have sounded suspiciously like a concocted one. The reference to cutting throats did not necessarily suggest that there was in their minds the knowledge that Netta Maul's throat had been cut a few hours earlier; it was commonplace bach geniality. Spearpoint persevered, however, asking, "And was the razor actually on the ledge at the time, or did Craven merely assume it was there because he knew it had been there the day before?"

Both Craven and Eachway affirmed positively that they had seen the razor on the ledge during the conversation. They admitted they had not seen it since. Tom Claypole and Wills, questioned, agreed that they had not seen the razor since Camelback had left, and Wills added, jokingly, that Camelback must have taken it after all.

"Perhaps," suggested Sharpe, "on second thoughts, he decided that he might want to cut his bloody throat before he got back," and they all laughed at his wit. Spearpoint smiled grimly, refusing to meet Sharpe's eye.

There was no shaking the story Camelback's bachmates told; they stuck to it loyally; but Spearpoint did not believe them. The photograph was handed round, and all agreed that Craven's razor was the dead ring of the compromising one; but none of them, not even the owner himself, could remember the maker's name on the weapon they were so familiar with.

As Spearpoint was about to dismiss the subject, Claypole made a suggestion which, whilst it failed to aid the Inspector in his immediate problem, threw an important light on another. "If you want further corroboration," he said, "ask Dr. Halibut. He was up here on Friday morning."

"Was he? What was he here for?"

"Came to speak to Camelback. I don't know what it was about. But he came along the verandah about twenty to eight, asking for Jim."

"I heard them talking," volunteered Craven. "But it was outside my room. Dr. Halibut didn't come in here, so he wouldn't have seen the razor."

"What did they talk about?"

"It was about golf. They were due to play off on Saturday, and it had to be postponed because of Jim's visit to Lau. They were just arranging a new date."

"Was that all? Can you remember any of what was said?" It occurred to Spearpoint that this visit of the doctor's might explain Camelback's assertion that he had called on him the previous evening.

Craven considered. "Of course, I wasn't listening particularly, but it went something like this. Dr. Halibut said he had heard Jim was going to Lau, so he wanted to know whether Jim was going to scratch, or whether they should wait till he returned. Jim said he would like to play off when he came back. Then Jim said, 'I was trying to get in touch with you last night,' and Halibut said he had been at the Club all the evening. And then he wished Jim a pleasant trip, and that was about all."

"And he didn't come into this room at all, so he couldn't have seen the razor?"

"No; as a matter of fact, I didn't even see him. I just recognised his voice."

Spearpoint dismissed the subject. He had learned that

Camelback had known, at the time of his interview with the police, that Halibut had been out all Thursday evening. If, therefore, he had not called on the doctor, he was safe in saying he had done so, and found him out. Spearpoint had been doubting Camelback's guilt only because of his idea that Camelback would hardly have risked saying he had called on Halibut and found him out if he had not done so, because if Halibut had chanced to be at home at ten o'clock, his story would have been immediately disproved.

On a shelf by the bedhead, Craven sported a row of cheap, red-backed novels. Spearpoint glanced along the titles with some interest, and even wandered so far from the matter in hand as to count the volumes; there were forty-seven of them, and they were all by Edgar Wallace. The bachelors regarded him with amusement.

"Interested in crime?" asked Wills, sardonically. "Like to borrow a dozen to learn how detectives work?"

Ignoring him, Spearpoint asked Craven, "These all the books you've got?"

"Quite enough, isn't it?"

"I asked you if these were all."

"Yes."

"I'd like to have a look at all the books in the place," Spearpoint announced. "Who else of you has any books?"

"I've got some Aussie books," volunteered Bob Eachway.

"But," added Wills, "they wouldn't interest you—you're too young."

"Has Camelback any books?"

"Has he hell? What would old Jim want with bloody books?" All four laughed in derision at the idea of their bachmate possessing any books. Nevertheless, Spearpoint visited every room, glancing at all the books they would produce for his inspection.

"I can't compliment you on your literary taste," he commented, finally. "What I was really looking for was some poetry. Any of you chaps interested in poetry?"

It was an ironical question, and it received four ironical

and negative answers: "Too right!" "Not half!" "Like hell!" and "Yes, teacher!" The last was from Wills, who added, "I know a little poem, teacher. Listen. 'There was an old man of St. Paul's, Who felt a——'"

"Any of you got a copy of Swinburne hidden away?" interrupted the Inspector.

"Who's he?" "Nevereardofim." "Was he the bloke who wrote 'The Jew's Lament'?"

Spearpoint gave it up, and asked them to call in the two Chinese servants, both of whom confirmed, in their clicking and faulty English, the fact that the razor had been missing for several days. Spearpoint again questioned the one who acted as laundryman concerning the clothes he had washed for Camelback on Monday, but he again failed to obtain the admission that any of the white suits had been stained with earth or with blood. Both Chinese denied that Camelback's shoes had been unusually muddy on the Friday morning.

The two policemen returned to town with their suspicions confirmed rather than shaken, but still unproved. As soon as he arrived, Spearpoint was informed by the sergeant on duty that the Inspector-General of Constabulary had been telephoning for the D.I. He called up his superior officer and received instructions to report progress immediately. He had been allowed time for the reply of the Auckland police, but now that that had arrived, the authorities considered that a solution of the murder should be promptly forthcoming.

Spearpoint accordingly hastened across the town to a certain residence in the select quietude of Domain Road; and, there, round a bare polished dinner-table, he found four august gentlemen in white shell-jackets, smoking cigars suited to their rank and passing the port in the correct direction.

Inspector Spearpoint, who had encountered these mighty ones in their offices, on the golf course and at the Club, had visited only one of them at home, and he instinctively glanced under the table to see whether the Colonial Secretary was wearing spats on this, as on all other occasions. The Attorney-General put up his eyeglass and regarded the policeman as if he were a most unusual phenomenon. The Inspector-General, however, waved him genially enough to a chair; and the fourth man, the host, offered him a cigar. Having removed the band, Spearpoint was astonished to find the Attorney-General, on his left, handing him a cigar-cutter; and he nearly bit the cigar in two when the Colonial Secretary offered him a light. The port arrived in due season, and they all settled down to be matey together.

Spearpoint gave first a brief précis of the facts he had discovered so far, and then explained how, in his opinion, they all pointed to one conclusion.

He admitted, however, that he had had no time to trace the volume from which the stanzas of 'Dolores' had been torn. Sharpe had examined the leaf in vain for recognisable fingerprints. The crumpled page passed from hand to hand round the table, exciting no comment on its verbal content. All these gentlemen had been more or less educated at English public schools and universities, and they viewed the sentiments of Algernon Charles dispassionately, without either interest or surprise. Swinburne was a poet that every educated man had heard of during his youth, and had not read since. The authorities had accepted him as a classic, so every conventional, educated man accepted him likewise, and ignored him. The page was considered purely as evidence. All agreed that it proved definitely that the crime was a white man's crime. There were not half-a-dozen Fijians or Indians in the whole Colony who could ever have heard of the poet, and it was not conceivable that any of the exceptions could have murdered Netta Maul. And much the same would apply to the half-castes; there were plenty of half-castes in Fiji who had been educated at schools in Australia and New Zealand, and who presumably possessed a nodding acquaintance with English literature, but it was unlikely that any of these would treasure a volume of Swinburne. This latter applied, also, to almost the whole white population.

The suggestion that the page had been stolen by an illiterate murderer to plant the crime on someone else was rejected for two reasons: first, because the lines were so appropriate that they could not have been chosen at random, but only by someone who was well acquainted with the poem; second, because the hair was hidden in an almost inaccessible part of the cliff where the murderer might have reasonably assumed that it would not be found. They concluded, therefore, that it was necessary first to find the book from which the page had been torn, second, to list the people with access to the book, and third, to list those of the latter who might reasonably be supposed to have read the poem.

"And," added the host, "out of those we have to pick a man so extravagantly sentimental that he would cut off the girl's hair, and hide it with a piece of poetry embedded in it."

The Attorney-General then remarked that he had an idea that there was an odd volume of Swinburne at the Fiji Club. There were a couple of shelves of miscellaneous books on the verandah, the relics of departed guests, and he thought he had noticed a Swinburne. The host thereupon telephoned the Club, and had a word with Mr. Dummfish, that incessant bridge-player, who obligingly left the table at which he was serving as dummy (a busman's holiday it was for him to be dummy in his leisure) and inspected the books; after several visits to the telephone to confirm what was required, he announced that the Fiji Club's bookshelf did contain a copy of the first series of Swinburne's *Poems and Ballads* in the Golden Pine edition, and that pages 165 and 166 had been torn out. He confirmed that these pages were part of the poem 'Dolores.'

"That's solved the first point," remarked the host. "Now point number two incriminates us all. Obviously all the members of the Club had access to that book."

"But," pointed out the Inspector-General, with a sly look at the Attorney-General, "only one of us knew it was there."

"Do you think I'd have mentioned it, if I'd torn out the page myself?"

"What is important," cut in the host, "is that Camelback had access to that bookshelf."

"But would he know of the poem?" asked Spearpoint. They were all agreed that Camelback would certainly have heard of Swinburne and that at some time or other he would have heard of 'Dolores,' but all doubted whether he would be so familiar with the poem as to be able to make use of it. Spearpoint admitted, truthfully, that, now he came to think of it, he had heard of the poem somewhere or other; but that, not being interested in poetry, he had entirely forgotten its existence; it was agreed that it was probably the same with Camelback. Two of the four confessed that, though they knew of the poem, they could not have named the author. "And," added the host, "I wouldn't mind betting that that young Whatsisname— Bellamy was right when he said he thought he was the only man in the Colony who knew anything about Swinburne. If only he had access to the Club bookshelf, I'd think things looked pretty black against him."

The Colonial Secretary had another idea. "Wasn't there a book about Adah Isaacs Menken published recently? I seem to have seen it somewhere."

"*The Naked Lady*," agreed the host. "I know there's a copy somewhere in this burg. I've seen it; but I can't remember where."

Spearpoint, who had hitherto taken little part in the conversation, cut in here. "Why," he said, not quite comprehending the reason for this turn of the conversation, "Claypole has a book called *The Naked Lady*."

"At the bach now?"

"Yes—I made them show me every book they had. I'm certain he's got one called *The Naked Lady*. He said

Carnarvonshire lent it to him, and it was about time he gave it back."

"Just the sort of book Tom Claypole would be reading."

"Well, Inspector, there's your case," exclaimed the host, sitting back with a smile of satisfaction.

"But I don't see the connection," objected the Inspector. "What has the poem to do with the book?"

"'Dolores'," the Attorney-General explained, "was written to a circus rider named Adah Isaacs Menken, who was famous for taking the part of Mazeppa—Byron's 'Mazeppa,' you know—being tied naked on the back of a wild horse. Of course, she wasn't really naked. But *The Naked Lady* made a good title for a biography of her. Camelback had access to the book, which would remind him of the poem. Of course, it's only circumstantial. You can't hang on that alone."

"No, but it clinches the matter, in my humble opinion," decided the host, with unintended irony. "There can be no doubt that Netta Maul fascinated friend Camelback, and he may have dramatised his situation into thinking she was Dolores to his Swinburne. It's a good enough case, to my mind."

A debate, in which Spearpoint took no part, followed as to whether they had sufficient evidence to arrest Camelback. The Attorney-General, the only lawyer present, was dubious, but he allowed himself to be overruled. The host was a masterful man, and no one attempted to controvert his argument:

"It's plain enough that Camelback did it. But all we've got is circumstantial evidence, and pretty thin evidence at that.—That's no discredit to you, Inspector; it was a brilliant piece of work, finding that hair. The fact is, the evidence doesn't exist; or, if it does exist, it can't be obtained. But, though the evidence is a bit slender, it's good enough; it's enough to make him stand his trial on. Everyone will believe he did it, on the evidence the Inspector has obtained. Even the jury that brings him in

'Not Guilty' will really believe he is guilty. We've got the man. That's the important point. If he gets off, it doesn't matter. (He'll have to leave the Colony, of course.) As a matter of fact, I hope he does get off. I don't believe in capital punishment—never did. It's no deterrent; and it's a savage punishment. If a man murders in hot blood, the thought of hanging won't deter him. And if he's planning to murder someone, and knows he'll be hung if he's caught, he'll take damned good care he isn't caught. There are scores of unpunished murderers every year— unsuspected murders, most of them. I don't care if Camel-back does get off."

"But suppose he doesn't get off?" interposed the Colonial Secretary.

"He'll get off all right."

"But suppose he doesn't?"

The masterful one shrugged his shoulders. "We'll have to hang him."

The Inspector-General looked grave, and pulled nervously at his moustache. "We haven't hung a white man in Fiji since God was a boy," he protested. "Never had occasion to. The Colony has always been free from real crime—at least, among Europeans."

"A paradise in the Pacific," murmured the host. "But our friend here thinks he will get off," and he nodded to the Attorney-General.

"It's a weak case," admitted the man of law, "and he'll have a very able man to defend him." He named the leading lawyer of the Colony. "Frankly, I don't think there's much hope of a conviction. We've got no evidence that he was out of his bed from two o'clock onwards; and every man Jack of them at 'Segai Na Marama' will swear blind they saw him in bed during the night."

"They'll be lying, of course."

"They'll be lying, and everyone will know that they are lying; but their story will be unshakable, just like that yarn about the razor. He'll get off, all right."

"Unless he confesses," suggested the Colonial Secretary.

"Unless he confesses," assented the Attorney-General. "But why the hell should he confess? He's got a watertight alibi—four fellows to swear to his whereabouts from twenty-past ten until the time the body was discovered."

"Gentlemen," said their host, cutting across this speculation with the authority of personality rather than that of office, "I think we all believe that Camelback murdered the girl, and we're all agreed that he'll probably get off if he's tried. But is that any reason why we should not try him? I think not. We're faced with these alternatives: either we drop the case, make no arrest, admit our failure to discover the murderer; or else we arrest Camelback, charge him, and prove to the satisfaction of everyone in the Colony that he did it—for the evidence the Inspector has gathered will prove that all right. No doubt about it. After that, it doesn't matter if he does get off. He'll have to leave Fiji. I think we should give the Inspector a warrant to arrest him the moment the *Whitman* berths."

"Suppose he doesn't get off," reiterated the Inspector-General; "suppose Spearpoint gathers fresh evidence; suppose, when he's been arrested, someone comes forward who did see him that night. Then we'll have to hang him. It's all very well for you," he told the host; "you haven't got to see it done. We," and he nodded across at Spearpoint, "we've seen men hung—those Solomon Islanders last year. And I don't want to see a white man hung."

"It's just a part of your job," the Attorney-General pointed out. "I've got to demand that he be hung, and I've got to do it to his face. And the Chief Justice has got to sentence him. I was playing golf with Camelback the Sunday before last. He beat me two and one. I came unstuck at the ninth, as usual. Until then——"

"He won't be hung," interrupted the host, firmly and confidently. "But I'll tell you what we'll do. We'll give him a chance. Instead of sending the Inspector to arrest him when he lands, we'll wireless Captain Stickithemud

and tell him to arrest him; and instruct him to let him
have the run of the ship."

"What's the point of that?"

"It may save us a lot of trouble," was the enigmatic reply.

"You mean, he'll confess?"

"Not if he's innocent."

"Well?"

"If he's innocent, he'll know we can't prove him guilty.
If he's guilty, he'll assume we can."

"Well?"

"He may prefer drowning to hanging."

"You're an immoral man," the Attorney-General told him.
The host shrugged his broad shoulders and laughed.
"The man's a murderer. We all know that. By the law
of the Colony, he ought to be hung. We all know that;
and he knows it too. But we don't want to hang him. If
we arrest him on the wharf, we may be compelled to hang
him. Arrest him at sea and give him a chance to save us
the trouble and the expense."

The plan was agreed to; and that night Spearpoint
slept his first untroubled sleep for a week.

CHAPTER EIGHTEEN

INSPECTOR SPEARPOINT
TEARS HIS HAIR

(*Thursday: 11 a.m.–1 p.m.*)

AT ELEVEN O'CLOCK next morning, Inspector
Spearpoint, sitting in his office and blithely taking over
the reins of his normal duties from Sub-Inspector Clubb,
received a telephone message from the cable office to the
effect that a cable had arrived for Bellamy of Marryam
& Cutt. He had forgotten that there was an answer to

come to the question of how Phyllis Bellamy had disposed of her husband's razor. Now that he was reminded of the matter, he assumed that it had been given to a Fijian, but he deemed it advisable to send Sharpe to be present when Bellamy opened the envelope.

Sharpe returned some quarter-of-an-hour later, wearing his most puzzled expression, and thrust a cablegram before his chief. "What do you know about that?" he asked.

Spearpoint read aloud. "Gave razor to Halibut visiting Doris feeling fine love Phyllis."

"Who's Doris?" he enquired, suspicious of the contractions of cabled messages.

"Cousin of Mrs. Bellamy's. She lives some way out of Sydney. Bellamy said she probably put that in to explain why she hadn't answered yesterday. The poor devil stayed awake all night thinking she'd been too ill to answer."

"Does he read this to mean that his wife gave the razor to Dr. Halibut?" demanded Spearpoint, determined to have every point confirmed.

"Yes. Funny, isn't it?"

"What the hell did she want to give it to Halibut for?"

Sharpe shrugged his shoulders. "Bellamy said he was friendly with them. Pal of her father's, you know."

Spearpoint sat and brooded over this unexpected development. Then he slapped the table, and stood up, and swore lustily. "Great starving cats!" he can be represented as saying. "We've been blind fools! Halibut! Why, in the name of Julius Caesar, didn't we think of Halibut?"

"Why should we? He wasn't there," Sharpe asked, bewildered. "He was at the Club all the evening."

"Was he? Where was he at ten o'clock? Cutt says he came into the card room just before ten, and that he was on the verandah reading some time after a quarter past. We don't know yet who it was who borrowed Conky's car; but suppose it was Halibut. He strolled into the card room to make certain that Conky was occupied, and then he borrowed his car, nipped round the town, and back again so as to be on the verandah by the time they had finished the rubber."

"But why should he do that? How could he know she would be outside his house at that exact moment?"

"He must have had an appointment with her. Consider: whoever it was took the car, it was a big man. The Police Medical Officer would have rubber gloves in his possession. Who knows Walu Bay better than old Halibut? Who's tall enough to clamber up that last bit of the climb into Humble's garden? Only Halibut! But they're not the important points—what we ought to have seen at once was the point about the hair. It was Len Rogers who wrote the poem about it! And that's why Halibut cut off her hair, so that she wouldn't be buried with it! Her hair ruined his nephew, and so he robbed her corpse of it! That's why he slashed her face, too! He made a job of her beauty, all right!"

"But didn't he say her throat was so unskilfully cut that he could have saved her if he had been on the spot in time?"

"Eyewash, my dear boy, eyewash!" Spearpoint was certain he was right. "The cut was on one side because he made it with her head held downwards, so that the blood would spurt on the ground instead of over him, and so he had to cut from the side, holding her as near to the ground as he could. That's why the cut only just reached the jugular. His knowledge of anatomy told him exactly how far he needed to go. And I'll tell you another thing," he added, as half the jigsaw puzzle fitted into place in his mind. "Do you remember this mysterious white-bearded Punjabi who's kept cropping up in this case? He was seen on the bridge at one o'clock, and in Tom Humble's garden at three o'clock. That was Halibut. He can speak Punjabi like a native; and do you remember him as Father Christmas? No, of course, you wouldn't be at the children's party. He rigged himself out in his cook-boy's clothes—on Thursday, I mean, not at the party—and put the false white beard on, and borrowed Conky's car for the second time, and all the rest of it. I've got a hunch that if we go up to his house now, we'll find hanging in his boy's room a pair of trousers with a black tin button missing." He made for the door, with the bewildered Sharpe on his heels. Then he stopped so suddenly that they collided, and, without apologising, said abruptly, "No; you'd better not come with me; you'd better go up to the Colonial Secretary's office, and see if they've sent that radio to the *Whitman* yet; and, if they haven't, ask them to hold it for a bit. If they have, say nothing; after all, though I'm as certain as can be that Halibut is our man, yesterday I was certain it was Camelback, and there may be some hitch here. And while you're up there, scout round and try and find out where Halibut was between ten and ten-fifteen last Thursday night."

Sharpe made off reluctantly, marshalling all his reserves of tact for the delicate task assigned to him. Spearpoint shot madly up the hill in the opposite direction. With scant ceremony, and quite illegally, he pounced on Dr. Halibut's Indian cook-boy, and demanded to see all his clothes. The cook was considerably taller than the average Hindoo, and though he was not so tall as his employer, it was possible that his clothes could have been worn by the doctor, especially when it is borne in mind that anyone masquerading as a Punjabi labourer does not need to pay meticulous attention to the cut and fit of his garments. The doctor was considerably broader in the beam than his cook, and if the former had indeed tried to don the trousers of the latter there should have been every likelihood of a button being forced off.

Consequently, when he found among the Indian's wardrobe a pair of khaki drill trousers, with caked mud on the knees, and without the top fly button, Spearpoint was assured that he had made a discovery of the first importance. And this opinion was confirmed by the fact that the remaining buttons were of a similar pattern to that found on the floor of the car. The pattern, however, was common enough. The cook possessed, among several others, a striped shirt bearing ancient mud-marks; and Constable Genghis had stated that the Punjabi he had observed by the creek had been wearing a striped shirt, hanging, Punjabi fashion, outside his trousers. The cook asserted that he had not worn either the trousers or the shirt for months, and that he did not know whether they had been muddy when he had last seen them. All the rest of his garments were clean and in good order; these, he said, were old things he had discarded.

His rubber shoes bore markings different from those in the garage; but when Spearpoint called for Dr. Halibut's plimsolls, he obtained the pair he sought.

"Where does Dr. Halibut keep his Father Christmas beard?" he demanded next.

The Indian obediently led the way into the doctor's bedroom, opened a trunk, and produced from among a pile of miscellaneous clothes and household linen, the beard and the long red robe. It was matted around the tip, as if it had been washed and put away without being sufficiently dried. The red robe was slightly discoloured, at the place where the beard had lain on it, and some of the colour had run and dyed the beard. Or was it blood on the beard?

"I'll borrow these things," Spearpoint announced, taking the trousers, the shirt, the shoes, the beard and the robe, and rolling them up together. "You can tell Dr. Halibut I've taken them. Got a piece of brown paper?"

As the parcel was being tied up, he had another idea, and said, "Here, Tommy, has Dr. Halibut got an inky pad? I want your fingerprints."

The Indian complied, grinning. Even to the Inspector's untrained eye, it was obvious that his print had some of the characteristics of Bellamy's.

"Did the doctor sahib ever get you to sharpen a razor for him—one with a black handle?"

"Yes, sahib, two, three times—I forget. Last month, and again, last week; and a long time ago."

Spearpoint dashed back to his office to compare the

Indian's print with the photograph of the one on the razor. It seemed to him to be just as likely that the weapon had been handled by the Indian as by Bellamy; what was certain was that Halibut had handled it. The Inspector's brain was in a whirl.

If his new theory was correct, and there could be no possible doubt of it, he had made a bad blunder in marshalling the case against Camelback and stressing it to his superiors; and although the decision to arrest had been theirs and not his, he could not doubt that the blame for the howler would be passed on to him. And the Inspector did not relish, either, the prospect of having to arrest and charge the genial and popular doctor.

Sharpe returned to find his superior in an unusually reticent mood; instead of exchanging information, Spearpoint said nothing of his own discoveries, and merely listened moodily to the report that they had been too late to stop the radio to the *Whitman*, and that Sharpe's enquiries had been negative. Dr. Halibut had not called in at the nearby Defence Club; he had not paid a visit to the Girls' Grammar School Hostel, next door to the Fiji Club, nor to the Bishop in Polynesia, just beyond, nor to the private medical practitioner opposite. He had not been seen at the Royal Palm Hotel, nor at the rival establishment on the other corner of Hercules Street. He had not taken a swim in the Suva Municipal Salt Water Baths, nor had he attempted to force illegal entrance to the Carnegie Library or to the Museum on the floor above it. In short, so far as Sharpe had had time to enquire, he had found no trace of the doctor at all. Spearpoint directed him to make further investigations in the afternoon, and sent him off to lunch.

Before going in to his own lunch, Spearpoint went methodically over all the items in the indictment of Camelback, and compared them with the evidence against Dr. Halibut. There were still a number of points that were obscure, but he came to the conclusion that Camelback was certainly innocent, and the doctor as certainly guilty.

The telephone bell rang, and he was informed that the Colonial Secretary desired to speak with him. As he waited, he wondered whether he should ask for an interview in order to explain his latest discoveries, or whether he should try to collect further evidence first. But he was given no opportunity to say anything; the Colonial Secretary deprived him of speech with his first sentence: "I thought you would like to know, Inspector, that we have received word from the captain of the *Whitman* in answer to our wireless, and that he says Camelback has confessed."

"Confessed?" shouted the Inspector, in amazement.

"Yes, confessed; and, what may be some relief to you, he has committed suicide."

"Committed suicide?"

"Yes. I thought you would like to know that as soon as possible. Your painstaking and careful work has brought this case to a successful conclusion, and I desire to congratulate you, Inspector."

"Er—thank you, sir," Spearpoint managed to stutter; and the Colonial Secretary rang off.

And Inspector Spearpoint gazed at the white beard and the plimsolls of Dr. Halibut, at the striped shirt and the trousers of the cook-boy, at the cablegram from Phyllis Bellamy; and then he went stamping round his office in bewilderment, tearing savagely at his hair.

CHAPTER NINETEEN

"BUT YOU CAN'T PROVE IT!"

(Thursday : 1–9 p.m.)

INSPECTOR SPEARPOINT HAD not yet recovered from the shock of the Colonial Secretary's message, when there was a bang on the door, and it opened wide enough to admit, some six feet up, the genial head of Dr. Halibut. Seeing the Inspector apparently unoccupied, the doctor opened the door further, and walked in.

"Well, old man," he said, "I thought I'd come and tell you the news before it's public property."

Spearpoint stared at him, and then grunted, "I know it. Colonial Secretary's just told me."

It was Doctor Halibut's turn to stare. "What?" he asked. "But he doesn't know yet. I'm not going to tell him until after lunch."

"You tell him? How should you know?"

"Well," laughed the doctor, "who would know if I didn't?"

Spearpoint sat down abruptly, put his elbows on the desk, and cupped his forehead in his hands. Halibut regarded him in surprise.

Presently the Inspector looked up, and said, slowly, "Now, let's get this straight. What are we talking about?"

"That's just what I was wondering. What were you talking about?"

"No, you first, doctor. What did you come to tell me?"

"Why, that I've decided to throw in my hand, and go home to Somerset."

"You mean you're resigning?"

"Yes; I think I've about done my work in Fiji. It's time I made way for the youngsters. I want to have a few quiet years in Somerset before I die."

"Oh, you do, do you?" enquired the Inspector, enigmatically. He had recovered his wits now. There was nothing unexpected in the announcement. The doctor was a bachelor and in his middle fifties; and ever since he had entered the Colonial Service he had been talking, more or less seriously, of his intention to retire to a villa on the outskirts of some unspecified market town in the West Country. The substantive Police Medical Officer was shortly due back from leave, and Halibut would be faced with the prospect of another spell in the provinces. "How soon do you reckon to go?"

"Next month; I'll take the leave that's coming, and I won't return. Shall I be sorry to leave Fiji, you ask—well, did you ever know anyone who was reluctant to see the last of Fiji?"

"Yes," retorted Spearpoint, brutally, eyeing the doctor closely, "Netta Maul."

Halibut winced as if struck; indeed, he had been struck. His genial grin vanished at once, and he turned pale. His jaw dropped, and for a moment he could think of nothing to say. Then he pulled himself together slightly, and muttered, "Yes, I suppose she—she would have been reluctant—had she known she was leaving it. But—but why drag her in?" he protested, plainly hurt at his friend's bluntness.

"You see," explained Spearpoint, slowly, "when you came in and said you had news, I thought you were going to tell me who had killed her."

"Oh, that!" returned Halibut, smoothly, perhaps a shade too off-hand in his manner. "They'll never find that out. Unsolved Mysteries of the Pacific, number seventeen."

"When you say 'they' you mean 'me'," the Inspector pointed out, grimly.

"Yes, so I do," Halibut admitted; "I'd forgotten for the moment it was your case. So full of my own affairs! But you've given it up, haven't you?"

"On the contrary. I made an important discovery only this morning. And yesterday—yesterday I found her hair."

"Her hair!" cried the doctor, startled. "Where did you find that?"

"Tied in a white linen bundle in the cliff overlooking Walu Bay. Care to see it?"

"How on earth did you come to be looking for it there?"

"I wasn't looking for it there. I was trying to find if there was a track up the cliffs. I found two tracks—and the hair."

"In a cleft in the cliffs, you say? How could it have got there, do you think?"

"Evidently hidden there by a very tall man—a man of over six foot. A man the size of Sharpe—or you."

"Well, that was a nice piece of work, old man. Congratulations. And where does this interesting discovery lead you?"

"It leads me to search for a certain tall, white-bearded Punjabi who was sleeping, or rather pretending to be asleep, in Morris, Hedstrom's colonnade by Naboukulau Creek and Renwick Road about one a.m. last Thursday night; and who was prowling in Tom Humble's garden, at the top of one of the cliff paths I discovered, an hour or so later."

"You think the murder was committed by a Punjabi?" asked the doctor, with interest, and without displaying any emotion at the revelation of how much the Inspector had discovered.

"I'm quite sure it wasn't."

"Then why search for a Punjabi?"

"Because I don't believe he was a Punjabi."

"I'm sorry, old man, but I don't quite follow your reasoning. If he wasn't a Punjabi, how will you find him by looking for a Punjabi?"

"To be more explicit, doctor, I was looking for a white man, over six feet tall, who speaks Punjabi fluently, who possesses, or has access to, a long white beard, a pair of dark trousers with one button missing and mud on the knees, a muddy striped shirt, and plimsolls of a peculiar pattern."

The doctor chuckled without any show of embarrassment, and observed, "Well, he ought not to be so hard to find."

"He wasn't," Spearpoint returned. "And I can tell you more about the man I was looking for. Just before ten o'clock last Thursday night he borrowed Conky Thomspon's car from in front of the Fiji Club, drove full tilt up Waimanu Road, arriving outside your house just after ten, and returned the car to its place outside the Fiji Club sometime between ten-fifteen and ten-thirty."

"It seems to me that your problem in finding the man is about as difficult as the riddle: what animal is it that has long ears and brays?"

"Quite. I found him easily enough. But I don't want him now."

"Oh!" There was a note of genuine surprise in the doctor's voice. "You found him, and now you don't want him? Why not? Wasn't he your man?"

"I thought he was," admitted Spearpoint, slowly. "I thought he was as soon as I learned that he was the man that Phyllis Bellamy gave her husband's razor to."

He handed the cablegram to the doctor, who read it carefully. With this, sparring was at an end, and they came to grips.

"In fact," said Halibut, looking up with a benignant smile, "you think I am the murderer?"

"Frankly," conceded Spearpoint, "I do."

"But you can't prove it," parried the doctor.

"This morning I thought I could prove it, but now——" And the Inspector shrugged his shoulders.

Halibut considered, twisting the paper into shapes, and then looked Spearpoint straight in the face. "What evidence have you against me?" he enquired.

"That would have come out at the trial."

"'Would have come out'?"

"Yes."

"You mean you've discovered some flaw in your chain, so that you can't prove it, and so all your case against me falls to the ground?"

"In a way. But there's a mystery that has only just appeared. It seems to clear you, though I don't quite understand how it can. Of course, I must assure you that I'm not sorry. I was hating the thought of having to arrest you, and I'm glad that I'm not in a position to do so at the moment."

"And you never will be," proclaimed the doctor, gravely and without malice; "because fortunately I am able to produce a convincing piece of evidence in my favour."

"What is that?"

"That would have come out at the trial," mocked Halibut, genially. "No—seriously: what I can produce is Bellamy's razor."

"But that's in Auckland."

"Pardon me: Bellamy's razor is in my desk up at the Medical Department. The razor we found with the corpse may be in Auckland, if you sent it there. They're very much alike, you know. That's why I got such a shock when it fell on the floor. I can tell you I made a dash up to my office to see if Bellamy's was still there."

"And was it?"

"It was. It still is. Care to see it?"

"Very much.—Can I drive you up there straight away? I suppose you can get in at lunch-time?"

So the District Inspector and the man he had suspected of murder rode side by side up the hill to the Government Buildings. They spoke little. Spearpoint asked casually, "Been up to 'Segai Na Marama' lately?" And the doctor answered, "Never go near the place."

"So you've not been there this past week?"

"Well, as a matter of fact, I was there the morning Camelback went to Lau, fixing a date for our tie," parried the doctor, thus, unintentionally, perhaps, failing to allay the suspicion that the razor he was about to produce was really the one missing from Craven's room.

When compared with the now celebrated photograph, the razor which the doctor produced as Bellamy's showed surprising resemblances, being not only of the same pattern, but worn and rusted to the same extent—apart, that is, from the recent rust, caused by the sea and the blood, in the photographed one.

"Mind if I take charge of this?"

"You're welcome."

"Do you mind telling me how she came to give it to you?"

"Certainly not. I was visiting there, one afternoon, not exactly professionally, just before she went to Sydney. I've known her since she was nothing visible, of course; and she's Carnarvonshire's patient; but I take a friendly interest in the children I've helped to bring into the world—so far as I can keep track of them, that is. She happened to mention that she'd given her hubby a safety-razor, and said she hated the idea of the old ordinary razor, didn't like to have one about the house, thought they were dangerous, wanted to get rid of the old one. Queer ideas some women get. So I said, 'Give it to me, child,' and put it in my pocket. And that's really all there is to it. I'd been intending to give it away to some-one, some time, and just put it in my desk until some deserving Fijian came along."

"Thanks." Then, as they reseated themselves in the car, Spearpoint asked, "And perhaps you'll tell me as well, why you borrowed Conky's car?"

Halibut laughed. "So you still think it was I who took the car?"

"Yes."

"I'm afraid you'll have to prove that."

"Apparently it doesn't matter. It was just my curiosity. I believe I know why, but the coincidence is a bit too extraordinary for belief.—If you care to wait a minute when we get back to the Station, I'll let you have back the Father Christmas beard and the other things I borrowed. You may as well take back the plimsolls and the striped muddy shirt and the muddy trousers with the missing button."

"Keep them, old man. They're no further use to me."

"They were useful to you, then?" jerked out Spearpoint, in one of his rare moods of repartee.

"The beard and the robes were useful," conceded the doctor, getting into his own car. "As for the shirt and the trousers, I must admit I don't know what you're talking about. I'll take the plimsolls, though."

However, he made no protest when Spearpoint handed him the whole parcel, but said instead, with a twinkle, "Tell me, Spearo, would you have hung me because my cook-boy had a button missing on his trousers? My dear chap, look at the next hundred Indians you meet and note how many of them are lacking at least one button on their trousers—fifty of them, I'll wager."

Spearpoint did not reply to this raillery; it was bluff, if intended as anything other than a joke, for most Fiji Indians wear their shirts outside their trousers, thus hiding their trouser buttons from view. He hesitated, his hand on the door of Halibut's car.

Halibut looked at him enquiringly, his usual friendly smile playing about his mouth.

"You know, doctor," Spearpoint said, awkwardly, "a man has to do his duty. It's not always pleasant. I never suspected you at all until I got the cable about the razor this morning. Then it all came to me in a flash. I didn't want to have to arrest you—there are few men in the Colony I'd have less pleasure in arresting; but a man's got to do his job."

"That's all right, old man," laughed the doctor. "You'd never have got a conviction, you know."

"I can't now, anyway."

"And why not now? Even before I produced the razor you seemed to imply that I'd been exonerated."

"We've got a confession," Spearpoint explained. "That was what the Colonial Secretary told me. I'm not at liberty to tell you more, though I suppose it will be public——"

Halibut broke in anxiously, "It's not Bellamy, is it?"

"No. You need not worry about him. It's another chap. He's confessed, and he's committed suicide, and consequently the whole case against you, which was circumstantial, I admit, but pretty damning, collapses.— But," added the Inspector, suddenly, "I'm puzzled, because I'm quite sure this chap didn't do it. There's one thing the murderer did that this chap could not have done. If he did it, he must have had an accomplice. And the accomplice made that little slip that every criminal makes, and gave himself away. We can only wait until we have a chance to study the confession.—Well, I won't keep you from your lunch, doctor."

"You're talking in riddles, but I suppose that's to be expected. But there is one thing I'd like to ask, old man. I've been rather interested in this case, you know, and I'd like to know the inside story. My natural curiosity. When it's all cleared up, will you give me the lowdown on it all?"

"I'll be very pleased to tell you as much as I can, doctor—when it's all cleared up," and the two men separated.

Spearpoint went in to lunch, wondering whether the doctor was as innocent as he had implied. He was by no means satisfied with the meagre facts that had come to light during the day. Halibut had avoided repudiating directly both the charge of murder and the suggestion that he had visited 'Segai Na Marama' during the week; but he had confirmed the evidence about his visit to Camelback on the morning of the trip to Lau. There was little love lost between these two, and neither would desire to avoid even a contest at golf at which a triumph might be obtained. They were, of course, on speaking terms, and disguised their antipathy in the way usual among civilised Englishmen; but Camelback had supplanted Leonard Rogers in Netta Maul's favour, and, assuming that Halibut had murdered Netta Maul because she had caused the ruin and suicide of his nephew, it was unlikely that he had forgotten Camelback's share in the tragedy. It was now by no means certain that the doctor had murdered her; the problem now was to ensure that Camelback's guilt and the doctor's innocence could be demonstrated in the light of the evidence to hand. Spearpoint was determined to accept no solution that did not explain all the facts. In deciding on Camelback's guilt the previous night he had overlooked one fact which, as he had mentioned to Halibut, did not support it. He would not overlook anything again.

Immediately after lunch, Spearpoint rang up the Inspector-General in order to obtain the exact wording of the message from the *Whitman*. It was brief enough: 'Camelback, arrested in accordance with your instructions, confessed and committed suicide in his cabin.' Spearpoint suggested that the skipper should be asked for more details, including whether there had been any mention of accomplices. He felt that he could await but impatiently the return of the ship in two days' time. His superior was very reluctant to agree; he had been greatly relieved at the confession and suicide, and viewed with some annoyance the possibility of an accomplice, which might involve an arrest, a trial, and the dreaded execution of a white man. But he finally assented at Spearpoint's earnest request, and the Inspector felt free to devote the rest of his afternoon to further enquiries.

Both Spearpoint and Sharpe spent the next few hours in intense and exasperating activity. Very few of the people they interviewed could give a consecutive account of their occupations during the preceding Thursday evening, exactly a week earlier. It was not even possible to ascertain with accuracy who had been present at the Fiji Club between nine and eleven p.m. At least two members who were thought by other members to have been there could not remember where they had spent the evening in question. Many of the people interviewed either refused to give information in an unofficial way, or else answered carelessly, with an indifference to the importance of the police enquiries which was at the same time intolerable and impregnable. Spearpoint's investigations into the movements of the members of the Club were resented, by some openly, by some covertly, and he was chaffed unkindly by all. But he persisted and received a good deal of information, some of it obviously bogus, some of it possibly bogus, and little of it of any value. For he thought it desirable to hide the fact that he was concerned solely with the movements of Dr. Halibut. However, he did finally discover a member, apparently sincere, who said he had entered the Club at five to ten, at which time the only person on the verandah was Dr. Halibut, who was standing up, near that part of the inner wall where the bookshelves were. He knew it was five to ten because, being a man of habit, he invariably went out for walking exercise at nine-thirty every evening, wet or fine, taking a route which, at his steady three-and-a-half miles an hour, brought him to the Club at exactly nine-fifty-five for a drink before returning home for bed at precisely ten-fifteen. 'Bellamy in thirty years' time,' thought Spearpoint, as he gratefully noted this piece of important evidence; he could not help mentally deriding this old stick, although he realised that if all men were like him, a police detective's job would be greatly simplified.

It was impossible to ascertain what time the doctor had returned to the Club, the earliest known time being that of his conversation with Mr. Montgomery Thomspon when the latter had left. Mr. Montgomery Thomspon had placed this at ten-fifteen because the doctor had told him it was—evidence now suspect. If Bettina Bloggins were to be believed, it had been nearer ten-thirty. Mr. Cutt had put it between ten-fifteen and ten-thirty. Neither Dummfish nor Carnarvonshire would place the time earlier than that.

Sharpe had met with an even less happy reception, and he returned to the Police Station with his natural high spirits somewhat depressed by the ribald and suspicious attitude of his questionees. Honest citizens of Suva, having nothing to fear from the police, cannot treat them with the reverence that they are accorded Away (that is, in the rest of the civilised world). They are too familiar with the names, faces, characteristics, and failings of their guardians to take them altogether seriously; and the (so far as they knew) unsolved murder of Netta Maul had become more of a joke than otherwise. No one appeared to regret her death, and only those who had actually seen her mutilated features could regard the affair with horror.

At dinner, Spearpoint's thoughts revolved round what had become for him the chief mystery of the crime: the hiding of the hair. This could not have been done by a Fijian or an Indian, for it was not conceivable that a pink man would invite the collaboration of a chocolate man for such a purpose. His conclusions led him to further investigations.

He drove up to the Fiji Club, and, after turning and coming to rest at the foot of the steps, scorched round the town to Dr. Halibut's house and back by the route he presumed the doctor had taken—Gordon Street, Renwick Road, Waimanu Road, Browne Street, Amy Street and Holland Street. Going as fast as he dared, he occupied eleven minutes over the journey. Assuming that Dr. Halibut had started at four minutes to ten, and had got back at twenty past—an absence of twenty-four minutes, which seemed to Spearpoint too long for safety —he would have had thirteen minutes for his stop at his house, or, in other words, for the murder of Netta Maul and the temporary disposal of her body in Paul's garage. How the doctor could have been absent for so long without being noticed, and how he could have performed the necessary work of the murder in less, was a problem which Spearpoint puzzled over without being able to solve. He decided to make a few more enquiries.

He drove slowly along Victoria Parade in the direction of the home of the Blogginses, and was saved the possible embarrassment of having to call by meeting Bettina a few yards from the gate. He pulled into the kerb and called her. She came, smiling frankly, and saying, "Now what does Mr. Spearpoint want with Bettina?"

"Mr. Spearpoint wants Bettina to help him with his investigations. How about coming for a ride with me?"

"Oh, Mr. Spearpoint," she answered, coyly, dimpling as she climbed in beside him; "my mother told me never to accept a lift from a man."

"And you always do what your mother tells you, don't you, Bettina?"

"Oh, yes, Mr. Spearpoint, always." She giggled, and then asked, daringly, "Are you one of those men who can drive with one hand, Mr. Spearpoint?"

He did not know how to reply to this, and played for safety by grinning at it.

"I say, where are you taking me?" she asked next.

"Right here," and he drew up under the cliff of the Fiji Club. "Now I want you to be a good girl and sit here quietly for five minutes while I fetch someone out to talk to you. You'll do that, won't you, Bettina?"

"I always do what I'm told, Mr. Spearpoint."

The Inspector, not without some misgiving, left her and ran up the wooden steps and into the Club. As he suspected, Conky Thomspon was sitting there with a half-empty glass by his side and an *Illustrated London News* on his knee.

"Hallo, Conky, I thought I'd find you here. I want you to come out to my car for a minute to have a little private talk with someone."

"Er—can't you—er—bring him in here?"

"Not a member."

"Oh, all right—er." The little man got up grudgingly, emptied his glass, and followed the burly Inspector into the road.

The car had disappeared.

"That little devil!" swore Spearpoint.

"Er—what—er—what's happened?"

"Must have driven off in my car for a lark. Blast and damn!" explained the Inspector. Knowing that Bettina had no licence, he had assumed she could not drive. He was wondering whether to let Mr. Montgomery Thomspon go, and to chase the fugitive, fearing that, having started the car, Bettina might be unable to stop it, when headlights came dashing towards them, swerving wildly. Spearpoint had to jump into the ditch to avoid being hit, and even as he jumped he reflected that the car was bound to crash. However, with a sudden application of the brakes, and a triumphant solo on the horn, it stopped, and Bettina hailed them. "There you are, Monty," she cried. "I can drive, see! I drove to Holland Street and turned right round there and drove back, see! He'll never let me drive, Mr. Spearpoint," she explained, with her most charming smile.

"Quite right, too. I've a good mind to run you in for driving without a licence. You nearly killed me, you little devil!" He was only mock-angry, being relieved of his anxiety for the car; besides it was difficult to be angry with Bettina,—even when she went into peals of laughter, saying, "You did look funny when you jumped into the ditch."

"Er—what—er," Mr. Montgomery Thomspon was muttering in the background.

"Now, look here," explained Spearpoint, dismissing the escapade. "I've brought you two together because I want to know exactly what time you met last Thursday night. It's very important."

"I told you at the time," protested Mr. Montgomery Thomspon, weakly. "Really, I can't remember little things like that a week after they've happened."

"And I told you too, Mr. Spearpoint. A gentleman should take a lady's word, I think."

"I'm a policeman, not——"

"You needn't say you're not a gentleman, Mr. Spearpoint. We know that."

"Yes—er—we do!" concurred Mr. Montgomery Thomspon, displaying extraordinary courage in the presence of the girl. "Really, I must protest at this——"

"Now, look here," cut in the Inspector. "The time you left the Club last Thursday night is extremely important. You'd look a poor fool if you went into the witness-box for one side and swore that you left the Club at ten-fifteen, and then the other side trotted out Bettina to swear you left at ten-thirty."

"Nobody would ever trot me out! Let 'em try!"

"Well—er—really, I'm not sure of the time."

"Bettina is. She says it was half-past ten."

"It was earlier than that, I'm sure."

"It was so! Didn't I tell you I'd been waiting half an hour? Didn't I say I'd made up my mind I wouldn't wait a minute longer?"

"Er—er, yes, Betty, that's what you said."

"Well, then, why can't you take a lady's word, Mr. Inspector Spearpoint—Esquire?"

"Then you knew all along it was half-past ten?" Spearpoint enquired of the little man, ignoring her.

"Er—yes, I suppose I did," he conceded, lamely.

"Then you must have left the Club at twenty-five past?"

"Er—yes, I suppose so."

"Dr. Halibut reckoned it was nearer ten-fifteen."

"Well, how should I know?" asked Mr. Montgomery Thomspon, desperately. "If Miss Bloggins says it was ten-thirty when I came along, then it must have been ten-thirty."

"Thank you, Monty," said Miss Bloggins, adding unexpectedly, "As a matter of fact, I put my watch on five minutes, just to make you think you'd kept me waiting half-an-hour."

"So he actually came at twenty-five past?"

"Yes, Mr. Spearpoint—but I wouldn't tell that to everybody; it's only because you're nice."

"Thank you, Bettina. And so"—turning to Mr. Montgomery Thomspon—"you actually left the Club about twenty past?"

"Apparently."

"Good enough. That's all, thank you, Mr. Thomspon. That will be very useful information. And I suppose Bettina may as well have her lipstick back now." Spearpoint took the bauble from his pocket and handed it to her. She accepted it unblushingly, saying, "Thank you, Mr. Spearpoint."

Mr. Montgomery Thomspon suddenly found a voice of unexpected firmness and said, "Bettina, do you mind telling Mr. Spearpoint what it was I wanted to see you about?"

"Why should I?" she stormed. "He wants me to give evidence! No one'll make me give evidence!"

Thomspon muttered, "Er—thank you," and retreated.

Spearpoint laughed and offered, "Can I drive you anywhere in town, Bettina?"

"How about a run to Nausori, Mr. Spearpoint?"

"I said in town, not fifty miles away."

"Nausori's only twelve miles, Mr. Spearpoint. Didn't they teach you geography at school?"

He did not know the answer to that, and, driving down Hercules Street to Victoria Parade, dropped her outside the Royal Palm. As he slammed the door after her, and engaged the clutch, he heard Stanley Pencarbon calling from the verandah, "What-ho, Bettina, who's your young man?"

And he could not help feeling an absurd gratification at her bantering and probably insincere reply, "He's a nicer man than any of you Aussies!"

CHAPTER TWENTY

WHO KILLED NETTA MAUL

(*Sunday evening*)

IT WAS TEN o'clock on Sunday evening, ten days after Inspector Spearpoint had had his last glimpse of Netta Maul alive. The Inspector sat on his mosquito-proof verandah, sweating in the tropical heat, in white trousers and open-necked cricket shirt. Opposite him, wearing a tie, but coatless, was the burly figure of Dr. Halibut. Between them, on a low tray, stood an opened bottle of Scotch, a siphon, glasses, cigarettes, and the previous day's issue of the *Fiji Times and Herald*; yet, despite these aids to the happy life, the doctor's face was troubled, and Spearpoint was plainly ill-at-ease. Only when he happened to glance at his curving abdomen did the Inspector's face lighten: it really did seem to curve rather less than it had a week before.

The newspaper, published on Saturday evening, had told the Colony the startling news of the confession and suicide of Jim Camelback. The editor had lavished his tallest type on the sensation, and had been enterprising enough to obtain interviews with both Inspector Spearpoint and Captain Stickithemud, as well as certain lesser members of the crew of the *Whitman*. It had published the exchange of wireless messages authorising the virtual arrest and reporting the suicide of Camelback; and also the official confession which had been considerately left by the murderer. This was the biggest scoop the *Fiji Times* had had since the Lautoka hurricane of 1931, and it had made the most of it.

But the two men had not yet mentioned the crime directly. A silence had followed the preliminary 'Say when' and 'Here's how,' and then Halibut had announced, "Bellamy tells me he had another cable to-day. It's a boy." The doctor had seemed as pleased as if it had been a son of his own.

"And how's Phyllis?"

"Fine. They're both fine."

"Good." Spearpoint had accepted the news with a twinge of envy; he wouldn't have given up Muriel for all the tea in China, but, all the same, he had wanted a boy.

The doctor had again broken the silence with, "Cecilia Snitch is not making the progress she should. She'll get better, of course; but this business has taken the heart out of her—she was the only real friend the girl had."

Spearpoint shrugged his shoulders, and made to speak, but the ten strokes of the clock interrupted him. As they concluded, he began, "I asked you along, doctor, because

I promised to tell you the inside story of this murder. You've read what the paper says? That's the official story. All Fiji will accept it as the truth. But it's not the real story; you know that as well as I do."

The doctor did not reply to this virtual accusation.

"Consider Camelback's confession," continued Spearpoint, picking up the paper; "it's a very curious document. It runs like this:

> 'I, James Thomas Camelback, being in my right mind, solemnly declare that I killed Netta Maul on the night of last Thursday. I struck her in anger, and did not intend to kill her; but I do not imagine any jury would believe that, and I prefer to anticipate the verdict of the trial I am told I must stand.
>
> 'James T. Camelback.'

After writing that he cut his throat with a razor which has since been identified as one taken from Craven's room, presumably in case he would need it for that purpose. He left no other confession or document at all.

"Now, I want to read to you what I said to the *Fiji Times*"; and the Inspector read out the seven hundred and fifty word statement in which he had marshalled all the evidence against Jim Camelback, and from which he had omitted every point in his favour.

When he had finished, he refilled the glasses, saying, "Well, doctor, what did you think of that?"

"I thought it was a very clever piece of work," answered Halibut, seriously. "You certainly discovered a great deal."

"We discovered more than that. We discovered enough to prove that Camelback didn't do it."

"You can prove that he didn't do it?"

"Yes."

"But you can't prove who did do it."

"Fortunately, no."

"I should be interested to know how you can prove he didn't do it."

"I know Camelback didn't hide the hair because I know he was not tall enough to reach the crevice it was hidden in. I couldn't reach it myself. I think that is conclusive proof that he was not concerned in the disposal of the body. In fact, I think it proves that he committed suicide by mistake."

"By mistake! You mean he cut his throat without intending to do it?"

"No, he meant to do it all right. And, to tell you the truth, I'm not sorry he did do it. At the time he killed himself, however, he was not in possession of a very important piece of information which, had he known it, would have proved to him that we did not have a water-tight case against him. Had he known that one fact, he would be walking about Suva to-day a free man, and another man would be on remand in a cell at Korovou."

"And what was that fact?" asked the doctor, uneasily.

"He was not aware that Netta Maul's body was found in a sack floating in the harbour. I told him she'd been found dead; I did not say where. And he sailed for Lau before the news got round the town. He thought she'd been found where he had last seen her, on the path between your garden and the garage where her throat was cut."

"How do you make that out?"

"His confession is plain enough. He says, 'I struck her in anger, and did not intend to kill her.' That obviously refers to the single blow—the punch on the temple, which made her sit down with a bump on your concrete steps, and knocked her out. They quarrelled; he struck her; she went down; he bent over her and found her senseless; he carried her off the road, and into the path, grabbed her handbag and hurried off to the Royal Palm, where he probably took documents which he thought would protect him from any threat of an action she might bring for assault. We shall never know what he took. After that, whatever his inward perturbation, he pursued his normal evening's occupation."

Spearpoint paused, but the doctor made no comment,

so he continued, "The slashing of her face—was that done before death, or after, by the way?"

"After," replied Halibut, promptly.

"Yes, I think that is so," agreed Spearpoint, "but what really killed her was the razor across the throat."

"The blow on the temple," amended Halibut.

"Too much blood. However, it doesn't matter; my point is that the slashing of the face and the cutting of the hair were not done in anger. They were done deliberately, fanatically, in cold blood, by someone who hated her beauty, and had planned to destroy it—to destroy it so that the very undertaker would look at her once-lovely face in horror, to destroy it so that her coffin should not contain the imperishable beauty of her hair."

"You must have been reading poetry," smiled the doctor, quite pleasantly.

"I'm not the only one," retorted Spearpoint, not put out. "My point is that this mutilation of her beauty was not done by Camelback. He would never have done it; he was no sentimentalist; he would strike her in anger; but he would never mutilate her features in cold blood. All that was done by the second man."

"So you think there was a second man, do you?"

"I'm quite sure there was a second man. And I know who the second man was. He was the man who borrowed Conky Thomspon's car from outside the Fiji Club just after five to ten, and who drove it hell for leather past me up Waimanu Road just after ten. He had been playing bridge with Willy Cutt, who always plays for cash, and he had not enough money to pay his losses, and did not like to admit that he had been playing beyond his pocket; so he took the car and dashed home for the cash. As he got out of the car he noticed Netta Maul lying unconscious in the place where Camelback had left her a few minutes earlier; and he was back on the verandah of the Fiji Club at twenty past ten, telling Conky Thomspon that it was not quite a quarter past."

"But you can't prove it," said Dr. Halibut.

"The second man," continued Spearpoint, more softly, and without looking at his guest, "—the second man once had a nephew. The nephew was a fine young fellow, and a poet, and some people said he was a genius. He fell in love with a certain half-caste girl, he wrote his best poems in her honour, he embezzled from his employers in order to give her expensive presents, and when she cast him off and took up with another man, he cut his throat. This girl took this fine young fellow and made a thief of him and ruined his career; and his love for her beauty cost him his honour and his life. The uncle determined to be revenged on her; he procured a razor—perhaps the very same razor with which the poet had killed himself—and he carried the razor with him always, waiting for the chance to cut the girl's throat without risk of detection. It may be that he carried with him also a pair of rubber gloves, which were a part of his professional equipment."

"How do you know he carried the razor and the gloves with him always?" interrupted the doctor, who had been visibly moved by the reference to the dead nephew.

"I don't know. I only guess. It is very likely, isn't it?"

"It is very likely," conceded the doctor; "but you can't prove it."

"I can't prove it.—But to continue: the second man saw the stunned body of Netta Maul lying in the path, and realised that his opportunity had come. He carried her into Paul's garage, accidentally leaving a small piece of her frock caught on a bramble in the hedge, and he cut her throat, performing the operation with sufficient skill to do the job effectively whilst at the same time making the cut appear as if it had almost missed the vital part. He did it skilfully enough to avoid getting blood on his hands or clothes. He left her in the garage, dead; and went back to the Fiji Club. A couple of hours later, he returned to the garage, disguised as a white-bearded Punjabi; he slashed the face then, and cut off the hair; and tied the hair in a bundle in which he also placed a page of poetry—a page torn from a book on the bookshelf of the verandah of the Fiji Club. Then he tied up the corpse and put it in a sack and followed out the routine I have already attributed to Camelback. He was nearly caught by an Indian constable on the bridge, but he heard the heavy footsteps in the distance, and, risking the discovery of the body in the car, feigned sleep in the colonnade on the other side of the road. When he climbed the cliffs later he did not come out by 'Segai Na Marama,' but in Tom Humble's garden, squirming over a final precipice that no one shorter than Sub-Inspector Sharpe can surmount. And he made the fatal mistake of hiding the hair in a crevice that no one shorter than Sub-Inspector Sharpe can reach. And, having thus disclosed his identity as the only white man in Suva who is taller than Sharpe, he retired to bed in Dr. Halibut's house."

"But you can't prove it."

"I don't want to prove it," answered the Inspector. "I'm thankful I haven't got to try to prove it. We've had a confession and we've accepted it, and the matter is over. Only two people know the confession is bogus. If the other fellow doesn't split, I won't. Sharpe may guess at the truth, but I don't think he will. I never told him of what I discovered at your house, but he did see Bellamy's razor after you had handed it to me. I promised you the inside story, and there it is. What do you think of it?"

"Very ingenious," conceded Halibut, cautiously.

"Of course, there are a few points I'm not sure of. I wonder if you can offer any theories to explain them?"

"You seem to be quite capable of inventing all the theories you need," retorted the doctor.

"What I wonder is: did the murderer want the body to be found or not?"

"Meaning the first man or the second?"

"The second."

"What do you think?" parried the doctor.

"I think not. I think he hoped the sharks would get it, but he destroyed her beauty in case it was discovered."

"That seems very probable."

"And I also wanted to know why he hid poetry with the hair when he hid it in an almost inaccessible spot. Was that done for sentimental reasons? Surely he never expected the hair to be discovered, even after the body had been?"

"Sentimental, I should say."

"Then the razor that cut her throat was the razor that had been used by the poet?"

"Not the poet Swinburne, of course. He wore a beard. —You seem to be able to explain everything. What you fail to explain is the extraordinary coincidence of the second man cutting the girl's throat immediately after Jim Camelback had knocked her senseless."

"That is a coincidence, but not an extraordinary one," submitted Spearpoint. "The second man had waited for two years for the chance to catch her alone and defenceless. The opportunity came at last, and he snatched it. It reminds me of a man in Sydney I was reading about in the paper last week: he walked under a ladder, and as he did so a pot of paint fell on his head and he slipped on a banana skin. You can't say that didn't happen merely because two accidents coincided; and you can't say that what I claim happened to Netta Maul didn't happen merely because the two attacks coincided. In fact, you can't honestly argue that my theory is incorrect."

The doctor did not answer the challenge.

"In fact," said Spearpoint, triumphantly, refilling the glasses, "you and I are the only people in the world who know who really killed Netta Maul."

"Yes," agreed Dr. Halibut, at last, "but we can't prove it."
